MADE FOR US

Abigail

It was time to celebrate.

After all my hard work, I was graduating at the top of my class.

Our family vacation was the perfect chance to relax.

Until I saw him get on the plane and my plans went out the window.

Tristan's everything I've always wanted but can never have.

One night was all we had together.

Now, I'm staring at the two pink lines wondering if I should even tell him.

Tristan

Six years ago, I was living for myself until I found out I had a two-year-old daughter.

Now, I love my life exactly how it is: me, my daughter, Penelope, and hockey.

Except—I've been in love with Abigail from afar for years.

She was the only one I trusted Penelope with.

One night with her is more than I deserve.

Now that I've had her, I know she was made for us.

BOOKS BY NATASHA MADISON

SOMETHING SO, THIS IS ONLY ONE & MADE FOR FAMILY TREE!

Hockey Series

SOMETHING SO SERIES

Something So Right

Parker & Cooper Stone

Matthew Grant (Something So Perfect)

Allison Grant (Something So Irresistible)

Zara Stone (This Is Crazy)

Zoe Stone (This Is Wild)

Justin Stone (This Is Forever)

Something So Perfect

Matthew Grant & Karrie Cooley

Cooper Grant (Only One Regret)

Frances Grant (Only One Love)

Vivienne Grant

Chase Grant

Something So Irresistible

Allison Grant & Max Horton

Michael Horton (Only One Mistake)

Alexandria Horton

Something So Unscripted

Denise Horton & Zack Morrow

Jack Morrow

Joshua Morrow

Elizabeth Morrow

THIS IS SERIES

This Is Crazy

Zara Stone & Evan Richards

Zoey Richards

This Is Wild

Zoe Stone & Viktor Petrov
Matthew Petrov
Zara Petrov
This Is Love
Vivienne Paradis & Mark Dimitris
Karrie Dimitris
Stefano Dimitris
Angelica Dimitris
This Is Forever
Caroline Woods & Justin Stone
Dylan Stone (Formally Woods)
Christopher Stone
Gabriella Stone
Abigail Stone
ONLY ONE SERIES
Only One Kiss
Candace Richards & Ralph Weber
Ariella Weber
Brookes Weber
Only One Chance
Layla Paterson & Miller Adams
Clarke Adams
Only One Night
Evelyn & Manning Stevenson
Jaxon Stevenson
Victoria Stevenson
Only One Touch
Becca & Nico Harrison
Phoenix Harrison
Dallas Harrison
Only One Regret
Erika & Cooper Grant
Emma Grant
Mia Grant

Parker Grant

Matthew Grant

Only One Mistake

Jillian & Michael Horton

Jamieson Horton

Only One Love

Frances Grant & Brad Wilson

Stella Wilson

Only One Forever

Dylan Stone & Alex Horton

Maddox Stone

Maya Stone

Maverick Stone

Made For Me

Julia & Chase Grant

Made For You

Vivienne Grant & Xavier Montgomery

Made For Us

Arabella Stone & Tristan Weise

Penelope

Payton

Made For Romeo

Romeo Beckett & Gabriella Stone

Mine to Take

Matthew Petrov & Sofia Barnes

Mine To Promise

Stefano Markos & Sadie

Cover Design: Jay Aheer
Editing done by Jenny Sims Editing4Indies
Editing done by Karen Hrdicka Barren Acres Editing
Proofing Julie Deaton by Deaton Author Services
Proofing by Judy's proofreading
Formatting by Christina Parker Smith

MADE
FOR US

NATASHA
MADISON

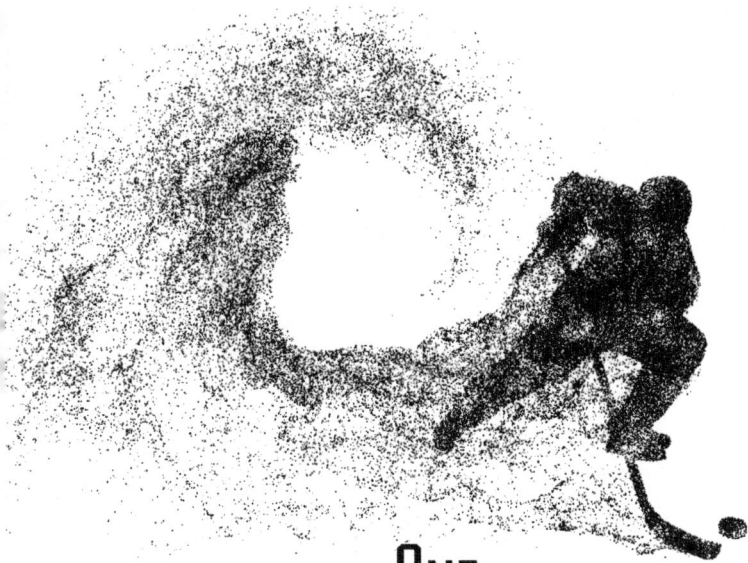

ONE

ABIGAIL

I LEAN OVER the empty white desk, unpinning the thumbtack at the corner of the picture as the soft music playing from my phone fills the room. Unpinning the other corner, the picture comes undone in my hand. I stare down at the picture of Gabriella, my twin sister, and me at our high school graduation. The two of us are in our graduation gowns staring at each other, sticking our tongues out. I can still remember it like it was yesterday, feeling the pit in my stomach knowing our time was soon running out. It was going to be the first time we were leaving each other, ever. We were going off to our respective colleges, neither of us knowing how one would survive without the other. I was off to Dallas to study nursing, and she was off to the West Coast. She was in love with photography, and LA was the place to be. She even contemplated Paris. The only thing was she didn't want to be anywhere close to the family.

I put the picture down on the empty desk before leaning over and unpinning another picture right next to the one I just took down, when my phone rings from the side of my bed. I make my way through the moving boxes to get to the cell. I look down, seeing a picture of my dad and me, "Hey, Daddy-o." I smile. "What's the dealio?"

He chuckles as I sit on the bed before leaning back on the pillows and putting up my legs on my unmade bed. "Hey, Abby," he says softly. "Whatcha doing, Buttercup?"

It's my turn to chuckle at him. Apparently, the story is he used to call us Buttercup because he couldn't tell us apart from the back, so he just went with calling us that nickname. "I'm almost finished packing." I look at the boxes all over my bedroom. It feels like I arrived at the empty room just yesterday. "I can't believe this is it." The wall that used to hold hooks to hang my jackets is down. The dresser that used to have little knickknacks on top is now bare.

"You busted your ass," he says, and I can see him smirking, "taking after me." I laugh right away. "Don't tell your mother." My parents met when my brother, Dylan, got an opportunity to attend my father's hockey school. From the way they tell the story, it was love at first sight. At least for my father.

"Your secret is safe with me. When are you guys coming down?" I look over at the window and see the sun has already gone down.

"We leave bright and early in the morning," he confirms. "Are you ready for tomorrow?" He's flying down with my mom to attend my graduation ceremony. The butterflies now fill my stomach. I've worked my ass off for this. The past six years are a blur, and it feels like I just moved out to college yesterday. I graduated after four years with a bachelor's of nursing and then did two years at John Hopkins.

It's my turn to smirk, and my heart speeds up. "As ready as I'll ever be."

"My daughter, a pediatric nurse." I blink away the tears. "So flipping proud of you."

"Okay, I'm going to let you go before you make me start crying. I have to get my makeup done soon, and I don't want to have swollen eyes."

"Okay, okay, fine," he says. "The moving truck is scheduled to be there on Saturday." I nod. "Then we can fly to Dallas and start house hunting."

"Dad," I say softly, "I was going to rent an apartment." I close my eyes, pinching the bridge of my nose.

"Negative. Can't talk now, heading to a meeting."

"We'll discuss it at dinner tonight," I tell him quickly before he hangs up.

I shake my head and look down, seeing he's already disconnected the phone. I toss my phone on the bed beside me, then get up and walk back over to the family board I did as soon as I moved into this studio apartment in Maryland, which is five minutes from campus, two years ago. I put my favorite pictures right in front of my desk, so when I looked up, all I saw were my people. I grab a picture of the whole family that was taken last year at the annual family vacation. There were so many people that Uncle Matthew had to call someone with a ladder to take an aerial shot. I stare at it for a couple of minutes, my mouth going to a smile without even knowing it. There is so much love in my family it's almost contagious. I put the picture down when my phone rings again.

Turning, I walk over to the phone I just threw down. "Hello." I press the speaker button when I see it's Gabriella.

"Well, well, if it isn't my older sister." She snickers.

"By three minutes," I add, walking back to the board to remove the rest of the pictures.

"Whatever. What are you doing?" she says, and I can hear she's walking outside when I hear car horns in the background.

"Doing last-minute packing," I tell her. "I have pretty much everything packed. I'm just packing my desk." Putting the phone down beside the stack of photos, I add, "Did you pack yet?" She surprised me two days ago when she called telling me she was moving. From the last conversation with her, everything seemed like it was going amazing in LA.

"Not even close. You know me, always late to the party. Anyway, I'm not calling about that. I'm calling to discuss this year's vacation. Did you get the itinerary?"

"I saw an email, but I figured someone would tell me something." I unpin a picture of my brother, Christopher, and me on the beach last time we saw each other last summer.

"Well, it's another little island. At this point, I think he had them build us houses." She laughs. "Either way, we have to celebrate."

"I agree." I unpin a picture of me with my nephew, Maddox, who is now taller than most of the men in our family at only sixteen. "We both should let our hair down."

"Speak for yourself," Gabriella pffts out. "My hair has been down for the past six years. But I'm happy you are finally going to let your hair down!" She snickers. "It's been tied up so tight that it's not sur—"

"Okay, well, this has been a great chat," I shut her down before she says anything else, "but I have to shower."

"Fine, I'll let you off the hook for now, but as soon as we get on that island, we are finding someone to finally get you to let loose. I don't know how you do it."

I roll my eyes. "You know, I've lived for the past six years without you beside me, and I survived."

"Barely," she jokes, and I laugh. "Good news is, I think I'm going to be staying in Dallas for the summer." I sit up all excited. "Do you think you could use a roomie?" Her voice goes lower and I have a feeling that her moving out of LA isn't just because of her work.

"Well, does this roomie clean up after herself?" I ask her, knowing full well that she doesn't. Even though we are twins, we couldn't be more different. I'm the clean, quiet one, she's the messy, outgoing one. I mean, I'm not going to say when we are together, we don't get into trouble, but the last six years I've learned a lot about myself.

"The roomie is somewhat cleaner than she used to be, and she also learned how to cook," she informs me, and I don't have a chance to say anything else because a horn honks in the background. "Okay, my ride is here. See you on the flip side," she says right before she disconnects the phone.

I toss the phone on the desk, shaking my head. "At least my move to Dallas won't be uneventful." I finish taking the pictures off the board, leaving the most special one for last.

I hold the picture in my hand, the subject the sole reason I picked pediatrics. Penelope. The little girl who I met while volunteering in the hospital in Dallas. Her black hair is in a ponytail and her eyes so crystal-blue it looks like you can see into her soul.

I had just gotten started in the nursing program and signed up to volunteer a couple of times a week. Little did I know, one day that decision would change the course of my life. She came into the hospital when she was a little over two years old. Her mother had died in the car accident when she was under the influence. It was a miracle Penelope survived because she had so many injuries, and she was all bandaged up. She had a cast on her arm and her leg, along with a slew of small injuries.

When I walked into her room, she was a little girl in a very big bed. I can't even put into words what I felt looking at her. My feet moved without my head even registering it as I sat beside the bed and held her little hand in mine when she woke up and cried for her mom. There was no amount of soothing I could have done, so I did the only thing I could. I held her in my arms, rocking her for much longer than I should have. Telling her she was coming, knowing I was lying to her. The little girl had lost her whole world, and her grandparents had come in trying to claim her, which ended up being more of a shit show. I would show up, even on my days off, just to spend time with her. To be honest, I was at the hospital every single day. If I wasn't in class, I was in the hospital, doing my homework in the little waiting area, just in case she needed me. It's hard to put into words the pull I had for her, but it was the easiest decision I ever made.

After spending a week in the pediatric wing with her, I knew that was where I wanted to focus my studies. I knew this was what I wanted to do. I knew I had to finish the nursing program and then I went a step further and focused on attending John Hopkins. Not sure if I would be getting in, but it was my top school, and luckily enough, I was accepted. Now here I am, getting ready to graduate tomorrow and collect my diploma. Another thing checked off my list with the next waiting to be checked off.

I knew there was only one hospital I wanted to work at once I graduated. I also knew not to get my hopes up high, but considering I was at the top of my class and I volunteered there, I was lucky enough to get an offer from them. So in one month, I will be officially walking in there as a registered nurse on the pediatrics floor.

I can't help the smile on my face when I think about it. I can't help but look back and run my hand over the picture. Penelope stands beside me with a huge smile on her face as she hugs my waist. It was taken not too long ago when I surprised my family at a Sunday lunch. I put the picture down with the rest of them and turn to grab an empty brown envelope. Getting up, I place it at the top of the box sitting right next to my chair. I put the cover on the box before taking one final look around.

By the time I crawl into bed, my body is exhausted, and the alarm for seven comes way too fast. I throw the covers off me before getting up and making myself a coffee before I walk over and start putting on my makeup. I have one hour to get ready before the car is set to pick me up.

I decide to wear my hair down and just curl the ends. My makeup is done in a matter of twenty minutes. After putting just some mascara on and a little bit of eyeliner, I walk over and grab the white dress that is the only thing hanging in my closet. I slip on the white spaghetti strap dress, making sure my boobs are in place. Grabbing my black high-heel sandals, I sit on the bed and fasten the straps around my ankles.

My phone rings from the bedside table, and I see it's the driver telling me he has arrived. I stand, putting in the diamond earrings my parents gave me for my twenty-first birthday, then grabbing the blue gown and yellow honors sash, along with my phone.

I'm walking down the stairs, and the minute I open the door, I stand here in shock. There is a huge bus in front of my building. I'm shocked as my whole family, and I mean my whole freaking family, is here. I can't help the tears that are coming down my face. "You didn't think I wouldn't be here." Gabriella is the first to run to me and takes me in her arms. "I'm not even going to tell you the shit show this morning was," she whispers, and then she's pushed away from me when Dylan just stands before me.

"How are you even here? Aren't you in the middle of playoffs?" I ask him, and all he does is smile at me.

"My baby sister is graduating," he states, "but I have to be back in Dallas by five tonight." He brings me in for a hug. "So proud of you," he says, and I cry on his shoulder, just like I did when I was younger. He was twelve, I think, when Gabriella and I were born, and from what I remember, he was my favorite person in the world. Now he stands here with Alex and their kids.

"Can I get a turn?" I hear my grandfather on the side, and all I can do is put my hands on my mouth as he stands here with my grandmother. Both of them just beaming with pride. "Before your father and Uncle Matthew hip check me out of the way."

I look over his shoulder, seeing my father standing beside my mother as she dabs her eyes. "You did all this?" I ask him, laughing as I hug my grandfather.

"He obviously had help," my uncle Matthew says from beside him. "Who else could wrangle up all these people?"

I stand here in shock, seeing all my aunts and uncles. "Now, can we get back on the bus so we can get good seats?" My father claps his hands. "Let's go, people. Got to get my girl to her ceremony."

Two

TRISTAN

"GO-GO-GO-go," the coach yells at us, and my leg swings over the board as I get onto the ice, skating back to try to get the puck in the neutral zone. My heart beats so fast it echoes in my ears, just as the sound of my breathing almost feels like it's in slow motion.

My legs feel like I've climbed Mount Everest five times, but the adrenaline in my body tells me to push harder. We are in triple overtime in game seven of the Stanley Cup finals. The line changes that usually go forty seconds we are putting down to thirty seconds to give all of us a chance to rest. But it hasn't been working. Both teams are fucking exhausted, but this is what you fight for all year. The Stanley Cup is somewhere in this building, just waiting to be hoisted up. The big question is, which team is it going to be?

"Change," the coach yells, and I skate over to the bench, swinging my leg back over, my legs almost giving out when I sit down. I try to focus on my breathing, working to get it back to normal. I reach out, grabbing a green Gatorade bottle and spraying water in my mouth before looking up at the Jumbotron. There are two minutes and seventeen seconds left of the triple overtime. Both teams have given it all we have.

I lean forward, my eyes watching everything happening on the ice. The feeling you want so much to help and you want so much to be the one who helps bring your team to that place is like the biggest monkey on my back. My legs start to shake now with nervousness as another line change is done. "We are going to try something different," the coach says, coming over to me as I sit next to my defense partner, Ben. "We are putting Grant in for Ben's place."

I look at Ben, who looks at me. "If there is anyone who will take my place, it's going to be Cooper. He's the best defensive player." I nod, agreeing with him. This season has been the best of my life, if I'm honest. I finally found my footing, which is crazy since I've been with this team for eight years. I was drafted to the team at eighteen and picked fourth overall. I thought I would be drafted and then immediately put on the team. I wasn't. You had to earn your spot, so for two years, I busted my ass to earn my spot.

Fighting for your spot is different than assuming you will have it. It makes getting on the team so much sweeter. Every single year, I trained hard and worked my ass off to make sure I belonged on the team. The whole team is filled with superstars, so I had to definitely keep up with them.

"Stone," the coach yells for Dylan, who looks back at him. "I want your line on there with Monti and Grant." A couple of eyes look back at the coach and then at each other. I'm sure everyone is wondering what in the world the coach is thinking. "Grant, you good to play back?" I'm sure the only thing on everyone's mind is, don't fuck this up.

"Yeah," Cooper says as we get up and make the line change. Not fast enough because the other team skates into the zone. It takes a second for us to get into position, but not before they get a shot at the net. My eyes fly to the little round black puck. The whole time, I hold my breath, hoping if they do score, I'm not the one on the ice. You always want to be on the winning line, but you also never ever want to be on the line that gets scored on. Even though no one ever blames you, you have enough blame inside yourself to go around. Steven, our goalie, sticks his leg out, and it bounces off his pad. I quickly get to the puck first, and the five of us now hustle back toward the other end. Cooper playing back by me, with Michael, Dylan, and Xavier skating ahead of us.

I take my time to skate up, taking the puck out of the zone, looking over at Michael and passing it to him. The three forwards skate against the two defensemen in front of them. I stay back at the center ice until they get into the zone, making sure I'm on it if the puck is intercepted. Monti skates up right along Michael and Dylan. Cooper stays back with me on the opposite side. His eyes watch the play at hand. Michael passes the puck to Monti, but Dylan skates up and intercepts it, just like the play we did in practice a couple of days ago. He skates into the zone, rushing for the goalie. The three forward players are all around him, leaving Monti empty. Monti glides closer to the goalie, who is not even watching Xavier. He's watching Dylan. He slides over to the corner to make sure he's got it covered, but Dylan passes the puck so fast to Xavier that there is no time for the goalie to slide across to the other side. The puck hits the center on Xavier's stick, and he slaps it toward the goal, making the goalie slide across the ice to the other side. Everything feels like it's going in slow motion, the puck suspended in air as it flies to the back of the net. The horn fills the arena, but it's drowned out by the crowd banging on the glass behind the net. I throw my stick down, and my gloves fly above my head as I scream at the top of my lungs. We did it! I can't even think right now. Xavier is the first to jump into the air with Michael, who jumps with them. Dylan skates to the net to grab the puck before joining them, followed by Cooper and me.

It takes a split second before the rest of the team surrounds Xavier as we celebrate with each other. "We did it!" somebody says over and over again, the whole team in a circle jumping up and down.

"Who's got your back?" Cooper yells.

We chant back to him, "I've got your back."

It was a little thing we started at the beginning of this year when Xavier signed with the team. He came from a team that didn't have his back and the team banded together to make sure he knew he wasn't in this alone. "Who's got your back?"

"I've got your back," we all yell.

The crowd's roar is even more deafening when they know we are doing our chant, something the audience has also come to enjoy. Winning the games in the playoffs is always amazing, but when you get to win in your arena, with the same people who cheer you on all year long, it is beyond words. I'm not even thinking about the thirty thousand fans outside now celebrating.

We stand together as a group, as we did all year long, before breaking and skating to the middle of the ice to shake hands. Gloves are scattered over the ice, helmets thrown off, sticks tossed to the side. I take a second to finally look up where I know my girl is. Penelope. With her hair in a ponytail, wearing my jersey as she jumps up and down clapping her hands. The fullness in my chest is off the charts as the tears start to sting at the back of my eyes. The emotions are all over the place. I hold up my hand to her, hoping she sees me.

I see my mother from the side lean down and whisper something in her ear. Then her eyes find mine, as she holds up her hand like mine, right before she blows me a kiss. I pretend to grab it and place it at my heart. This little girl, who is eight years old, weighs about fifty pounds, and is almost four feet tall owns me right down to my bones. She smiles so big at me, and then I see her walk over to Abigail, and my heart stops beating in my chest as I watch the two of them together.

Abigail stops what she is doing right away to lean down and listen to what she is saying. Penelope points at me, and I just stand there and hold up my hand again. Abigail smiles and waves as she puts her arm around Penelope and kisses her head. I shake my head away from the thought that I'm jealous of the kiss my daughter just got.

Instead, I skate to the middle of the ice, getting in line, and shaking the other players' hands. I look over to the side, seeing them opening the Zamboni door, where they are rolling out the red carpet and setting up the tables for the MVP of the playoffs, as well as the Stanley Cup.

I finally get to the end of the line and skate over to the bench, grabbing a Stanley Cup hat. I look over and see Chase, the team doctor and one of my best friends, leaning against the side with a matching hat on his head. He comes over to me with a smirk on his face. "Well, would you look at that." He takes his hat off his head and points at it. "Stanley Cup Champions."

I can't help but chuckle. "Is that what it says, Doc?" I joke with him, putting the hat on top of my head

"Great freaking game."

"It was a Xavier," I tell him, and he comes over and taps my shoulder.

"It's like you are all grown up now," he teases me like he always does.

When he joined the team, I had just turned twenty, and then I got hurt. He really stood by my side through it all. He worked right alongside me, and then I found out about Penelope, and to be honest, he was the big brother

I never had. I knew if I ever needed him, he would be right there beside me and vice versa.

I hear chatter beside me when Cooper, Chase's brother, teases Xavier. "The hero of the game. I still don't like you kissing my sister." That makes me laugh even harder.

"Who is going to tell him that I'm sure he does more than kiss her?" I say loudly, and Xavier looks at me and smiles.

"Yeah, I do," he confirms, putting on his own cap. Having Xavier on the team has been one of the best experiences I've had. He is one hundred percent so open about everything that it makes you be open as well. It was hard to come in sometimes and not be okay but pretend to be okay because you never really want to burden people. Once he was here, it was so refreshing to come in and be like 'I'm so fucking tired,' and you also found that a lot of other players were feeling the same.

I hear the president of the NHL, Paul, speak, and then the boos start. "Looks like it's about that time," I say, looking over at Xavier, who just smiles.

"It's about that time for us to raise the Cup," he says, and we skate over to the rest of the team.

"Congratulations to Dallas on yet another Stanley Cup win," Paul starts, and the crowd goes wild. "The award for the most valuable player of the playoffs. This person has shown perseverance on and off the ice. He is one of the top leading scorers in the playoffs, and he sure scored the big one tonight. Your award winner, Xavier Montgomery."

The minute I hear Xavier's name, I look over at him, putting my fist in the air and screaming, "Go get it!"

He skates over, grabbing the trophy as Cooper puts his arm around me and leans in. "Got to say, you're a good wing partner."

I shake my head. "I think I'm the one who should be saying this since I was the one who was actually playing where I was supposed to be playing."

He just laughs at me as I take in the scene before me. Xavier is giving an interview as I

look around and see the crowd on their feet, their phones in their hands as they capture this moment. Looking over, I see Penelope is now with my father, who holds her in his arms. My mother stands beside my younger sister, wiping away the tears from her face. She looks at Penelope, who just puts her head back on my father's shoulder.

I look over at Nico, who catches me looking and smiles at me with a nod. When he pulled me into his office some six years ago, I thought he was going to tell me he was thinking about trading me. I thought my injury was taking too long to heal, even though I was on the ice when he pulled me off. I thought for sure he wasn't interested in waiting. What I wasn't expecting was to be ushered over to a lawyer's office.

The last thing in the world I thought I would hear was that I was a father and I had a baby girl who was two. I sat there speechless as I listened to them tell me the mother of my child had died. I held my breath as I was asked if I recognized her, and I was ashamed that

I didn't. I was a young kid on top of the world, I was with women, and I didn't even know their names, and to be honest, they probably didn't know mine. But they did know I played hockey, which is the only thing they actually cared about.

Even when they showed me a picture of her, nothing rang a bell. But when they showed me a picture of Penelope, it was like I was looking into my sisters' eyes as well as my own. I knew right then and there that she was mine. I did the DNA test right away, but I also made them bring me to her. Chase was right there beside me, telling me it was going to be okay.

They had told me she was hurt, but she would be fine. But nothing could have prepared me for what I saw when I walked into the room. It will be forever engraved in my memories, looking at her sitting in the middle of the bed—right next to Abigail—who was making her laugh. I knew the minute she looked over at me that I would love and protect this little girl with everything I had. I knew right then and there she was mine. I knew right then and there what they said about the love for a child. A love you can't explain because there are no words that can do it justice. A love that is unconditional and pure. She looked at me and held out her little hand to offer me one of her Goldfish crackers, and I am not ashamed to say I sobbed like a baby.

Everything after was in warp speed. I called my parents, who came right down. My bachelor pad was now a single dad home. The PlayStation 5 was tucked away and in its place was a pink plastic play kitchen. I also had to live with the guilt I wasn't there for her. A guilt that was really hard to look past, so I did what I could to make sure every single day she knew how loved she was.

The two of us grew up together, and she is honestly the best thing I've ever done in my whole life. Even more than this right here.

I hear Wilson from beside me. "You know what he's doing tonight?" he says while he looks at Cooper. "He's going to be sleeping with your sister." He beams with a smile. "Just like me." Cooper just glares at him.

"If you say a word," Michael warns beside Dylan, and I roll my lips, trying not to laugh. "I will throat punch you on the ice." The minute he says that, I spit out the laughter.

The Stanley Cup comes out, and Cooper skates over as the team's captain. He shakes Paul's hand as he announces the Dallas Oilers are Stanley Cup Champions.

He takes the Cup, and slowly every single person gets their chance with it. I'm not even going to lie. I did a quick turn and then turned to look over to see if Penelope was here.

I see her finally standing behind the bench, holding on to Abigail's hand. "There he is." Abigail points at me.

Making my way over to her, she walks onto the ice where the carpet is, the whole time holding Abigail's hand. As soon as I get close enough, Penelope jumps into my arms and wraps her arms around my neck. "You did it, Dad," she says, putting her hands on my shoulders, and I can't help the tear that falls down my cheek. "I want you to know I would have been proud of you, no matter what."

"That is good to know," I tell her as I lean in and kiss her neck as she squeals, then put her down on the carpet.

I make the mistake of looking at Abigail. God, she has to be the most beautiful human person out there. Every single time I've seen her, it's like she gets even more beautiful, which is impossible. "Congratulations," she says, and I make another mistake and lean down to hug her. Wrapping my arm around her waist, I take in how perfect she feels for me. I also know that she is so out of my league this crush on her has to be the stupidest idea I've ever had. I kiss her soft cheek and look into her green eyes. "You were amazing," she says with a big smile on her face.

I'm about to say something to her when I see Xavier at the corner of my eye get down on one knee. Abigail gasps and holds my arm, squeezing it. "He's really doing it," she declares, and all I can do is look back at Abigail and then Penelope. I am having the second happiest day of my life, and with the exact people I want beside me. Too bad I don't have the balls to admit that out loud.

THREE

ABIGAIL

"WHEN YOU SAID you had a couple of boxes," my brother, Christopher, huffs, carrying a box inside the house and placing it in the middle of the family room, "what you failed to mention was you have a fuck ton of boxes." He puts his hands on his hips, looking over at me as I stand in the kitchen. He's in gym shorts and a Dallas Stanley Cup T-shirt. He's wearing one black flop and a white flop on the other foot, and I don't even think he's noticed that he's a mess.

"I'm moving into my house." I try not to laugh at him as he looks up at the ceiling and breathes in and out. "What did you think I had… three boxes?"

He looks back at me, but because he's wearing sunglasses, I can't see where he's actually looking. "Christopher," he mimics me, "can you come help me move a couple of boxes?"

"One," I say, holding up my finger at him, "you were drinking, so the fact you think you remember anything I said is comical." He shakes his head. "Two, I said can you come and help me move into my house."

"Why the hell wasn't this done when you moved to town a month ago?" he asks, taking off his sunglasses and then, seeing how bright it is in the room with all the curtains opened from the wall-to-wall back windows leading to the backyard, puts them back on. He walks over to the steps on the right side and sits down on the middle one, putting his elbows on his knees and hanging his head in front of him.

"How the hell was I supposed to know Dallas would be in the playoffs for eighty-five years?" I throw up my hands and walk over to the fridge, opening it to grab myself a bottle of sparkling water. "Don't bother renting movers," I mimic every single man in my family, "the whole family is going to be there. We can help you move." I unscrew the white cap off the green bottle hearing the hiss of gas. "The whole gang of us can come and help you." I take a sip of the cool bubbly water, mumbling, "Bullshit." Right after

"Hello, hello, hello," Gabriella comes through the door shouting. Her hair is piled on her head, and she's wearing black yoga leggings with a matching sports bra and her own sunglasses on the top of her head. Following is my cousin, Matty. His actual name is Matthew, but because our family has no originality, they just keep naming us after family members, so we have called him Matty to not confuse anyone. Who is also carrying a box that says *towels*. I try not to laugh at him since I'm sure there was a heavier box outside, but he took this one instead. He too is wearing the same thing that Christopher is wearing, just the same color shoes.

"Can you tone it down just a touch?" Christopher whines, holding his hand up and moving it up and down. "There is an echo in the house."

"There is no echo in the house." Gabriella shakes her head, looking him up and down and pointing at his shoes. He finally looks down and must see that they're two different colors, but he takes off his sunglasses anyway to make sure.

"Where is everyone?" Matty says from beside Gabriella, looking around.

"My guess is they are sleeping." I look at my Apple Watch and see that it's just a little after eight thirty in the morning.

"Didn't you tell everyone to get here bright and early?" Matty walks over to his partner in crime and sits beside him.

"What time did you guys go to bed last night?" Not only did my brother and cousin make the playoffs but they also won the Stanley Cup. The past ten days have been one celebration after another. It's been a whirlwind since they won the Cup. Then the party at home. Then the parade and street party. Then the team party, it's just been one party after another. Finally, yesterday was the last event they were doing, and in five days, we are finally going on vacation.

"I haven't," he says. "I left Dylan's at four and decided it would be better to just stay up."

"We went over to my house," Matty adds, "and decided to make breakfast." I just stare at him with my eyes big. "Let's just say my mother was not a fan of the pans hitting the floor. So she kicked us out."

"We tried to sneak into Uncle Matthew's house, but the alarm went off. Also, did you know that he sleeps naked?" Christopher informs, cringing.

Matty just laughs beside him, shaking his head. "He was not a happy person."

"Okay, how about I order some food for you two?" I suggest, walking to my phone. "You just bring the boxes in, and I'll organize them." I open the Uber Eats app. "What do you want?"

"Pancakes," Christopher rattles off, "scrambled eggs, bacon, sausage, fries."

"I'll take two of that," Matty says, pointing at Christopher.

"Does anyone want a mimosa?" Gabriella says, and the guys just groan, "Don't drink with the big boys if you are straight out of daycare."

Christopher gets up and looks at her. "That makes no sense." He holds out his hand to help Matty up, who just swats his hand away.

"I can do it myself," Matty declares, getting up and then falling back down on the wooden step, hitting his elbow. "Motherfucker." He rubs his elbow and gets up. "Can we just get this over with?" He takes out his phone. "Where the hell is Stefano?"

"I'm right here," my other cousin, Stefano, says, dressed in blue shorts and a white shirt, holding a box in his hand. "There are a million boxes outside."

"Listen"—I look at the three of them—"if it's too much work for you guys, I can always call the girls." I look at Gabriella. "Last time, it took us forty-five minutes to unload Zoey's things."

Stefano looks over at Christopher. "We can do it." Christopher nods at him. "Dude, why are you wearing two different shoes?"

"It's a fashion statement," Christopher grumbles, making Matty laugh.

"Yeah, it's an 'I got dressed in the dark look and didn't notice,'" Matty explains. "Let's go and beat the record." They all walk out of the house.

"It took us seven hours to do Zoey's house," Gabriella reminds me, folding her arms over her chest and looking over at me. "Well played."

I nod my head. "I must get it from Uncle Matthew," I say, turning back to the phone and ordering five of everything the guys said they wanted.

It takes them three hours to get all the boxes inside the house, but that's because they stopped to eat for an hour. The three of them leave, heading straight to each of their respective houses to sleep.

Gabriella and I work side by side, unpacking the whole kitchen, which takes us the longest time. By the time I walk up the stairs to go and tackle my bedroom, I'm honestly exhausted. As soon as I step into my bedroom, I take off my flip-flops and walk over to the white side table, putting down the glass of water I brought up. The bed is still unmade from this morning, so I just throw the cover back on it. I walk over to the tall brown boxes and open one to see all the clothes hanging. Walking over to the white door to the side of the bed, I open the door and turn on the light. It takes me a full hour before everything is hung up, and I'm walking to my en suite to start a bath. My head hits the pillow about twenty minutes later, and I only wake up when I hear the soft alarm ring.

I slept thirteen hours, and when I wake up, I feel like shit. My whole body aches, and I wonder if it's because I've been burning the candle at both ends. Between moving here and then the partying, I'm exhausted. I get out of bed, and the minute I do, my body shivers. I put the back of my hand against my forehead, and I feel like I'm on fire. Getting up, I walk over to the bathroom and take my temperature, and only when I try to swallow do I feel like razors are going down. "Shit," I curse, opening my mouth and looking in the mirror. I walk over to my phone and call Chase, who answers after one ring.

"Hello," he greets, and I can hear that he's in the car.

"Hey," I reply. "I have a fever of one hundred and one, and I think I see white spots at the back of my throat."

"We leave in three days," he says out loud.

"What do you want me to say, Chase?" I ask him. "Should I tell strep throat to come back while I'm on vacation."

"Are you home, smart-ass?"

"I am," I confirm. "I can come to you."

"No," he says, "I'm on my way over to the rink. I'll

stop at your house first."

"I thought hockey was done after you won the Cup," I state, and he just laughs.

"I have to clean out my office and make sure that everything is ready for next season. I'll be there in ten."

I hang up the phone and walk back to the bathroom, taking my temperature again and seeing it hasn't changed. I groan and make my way downstairs. I'm about to make a coffee when there is a knock on the door. I walk over and open it, seeing it's Chase.

"You look like shit," he greets me, and I just nod.

"Thanks." I roll my eyes. "I wonder why because I feel like a million bucks," I tell him, and he walks in with his little black bag.

He looks around. "Did you already unpack everything?" he asks, and I just look at him.

"I start work when I get back," I inform him. "So I didn't want to come home from vacation and have to unpack everything."

"Sit down," he urges, pointing at the stool in the kitchen tucked under the island table.

I sit down as he opens his bag and takes out blue medical gloves. "That's a bit too much," I say, and he laughs and feels under my chin toward my ears.

"Your lymph nodes are a bit swollen." He opens his bag and takes out a tongue depressor. "Say ahh," he says, "and stick out your tongue."

"I know what to do." I glare at him, sticking out my tongue. He presses down on it with the stick, making me gag. "You did that on purpose."

"Did I?" He just looks at me. "You definitely have strep throat." He looks at me, and I point at the sink. He turns and walks over to the sink, opening the bottom door and throwing out the stick and the gloves. He washes his hands right away. "I'm going to give you Zithromax since it's a five-day dose. You'll start to feel better after day three."

"Wow, you would think I didn't go to nursing school," I remind him, and he just smiles at me.

"But are you a doctor?" He walks back to the black bag and grabs his white script pad.

"I don't know if you heard," I share with him as he fishes around his bag for a pen, "Nurses are higher up there than doctors." He just looks over at me as I shrug. "Don't hate the player. Hate the game."

He throws his head back and laughs out loud. "That doesn't even make sense."

"What is all this noise?" Gabriella whines from on top of the stairs. "I'm trying to sleep."

"Your sister has strep throat," Chase tells her, and she just gasps.

"Am I going to get it?" She puts her hand to her throat, somehow trying to shield herself. "We leave for vacation in a couple of days," she groans.

"You don't think I know that," I hiss at her. "You think I want to go on vacation sick?"

"Maybe I'll go and stay with Mom and Dad."

"Yes, do that," I tell her as Chase rips the paper off the pad. "I'll drive you."

"This was fun," Chase says. "Also, don't forget that

this can mess with your birth control." Gabriella laughs, and I just glare at him as he holds up his hand. "I have to tell you."

"Honey," I yell up the stairs, "got to pick up condoms on the way back home today."

He just looks at me with big eyes, going from me and then up to the bedroom, "I'm joking, dickhead." I push away from the counter and walk over to the stairs. "Now, I'm going to go and get this filled, and I'm going to sleep until I have to pack."

"Are you going to pack your fake boyfriend to go with you?" Gabriella rolls her lips.

"He's busy," I deadpan, walking up the steps and flipping her the bird. "He'll be hanging with your boyfriend all weekend." It's her turn to glare at me. Something she hasn't mentioned since she's been back is the guy she was sort of kind of, kind of, not sure she was dating, "Don't mess with the big boys if you are."

"Shut up," is all she says. The only thing I can think of is that if I did have a boyfriend, it wouldn't be the guy I've always wanted because he doesn't even know I exist.

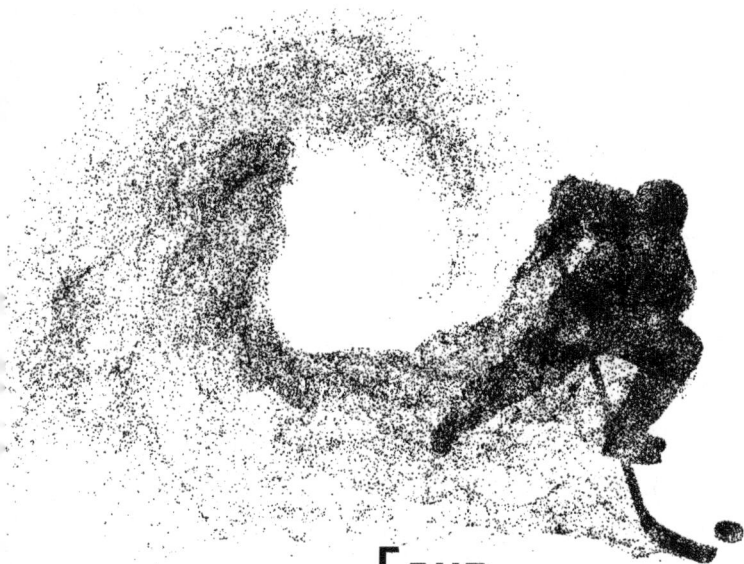

Four

Tristan

I PULL INTO my parking spot and get out of the SUV, my head still throbbing from ten days ago. I take the keys in my hand and press the button to lock the doors at the same time Xavier comes in and parks his car.

Looking over at the SUV, I decide to wait for him. When he gets out of the car, he looks just like I feel. "How're you feeling?" I ask him, and he just shakes his head, making me laugh.

"I don't think I've ever drank so much in my whole life."

I chuckle. "Well, it's not every day you are a hero and lead your team to win the Stanley Cup." I roll my lips, knowing this is all he's heard for the past ten days. Every single time he corrects everyone and says it was a group effort. "Do you have a cape on under that shirt?" I ask him as I pull open the metal door leading into the arena.

There are people everywhere, and I don't know why I'm surprised since today is clean out your locker day. Usually, it is done as soon as you finish the season, but after winning the Cup, there have been so many fucking parties there was no time to do anything. Thank God my family is down and watched Penelope at night because I don't know how she would have kept up with all these parties. "I'm going to go home tonight." I look over at him as we walk down the blue carpeted hallway. "And I'm going to sleep for fifteen hours."

He laughs at me as we walk into the changing room, and I see we are the last two to arrive. "Boys," I greet, nodding as I take in that most of the guys are just sitting down with either water in their hands or Gatorades. The night we won the Cup, I think we left the arena at seven in the morning. The families stayed and took pictures on the ice with us, but then when we went to the locker room, it was chaos, to say the very least. I think it finally sank in that we won, and everyone got their third or fourth wind. The champagne was flying all over the place, and the amount of beer that was drunk was insane. One of the guys actually did an interview while drinking a can of beer, and the interview made no sense whatsoever.

"I'm not drinking for the next six months," Dylan announces, downing the rest of his water in the bottle. He closes the bottle and tosses it in the big bin in the middle of the room and misses it, making us all laugh. "I literally have no strength in my whole body."

"Did you hear what your brother did?" Cooper looks

over at Dylan as I sit down in my place right next to Xavier. I get up after sitting for two minutes, grabbing a bottle of water and then looking over at Xavier, who just nods at me so I get him his own bottle.

"My brother?" Dylan points at himself.

"He tried to sneak into my father's house two nights ago." He laughs, and Dylan just shakes his head. "My father came running out of the bedroom while the alarm was blaring."

"Why the hell did he try to break into the house?" Dylan just shakes his head. "Idiot."

"No idea," Cooper says, "but he and Matty were busted and then spent the whole day helping Abigail unpack." The minute I hear her name, the tightness forms in my stomach as I try not to listen to what they say. It always feels like I'm stalking her. Taking out my phone, I open it up to see we got an email from Nico with all the pictures we took the night we won.

Sliding through them, I see the winning goal captured frame by frame. "Did you see this?" I look over at Xavier, showing him the picture, who just shakes his head. I slide through and find a picture of Penelope and me. "Look at her smile," I say, showing Xavier the picture. "She had the best time." I swipe again, seeing a picture someone took of me, Penelope, and Abigail. I press the save button and then slide through until I see the parade pictures.

"It's a blur," I state. "The past ten days have been a blur, and I really wish I remembered most of it."

The guys all laugh as they get up and start packing their lockers. I get up, putting my phone away, before walking over and grabbing a garbage bag to throw shit out. "What are you doing after this?" Xavier asks as he leans over and throws some of his stuff in my garbage.

"No idea," I say truthfully. "I'm going back home in a couple of weeks to stay at my lake house and start training. You?"

"Family vacation," he replies, opening his backpack and tossing in some of his hockey tape. "Why don't you and Penelope come?"

I look over at him. "I don't know." I chuckle. "It's a family vacation."

"And you've been a part of that family longer than I have. You are practically there every Sunday for lunch." He points out a little fact that I usually forget since it's become a ritual with Penelope and myself.

"Yeah," I agree. The minute I found out about Penelope, the whole Grant-Stone family was behind me. There was never a moment they judged me or made me feel like a horrible person for any of it. I mean, it took Julia a while to warm up to me, but that is only because she was the one who was the caseworker for Penelope. "Maybe." I think about how much fun Penelope would have. She loves her time at the lake, but she would really love to go to the beach. "Are you sure this is okay?" I look back over at Xavier, who just nods his head. "It's a family vacation. I don't want to intrude."

"Please," Xavier pffts me. "Cooper," he calls over to Cooper, who is tossing all his shit into his equipment bag. I don't even think he's looking at what he's putting in there. "How many people coming on the family trip?"

"Fuck if I know. I think we were up to eighty," Cooper answers, shaking his head.

"So would two more matter?" He motions over to me, and he just laughs.

"Fifteen more wouldn't matter at this point," Dylan interjects as Michael laughs.

"I'm dreading this plane ride," Michael groans, looking over at me. "Just make sure you bring earplugs."

I think about it for a second, and perhaps I should have thought about it a little more, but I can't help myself. "This sounds like so much fun. What's the worst that can happen?"

The whole group of guys moans when I say that. "Well, one year, I woke up, and my brother was wakeboarding naked," Cooper says of Chase, "and then my daughter drew a picture at school about it."

"One year," Dylan holds up his hand, "Wilson and Franny got caught doing it against a tree."

"We didn't get caught," Wilson says, laughing, "and we weren't doing it." He just smirks. "I was feeling her up, and her ass got stung by a bee."

"That's my sister," Cooper groans and pretends he's going to vomit.

"One year"—Michael puts his hand up—"Alex ran away from Dylan."

"She didn't run away," Dylan denies. "She was giving me space."

"She took a plane and left the island," Michael points out. "That's leaving you."

Dylan just flips him the bird. "One year, Michael fell

asleep in one of those hammock things and had a glasses sunburn on his face." All the guys laugh, even Michael.

"Needless to say, you never ask what can go wrong because with my family," Cooper says, "the possibilities are endless. Especially now that Matty and Christopher are allowed to drink."

"They got shit-faced two years ago," Wilson adds. "We found them throwing up in the bushes."

"Well, that sounds like a great time," I say, "if it's not too much trouble."

Cooper picks up his phone and dials someone, and as soon as I hear Matthew's voice, I just listen. "Dad, Tristan and Penelope are coming with."

"Perfect, we have five extra houses, just in case," Matthew replies, and I look over at Xavier.

"Just in case?" I whisper, and Xavier just shakes his head.

"Don't make me judge my future father-in-law," he says, and I laugh. It takes us about three hours to clean out the lockers, and the boys take one more picture before we all walk out.

When I finally pull up in the driveway, my phone pings with an alert and an email comes in from Matthew with all the trip details.

Grabbing the bag from the back seat, I walk up the path and open the front door. "I'm home." The door to upstairs is closed, so I know she isn't upstairs. I walk into the house, putting my bag right at the entrance to the dining room that we only ever use during the holidays. "P," I yell her name and still hear nothing when I walk into the huge family room. It's the whole reason I bought this house. It's in the middle of the house, attached to a giant kitchen with an even bigger island. It's where we spend most of the time.

The massive U-shaped couch in the middle of the family room took me six months to get since it was custom made, and it feels like you're in a bed every time you sit on it. The whole reason for that was because we love to do movie nights, and if we fall asleep, she won't get a sore back. I look over to the back door, seeing splashes coming from the pool.

I smile as I walk out and see her jump into the pool. "Hey," I say to Roxanne, the babysitter, who is sitting on the side of the pool watching her. My parents just left after spending the past two weeks here. I hated to see them leave, but I know in a couple of weeks I'll be with them for the rest of the summer.

"Hi." She smiles at me. Roxanne has been with me for the past six years. My mother hired her when she came down, and she is the one who watches Penelope when I travel and for home games.

"Is she tired?" I ask, and she just smiles. I know she's probably running on fumes at this point. "You can take off now," I urge her, and she gets up, walking inside.

"Daddy," Penelope squeals when she comes up from under the water, "did you see my jump?"

"I did." I kick off my shoes and socks and walk over to the side of the pool, putting my feet in while she goes around in circles. "Did you pack your things for the lake?"

She looks over at me and just smiles. "No." She shakes her head. "I thought you said we would do it together."

"No," I remind her, "I gave you a list of everything you needed to pack."

She laughs. "I forgot," she lies to me, and she smiles. "But we can do it together."

"Fine," I huff. "I was talking to Xavier, and he invited us to go to the beach," I inform her, and her eyes light up even more. "You didn't want to go to the beach, did you?" I get up, standing by the pool as she comes over to the steps.

She walks up the steps, leaking water everywhere. "I do, I do."

"Good, because we leave in two days."

"Yay!" She jumps into my arms like she always does, and I catch her, my shirt soaked from her. "Thank you, thank you, thank you." She kisses me on the cheek every single time she says thank you. She wraps her arms around me. "Is Parker going to be there?" She mentions Cooper's daughter who she is always with.

"She is," I confirm as she wiggles out of my arms. "Let's go pack."

She holds out her hand for me. "Can we have pizza?" she asks at the same time as she puts her hand in mine and looks up at me. Her blue eyes sparkle as her hair drips all over the place. "Can we build sandcastles?" I walk her over to the chair where her towel is. She lets my hand go to wrap the towel around her. "Can we do mermaid tails?"

All I know is I would give her my whole world. "We

can do whatever you want," I tell her, leaning down and kissing her nose.

"Is Abigail going to come also?" she asks, and I look at her.

"I think so." I think about the picture I saved earlier today of the three of us. " That would be nice," I tell her, but she just ignores me and walks inside, leaving me with my own thoughts. "Yes, that would be nice."

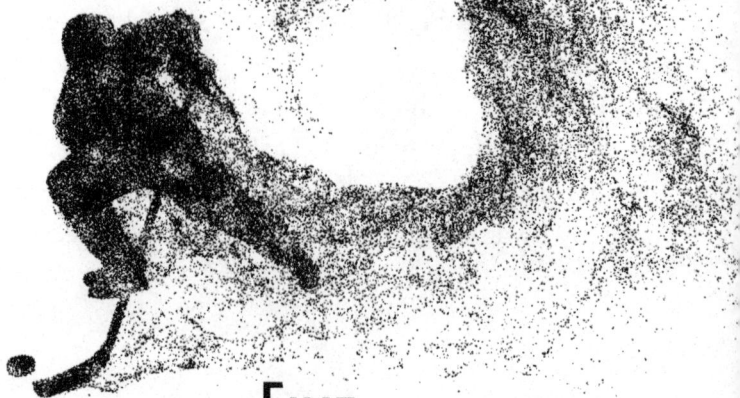

FIVE

ABIGAIL

"THE CAR IS going to be here in ten minutes," Gabriella yells from her bedroom. "Which means we have nine minutes to get downstairs."

I huff as I zip closed the suitcase. "Or we can get downstairs before the car gets here and be early," I yell back at her as I pull my luggage off the bed and onto the floor. I push it toward the door and it stops right at the door.

"You are already a buzzkill," Gabriella accuses from my bedroom doorway. "This is a vacation, which means we go on island time."

I can't help but laugh at her and look at her outfit. She's wearing cream-colored yoga shorts and a yoga bra with an open, white linen button-down top, with white sneakers, "I'm not a buzzkill. I'm just saying it would be nice if we…" I toss my earphones into my blue Christian Door purse. "And by we, I mean you, were on time."

She huffs at me, "You know there are like a million people going, right?" She puts her hands on her hips. "And you know it takes a good hour for us to even load up the plane."

"Which is why we are leaving forty minutes later than everyone," I point out to her, "but we should still be ready when the car gets here."

She throws up her hands. "I'm ready." She looks me up and down. "Are you ready?"

"What is wrong with what I'm wearing?" I look down at blue jean shorts and my oversized gray-and-white striped linen shirt, tied loosely at the waist, and the sleeves rolled up to my elbows.

"Nothing if you aren't trying to pick up anyone," she says, turning and walking back to her bedroom.

"We are going on a plane with our family members!" I shout at her retreating back. "Who the fuck am I trying to pick up?"

She looks over her shoulder at me. "The pilot."

"Who could be a woman." I can't let her have the last word, obviously.

"Don't forget to pack condoms," she fights back with words. "Wouldn't want you to get knocked up on your first try."

"You are such a bitch," I tell her, and she just smirks.

"Takes one to know one." She holds her arms over her head and puts her hands together in the shape of a heart.

"Why are you even living in my house?" I ask, and

all she does is laugh at me. I grab my Dior bag and then carry my luggage downstairs. "Four minutes," I yell and hear wheels rolling across the floor. Gabriella comes out of her room with one suitcase in front of her and another behind her.

"I'm coming," she declares, getting to the top of the stairs, picking up one bag, and carrying it down before walking back up and repeating it for the next one. When she finally gets back down the stairs, she is panting.

She walks over to the fridge, grabbing a bottle of water. "You are bringing two suitcases?" I ask her. She just nods while she drinks half the bottle of water as if she just worked out for an hour instead of twenty-six stairs.

"Remember the last time I brought one suitcase and I was missing all sorts of stuff?" She looks at me, and I just shake my head. "This time, I brought backup plans." She points at me. "And I'm not sharing."

"Fine by me," I walk to the door when I hear someone in the driveway. "I'm planning on being in my bikini all day and having one outfit per night."

"Same," she agrees, coming to me, and I just look at her. "Okay, fine, I will go to breakfast in one outfit and then bikini and then dinner." I tilt my head to the side, and she throws her hands up, "Okay, I have outfits in case there is someone I need to impress." I just laugh at her. "Let's go." She ushers past me. "We are going to be late." She stops mid-step. "I'll bring my camera,"

I walk out after her, and the heat hits me right away. "It's so hot," I mumble as I close the door behind me but then rush back in to make sure I closed and locked everything. I jog up the steps to Gabriella's room, seeing it in a total mess. But I just walk toward the bathroom, making sure she didn't leave anything on. I do a quick sweep and then walk back out, closing and locking the door.

I see the black car with the trunk already closed and the driver waiting for me by the door. He opens the back door for me as I slide in. "Did you go back and make sure I didn't leave anything on in my bathroom?" Gabriella asks, looking up from her phone.

"No," I lie to her, and she just laughs.

"Maury said that's a lie," she jokes with me. "You forget." She turns and continues on her phone. "I know you better than you know yourself." I'm about to say something to her when she just looks over at me and smiles so big it fills her whole face. "Also, I was ready before you." I snicker. "Was I not in the car before you while you did what you did?"

I don't bother answering her while I buckle my seat belt and the car starts moving. My phone beeps in my purse. I open my bag, grabbing it and looking down to see that Christopher texted the family chat.

Christopher: *I'm on the plane.*

Gabriella: *Congratulations, you have activated Squid Games.*

I snort out.

Christopher: *It feels like Hunger Games on this plane.*

Me: *How many people are left to board?*

Christopher: *No one, we are closing the doors now.*

Your boarding pass has been canceled.

"He's hilarious," Gabriella says to me while her fingers go nuts.

Gabriella: *Good, so we'll fly in our own plane. Bottom line, you still lose.*

Christopher: *I really think our family needs to stop producing children. It's like the Gremlins in here.*

Me: *You were one of those Gremlins at one point.*

Dylan: *Did you just call my kids Gremlins?*

Gabriella: *He did*

Me: *You should kick his ass.*

Alex: *I thought I left this group chat.*

Me: *Dylan added you back in.*

Alex has left the group chat

Dylan has added Alex back to the group.

Me: *You can run, but we'll find you.*

I toss my phone back in my bag when the car stops, and I look over to see the huge charter plane waiting. The stainless-steel stairs are pushed up against the door, which is open. I see four cars in front of us as various people get out of them. The porters are there with luggage carts unloading the trunks of the cars.

I open the door and step out, squinting with the sun hitting me in the eye. I slam the car door shut at the same time as Gabriella does. "You guys are late," my uncle Matthew declares, coming over to us.

"How are we the ones late when there are four other cars here at the same time?" I ask him as I walk over to him and give him a hug. "Oh, Uncle Matthew, Gabriella wants to know if there will be condoms given out in our room." I look over at Gabriella, whose eyes go big. "She really wants to be safe."

Matthew looks at me and then at Gabriella. "I thought after I survived Zara and Zoe, I would be safe from having a heart attack." He looks at Gabriella. "She's joking, right?"

"About having safe sex?" Gabriella replies. "Absolutely, it's so much better playing Russian roulette with my ovaries."

I can't help but laugh out loud as Matthew's vein in his forehead goes bigger. "Get on the plane," he grits between clenched teeth

We walk away laughing, stopping when we come face-to-face with Dylan. "Why are you late?" I look over at him, and he just laughs.

"This isn't our first rodeo," he reminds, as Alex looks at Maddox and says something to him. He's wearing blue shorts with a white shirt, a Stanley Cup baseball hat turned backward, pushing his 'hockey flow' hair back, and gold aviator sunglasses cover his eyes. He bends down and kisses her cheek. "I'll be fine, Mom." He smirks at her. "I'm going to hang with Christopher and Stefano."

"Absolutely not," Dylan declares, putting his hand on his hips, and I see they are dressed alike, just Dylan isn't wearing a hat.

"The legal drinking age on the island is eighteen, which means..." Maddox smirks at Dylan.

"Which means I'm going to be watching you like a hawk," Dylan warns him.

"You look like my father"—Alex tries not to laugh at Dylan and the way he stands there—"and Uncle Matthew all wrapped in one."

"Dad, what's the worst that can happen?" Maddox asks.

"One year, your father and Uncle Michael got so drunk your father fell asleep in the bathroom," I start to say, and Dylan just groans out. "I went to the bathroom and thought he was a home invader and kicked him right in the balls."

"Dad, you didn't?" Maddox says out loud, gasping.

"I was eighteen, and you should learn from me," he advises, and Maddox just shakes his head.

I walk toward Maddox. "I'll take care of him," I reassure, putting my arm around his waist. He places his hand around my neck, and we turn around and walk toward the stairs. "Would you go easy, please?"

He just laughs. "Always," he says, jogging up the steps to the plane. I walk up the steps, holding on as the wind now blows my hair across my face. I turn the other way when I get to the top, pushing it away from my face as I step into the plane.

"Hi," the flight attendant greets me with a smile. "Welcome aboard."

"Thank you," I reply, turning and looking into the plane. There are three seats on each side of the plane and even in the middle.

I look around, and my eyes find him right away. The minute I look at him, everything inside me stops as my head screams, *"What in the actual fuck?"* I try to get my heart beating a normal pace, but when he's around, it's very fucking hard for me. The sound of my heart beating erratically now echoes in my ears. I try to look around to make sure no one can see the internal freak-out I am having. I need to sit down before he sees me and talk myself off the ledge.

"Abigail." I hear Penelope say my name. I blink a couple of times and put on my game face. A face I've been perfecting for the past six years. From the first day I met him, there was something special about him. I just didn't know what it was. I was lucky enough to witness the first time they met. I saw magic happen before my eyes. He was scared shitless, but he also knew what he needed to do. His becoming the best dad I've ever seen made me fall more and more in love with him.

Penelope gets up and comes over to me, hugging me around my waist. I smile down at her. "Well, what do we have here?" I ask her as she puts her head back and looks at me.

"We are coming with you," she says and then grabs my hand. "Do you want to sit with me?"

I look up, seeing Tristan's blue eyes watching us. "Of course," I agree, faking it. I mean, not faking that I want to sit with her but faking that I'm happy about it. There is absolutely nothing I wouldn't do for her. She owns half my heart, and sadly her father owns the other side, and the best thing is, he has no clue either. No one does. I've been perfecting masking my feelings for the past six years. To be honest, the only one who has homed in on it has been Gabriella, who has been sworn to twin secrecy.

I walk down the aisle smiling and stopping to kiss my grandparents before walking two rows farther toward Tristan, who is now standing in the aisle. "Hi," he greets me, smiling, and I don't know why I expect him to lean in and kiss my cheek. But he doesn't, which then makes me wish he had.

"Hi," I say to him, putting on a smile. "This is a nice surprise." I try not to stutter as my mouth goes dry.

"Yeah, we decided at the last minute," he shares as I look at him. *A little warning would be nice,* my head says to itself.

"Can I sit at the window?" Penelope asks, walking into the row, sitting down, and looking out the window. "Abigail, sit next to me."

I smile at her. "There isn't anywhere else I wanted to sit anyway." I look over at Tristan, who just looks at me. I tuck the hair behind my ear, putting my bag in the overhead bin.

I step into the aisle and sit in the middle seat, telling myself the minute I can escape, I'm going to. I sit in the middle seat and grab the seat belt when I feel him sit next to me. The smell of his aftershave makes my stomach flutter. I can feel him looking at me, but I tell myself he's looking at Penelope, and I'm just in the way.

I buckle my seat belt, ignoring the pull to look back at him and instead look at Penelope. "This is going to be a great week," I say, feeling that I'm two seconds away from throwing up.

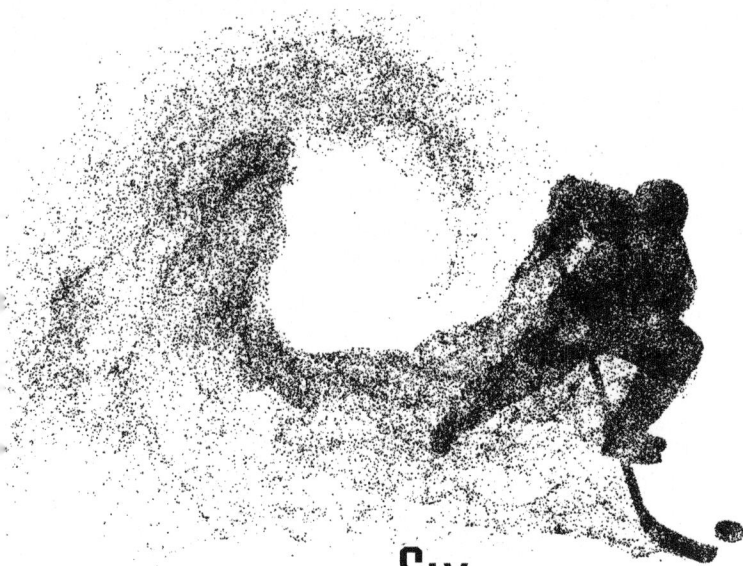

Six

I SIT NEXT to Abigail and buckle my seat belt, ignoring how my heart is pounding. Ignoring the way my eyes fly to her legs. Ignoring my head yelling at me not to look at her. But I fail at it all, and I turn to watch her. She looks at Penelope. "This is going to be a great week," she says, and I have to slow down the nerves that have now worked their way from my stomach to my throat.

I've been on the ice with the biggest and baddest there are. I've even been in some fights in the middle of the ice, but it's nothing compared to how nervous I am as soon as I see Abigail.

The whole night I tried to tell myself that going on this trip was a bad idea, but then the other side of my brain would tell me what a great fucking idea it was. It was a fucking nightmare, I barely slept.

Did I walk on the plane and immediately look for her? Yes. Did I immediately get disappointed she wasn't here? Yes. Did I ask if she was coming? No. Did I sit down and watch the door like a hawk? Yes. Did I see her walking toward the plane with Maddox as they smiled at each other and think she's gotten even more beautiful in the past two days? Yes. Did I wish I could tell her? So much yes.

"Anyone need a tissue?" Christopher asks from five rows over, laughing. He looks around the plane, and I see a couple of people snickering when he spots me. "Tristan, you good?" he asks, and my heart sinks, thinking he knows how I feel for his sister.

I lean over. "What's happening?" I ask under my breath.

"Every time someone new joins the family, they cry when they meet my grandfather," she fills me in. "Started with Wilson and then Xavier."

"So as soon as you marry into the family, you start crying?" I ask her, joking, and she can't help but throw her head back and laugh. I picture leaning in and kissing her lips, but the image quickly evaporates from my head when I hear Dylan.

"Regret coming yet?" he asks, and I just shake my head. *I might regret it at the end of the week,* I think to myself, *but not yet.* He slaps my shoulder before walking two rows back and then sitting down in the seat, waiting for Alex to join him. She stops to kiss her grandfather and grandmother before making her way to Dylan.

"It's not always like this," Abigail shares from beside

me, and I turn to look at her. She sits with her head back on the rest, and the way the sun is coming in, it hits her eyes and makes them even lighter.

I laugh a little. "I've been around them for the past six years," I remind her. "If I were going to run away, it would have been way before now." I lean back in my chair, folding my arms over my chest. "Besides, your family has been nothing but supportive and by my side this whole time."

"Oh my." I hear from the aisle and turn to see Gabriella. Even though she and Abigail are identical twins, I can tell them apart. Abigail has a bigger smile than Gabriella, and her eyes are warmer than Gabriella. Abigail also has one eye with a fleck of green in it. "I didn't know you were coming on the trip." She looks at me and then looks at Abigail. "Fun." She continues walking toward the back.

Matthew gets on the plane next, followed by Max, as they start doing a head count. I close my eyes for a second, and when I open them some forty minutes later, the plane door is shut, and I look over and see Penelope and Abigail are coloring together.

She smiles at Penelope, and my heart feels like it grows tenfold in my chest. She tucks her hair behind her ear, something she always does. Something she isn't doing to be sexy, but it just is. I take one long look at her before I turn around and tell myself, yet again, this is a bad idea.

This family has helped me from day one, and what do I do? I am lusting over one of their family members.

They invited me in, and all I can do is sit here thinking about Abigail in ways I should not be thinking about her.

"If you want to rest," Abigail starts, looking up at me from her coloring page, "I can watch Penelope." I don't say anything because the words are all jumbled in my throat. All the words that want to come out are me telling her that she is beautiful or she smells amazing or I want to kiss her. "I know that the last couple of days have been hectic, and from what I've been hearing, not many people got much rest."

"It wasn't that bad." I watch her color the paper and then show Penelope, who smiles at her and shows her the picture she's doing.

"I didn't even attend all the events you did, and I ended up getting sick," she informs me, and I am worried for her.

"What happened?" I ask, my tone going softer than I want it to.

"Nothing major, I just think with the whole moving and then not sleeping when I should've been sleeping, and then partying, I was burning the candle at both ends, and I got sick," she says as if it's nothing. I want to ask her what kind of sick she was. I want to ask her if she is okay right now.

"Do you need anything?" I start to unfasten my seat belt, ready to get up and make sure I can get her something. "I think I have water," I say, leaning forward and grabbing the black backpack I always bring when we travel.

She puts her hand on my arm, and I swear to God,

my whole body zaps to life. I haven't touched or been with anyone in the six years since I became a dad. My dating life was put on the back burner. Then every single time I tried to put myself out there, there was always something missing, or better yet, they weren't Abigail. "I'm okay," she assures me, and Penelope looks at the bag in my hand.

"Dad, can I have the iPad?" she asks, and as much as I don't want to pull my arm away from her touch, I have no choice. "Do you want to watch *Encanto* with me?" She looks at Abigail.

"Why don't we leave Abigail to rest," I redirect, and Abigail just laughs.

"I love *Encanto*," Abigail says. Her eyes light up as she sings, "We don't talk about Bruno."

I chuckle as I pass the iPad to Penelope and then hand her the small white square AirPod case, "You have one," Penelope says, handing her an earbud and then putting it in her own ear. I lean back and close my eyes, just to rest them, and the next thing I know, the plane is touching down, and applause fills the air.

I blink open my eyes and look over and see Abigail with her hand over Penelope's shoulder as they look out the window. "Daddy," Penelope says, her eyes bright, "we saw the crystal-blue water, and Abigail said it looked like our eyes." She points at the same eyes we both have.

I smile at her and then look over at Abigail, who just smiles at me. "Did you sleep well?"

"I guess so." I take off the baseball hat on my head, putting it on my knee before running my hands through my hair. As soon as I hear the ping for the seat belts, the whole plane basically springs to action.

I look over at Abigail, who holds the iPad as she hands it to me. "Thank you," I say, grabbing the iPad and then the black bag to put it back in. I get up from my seat and stand, stretching before I feel Penelope next to me.

"Daddy, can we go to the beach today?" she asks, and all I can do is lean down and kiss her head.

"We better," I reply, smiling at her and then looking over at Abigail standing up and trying to get her bag out of the overhead bin. I don't even think about it before I'm leaning forward over her, her back to my front, as I reach over her to grab her bag. "I got it." I look down at her as she looks up, and I suddenly realize how close I am to her.

"Um," she stutters, "thanks." She turns and quickly walks away from me. I swallow down the embarrassment of my cock being so hard. The minute I leaned over her and felt her ass on my cock, it was just like the switch was turned on, and my cock was ready for whatever was coming its way.

I place her bag in front of me, hiding my cock in case someone looks at me. God, this is going to be a long fucking week. My eyes are stuck to her ass as she walks in front of me, which makes my cock even harder if that was possible.

We slowly start to leave the plane. It's so bright I have to close one eye when I step out onto the stainless steel. Abigail holds on to the railing with one hand and never lets go of Penelope's hand.

As soon as I step foot on the tarmac, I look over and see three huge buses waiting for us. "Holy…" I say, putting my hand in front of my eyes to block the sun. "This is quite the production."

I look over and see Dylan is next to me. "It might look like it's madness, but it's actually a well-oiled machine."

My eyebrows pinch together, confused. "Trust me," he reassures, putting his arm around my shoulders and trying not to laugh. "You are going to hear some yelling, and someone is going to swear at least five times." I look over and see Matthew throwing up his hands in the air.

I also see most of the women are on one side, ushering the kids onto a bus and out of the sun. My eyes find Penelope, who is now holding hands with Emma and Parker. "Don't worry, the kids get on one bus where there is food and snacks," Dylan informs me.

The porters are in the back of the plane, grabbing the luggage as they load them onto a trolley and then drive it over to the buses. I make my way over to the bus I saw Penelope walk into. The door opens when I get close enough, and the air-conditioning hits me right away. I walk up the steps of the same bus we use when we are at away games. I scan the seats looking for Penelope and see her sitting with Parker.

Erika and Alex are sitting behind him, and of course, my eyes roam the rest of the bus looking for the other woman I always seek out, who sits in the row across from Penelope with Gabriella.

I sit in front of the bus, watching the madness outside. I grab the bottle of water from one of the trays beside me with the snacks, putting Abigail's bag on my lap, being careful not to lose it.

Forty minutes later, we are pulling up to the hotel or, as I'm told, a private resort. When the bus stops, I get up, walk out of the bus, and make sure the kids don't run off. A woman and a man are holding a clipboard each.

"Name?" the woman asks.

"Tristan and Penelope Weise," I reply. She smiles at me and hands me an envelope with two key cards inside, suite number eight written on the front. "Thank you," I say, nodding at her and then calling, "Penelope." She turns over toward me. "Come on." I motion with my head and she skips over to me.

"Your luggage will be delivered to your room within the next thirty minutes," the woman says to me. "If you walk through the lobby and toward the back, you will find signs on how to get to your room." I look around at everyone grabbing their own card.

"Let's go get changed, and we can meet everyone at the beach," I tell Penelope as we walk into the lobby and then see the big buffet area where the meals are served. Three signs are telling you which way rooms are. Walking past the massive pool, over a little bridge, I make my way over to number eight. Each numbered hut looks like its own personal house.

I stop at the big brown door with the number eight on it. "Are you ready?" I ask her, taking a key card out and sliding it over the sensor near the door handle. The click allows me to turn the handle and push open the door.

I hold the door on top while holding Abigail's bag

in my hand. Penelope walks in and shrieks, "Daddy, there is a pool in front of our back door!" She walks into the room, and I step in with her. A living room area faces a wall of windows. "Can we go into the pool?" She jumps up and down as I place my bag on the couch and Abigail's next to mine.

I open the back door and see the pool she was talking about is really the ocean. I slide open the door and walk out onto the patio, seeing that every single room has its own patio leading to stairs that take you straight into the ocean. "That isn't a pool. It's the ocean," I inform her.

I take a second to look around and hear a commotion coming from the patio beside us. "It's open." I hear, and then I see her walking out, the wind picking up as her hair flies around her head.

"Shit," I mutter under my breath, of course she would be in the room next to us. She must feel me staring at her because she looks over at me, and her eyes go big. "Hi." I hold up my hand, now counting the days until we can leave.

Seven

Abigail

I WALK OUT of the glass patio door, and the heat hits me right away. I can't help but smile when I see the patio has two lounge chairs facing the crystal-blue water. The sound of the water hits the side stairs that lead directly into the shallow ocean.

The warm wind suddenly blows my hair into my face as I turn my face toward it to push back my hair. I can feel eyes on me, and when I look over, I see the one man I've been trying to get away from. My whole body has been on alert from the time I sat down on the plane

My eyes go big, and I see him mutter something right before he puts up his hand. "Hi," he greets.

I automatically lift my arm up to wave back to him. "Hi." My heart speeds up, and it suddenly feels like it's going to come up to my mouth. *This is getting way out of hand*, I think to myself.

He snaps his fingers. "I have your bag," he says, turning and walking back inside. I put my hand on the railing, my head falling forward as I try to calm myself down.

"What in the hell?" I say. I'm about to turn around to call for Gabriella when I hear creaking coming from beside me. I look over and see him walking over to me, holding my bag in his hand. On the plane, the minute I reached out to grab it, I felt him behind me, and I swear to God, my body felt like it was going to go off. I thought for sure he would see the way my nipples perked up for him. Just looking down at myself, I felt my face turn a beet red. I literally felt like I was on fire. I couldn't even look over at him. I hightailed it off that plane and then into the first bus with all the kids, thinking I had somehow escaped him. But the door opened, and he walked onto the bus, and I literally yelled out, "What the fuck?" So I stayed back and let all the kids walk off the bus, then quietly slipped out of the bus and walked over to the guy holding a clipboard. The whole family was trying to gather up their kids and figure out what to do, and I had already secured my key and was making my way to my room with Gabriella.

I push off from the patio and walk over to the right, where the patio is separated by a little empty space. He leans over and hands it to me. "There you go." He smiles at me, and all I can do is nod at him.

"Thank you, I didn't even realize I didn't have it." I chuckle nervously, then hear the patio door slide open in behind me.

"Holy crap," Gabriella says, walking out onto the patio, "look at this view." It takes her a minute to look over and see us. "Oh, well, hello, neighbor." She holds up her hand.

"I was returning her bag," Tristan explains to Gabriella, who smiles and nods at him.

"I'm ready," Penelope announces, coming out of the house. "I need sunscreen." She looks over and comes over to see us. "Dad said we can go to the beach."

"That sounds like so much fun. Apparently," I say, putting my hand over my eyes, "they said that if you walk around there." I point at the stairs and to the left. "It takes you to the big beach."

"Oh, good to know," Tristan says. "Let me go get changed, and we can go to the beach. Come on, let's get some sunscreen on you before anything." He puts his hand on Penelope's head as they turn and walk back into their villa.

I take a second before looking over at Gabriella, who just looks at me rolling her lips, trying not to laugh as she folds her hands over her chest. "We need to move," I inform her, not giving her a chance to laugh in my face.

I walk past her, back inside our two-bedroom villa, which I think is exactly the same as Tristan's. I close the door, walking over to the big welcome basket in the middle of the living room table. I grab the bottle of champagne as the door slides open again. "Oh dear," Gabriella says while I peel off the foil and untwist the little wire that holds the cork down. I throw it on the table and then pop the cork, bringing the green bottle to my lips when it starts to pour out. "So we aren't using glasses?" Gabriella just walks over to the single couch and sits down, crossing her legs as she looks at me.

I gulp as much as I can before the gas, and the bubbles feel like they're going to come out of my nose. "I don't know who we need to call, but we can't stay here." I wipe my mouth with the back of my hand.

"What would you like us to tell Uncle Matthew?" Gabriella put one hand on the couch before she decides to get up and grab a glass of champagne for herself. She holds out the glass, waiting for me to pour her some. I pour her as much as I can before it bubbles over. "Hey, Uncle Matthew." She takes a sip. "We are going to have to change places because Abigail is secretly in love with Tristan, and it's going to be really hard for her not to stick her face to the wall and try to listen to him sleep."

I can only glare at her. "One, I would never press my face against the wall." I take a sip of the champagne. "And two, I'm not secretly in love with anyone."

"So are you openly in love with him?" She finishes off her glass of champagne as I flip her the bird. "That's what I thought." She holds out the glass for another refill. "Or here is a stupid idea." She just grabs the bottle from me. "How about you tell him how you feel?"

I gasp, "Are you insane? I am never ever going to tell him how I feel. Telling you was the biggest mistake of my life." She just laughs at me.

"I knew how you felt even before you knew," she teases, putting the bottle of champagne down. I'm about to answer her when there is a knock on the door.

"Don't answer that," I whisper, and she just looks at me.

"He knows we are here," she states, walking over to the door, and I sit down on the couch. "Thank you so much." I hear Gabriella say. "I can take that," she says, and I hear the door close and then the sound of wheels over the tiled floor. "It was our luggage." I breathe out a sigh of relief, getting up. "Are you sure you are going to be okay?" She is the only one who knows how I feel about Tristan. It's not like I told her. She sort of guessed it one day. She didn't guess right away, and that was only because we didn't live together.

But the minute she came to town for Christmas and came with me to volunteer at the hospital, it was almost as if she knew right away. It's a twin thing, just like I know there is a reason she moved to Dallas, and it's not because she got bored with LA. I thought I held the secret really tight, but then when he was in the same room with us, it took her point one second to guess. She didn't out me right in front of him. No, she waited until we were alone, where I couldn't hide from her. The minute she guessed, it was almost as if the dam broke, and I finally admitted what I was hiding. She sat there and then put her arm around me when I sobbed, knowing there was no way I would ever do anything about my feelings.

That weekend I decided it was just a crush, and I pushed back my feelings. Every single time I would see him, I would tell myself I didn't really like him that way. I would tell myself it was all in my head, and then two minutes in the same room as him, and I felt like a stalker. I would look over at him all the time. But then I somehow convinced myself it was because I was just drawn to Penelope and not her father. Besides, there is no way my feelings will go anywhere. He will never see me like that. I mean, surely, he didn't see me like anything besides the girl who helped his daughter get better. Then I became the younger sister of his friend. Then I slowly got into the lane of a family friend, where apparently I'm still at.

"Yes," I say, more confident than I actually feel. "It'll be fine. I'm sure he'll be hanging with the guys anyway."

"Why don't we get into our suits," Gabriella says, "grab a couple of cocktails, and go lounge by the pool?"

I clap my hands, getting up, and know this is the exact distraction I need. "That sounds wonderful," I agree, walking over to my suitcase. I wheel it into one of the bedrooms, and riffle through it until I can find the top and the bottom. I slip out of my shorts and into my white bikini. Grabbing a white linen button-down shirt as a cover-up, I walk into the living room, seeing Gabriella come out of her room with a black bikini. "Ready?"

We walk out of the villa and head back to the pool, finding it empty. "Where is everyone?" Gabriella asks, turning around and then looking down the pathway to the sand. "Ah, at the beach."

"Might as well just go there," I say to her as we walk around the pool toward the pathway to the beach. I can hear music and noise as soon as we take a couple more steps toward the beach.

"I forgot my camera," Gabriella says, "I'll meet you at the beach." She turns around and heads back to the villa. Turning, I make my way toward the beach, my feet sinking into the hot sand as soon as I step onto it.

I take a look around, seeing there are about twenty daybeds all lined up in four rows facing the beach. A tiki bar is set up next to the water, with Franny and Erika waiting for drinks. The kids are running around the beds, heading toward the water and then running back.

Lounge chairs are scattered around the beach. As I make my way down to one of the beds, I see my mother. "Hey," I greet her, sitting down on the side of it as she lies next to my father.

"Where is Gabriella?" My mother looks at me and then looks back at the villa.

"She forgot her camera," I inform them. I'm about to get up to go get a drink when I hear my name being called.

Looking up, I can't help but smile when I see Penelope coming toward me. "Abigail," she huffs as she holds a plastic shovel in her hand. "Will you come and help me build a castle?" Her eyes light up even brighter, and there is nothing I wouldn't do for this kid.

"Ohhh." I shrug off my shirt. "I love building castles," I tell her as I get up and hold out my hand for her.

"Daddy is waiting for us," she says, and I look up to see him standing there wearing a pair of swim shorts and nothing else. I really wish he didn't look so good in everything!

"Hey," he says when I walk down close enough to him, "I'm really sorry." I tilt my head to the side as Penelope runs off to grab a pail. "I told her to leave you alone."

I smile at him. "It's okay. I love spending time with her. Why don't you go and spend some time with the boys?"

"No way." He shakes his head. "I'm not letting you guys have all the fun." I can't help but laugh as I walk over to where all the plastic pails are. I look down and then up when I feel him staring at me. "Sorry." He shakes his head, chuckling, then looks back up at me. "I really like your laugh."

Eight

Tristan

"NO WAY." I shake my head at her. "I'm not letting you guys have all the fun." She throws her head back and laughs, and I swear it's like music to my ears. It's the best sound I think I've ever heard after "I love you, Daddy." I can't help but watch her as she walks over to the plastic pails. She looks up and catches me staring at her, and I have to think of a reason that doesn't sound dumb. "Sorry." I shake my head chuckling, looking down at the pails, then looking back up at her. "I really like your laugh." The minute the words come out of my mouth, I want to groan and kick myself in the ass. I could have said anything else, *anything else*. I could have said literally anything else, but the truth came out. "It's a pretty laugh."

She nods her head. "I've never been told I have a

pretty laugh before." She bends over and grabs a pail and I, for some stupid dumb reason, watch her every move. She bends down, and the white bikini bottom rides up her ass cheeks. My mouth waters as I take her in, and I wish I was wearing my sunglasses so I could ogle her without anyone catching me. "How are your castle-building skills?" She stands, looking at me.

"On a scale of what?" I walk over and grab my own pail.

"Of one to ten," she states as she takes the heel of her foot and makes a square in the sand.

"Negative one," I tell her as I just watch her. "What about you?" She looks up at me. "You look like a professional."

She laughs. "Not sure what you think a professional is." She finishes doing the square. "But I have had some practice with Emma and Mia."

Penelope comes running over. "What are we doing?" She looks at me and then at Abigail.

"Well, Abigail has built castles before," I say, pointing at her, "and she was going to tell us how to do it."

"Really?" Penelope asks with her eyes big.

"Yes," Abigail confirms and looks at my daughter. "Do you think you have what it takes to make the best sandcastle in the world?"

"Yes," Penelope assures her and looks over at me. "Do you think you have what it takes?"

"I think I'm going to try my best and hope that I do." I put my hands on my hips, looking back over at Abigail. "Okay, what do we need to do?"

"There are five steps to making the best sandcastle out there," she starts, and I roll my lips. She points the shovel at me. "I googled it." I hold up both my hands. "Step one I already did," she says, pointing down to the square she did with her foot. "This is how big our castle is going to be." She looks at Penelope, who just nods. "Step two." She smiles. "We get to make a huge pile of sand." She gets on her knees and fills up her bucket. "Then put it in the circle. We can use buckets or even our hands, but we need to get a huge mountain."

"We can do that," I say, looking at Penelope. "How about you fill them, and I carry them." She gets on her knees and fills her pail as I fill my own. We do this for I don't even know how long, but when I look over, we have a decent-sized mountain.

"Is that enough?" Penelope asks as she stands by the mountain.

"That looks good to me," Abigail praises. "Ready for step three?"

"Yes." Penelope claps her hands, jumping up and down. "We are so close."

"We are going to have to add water to the mountain," Abigail explains to us. "This way, the sand will become thick like concrete, and we will be able to make a nice foundation for the castle." She walks to the crystal water and grabs a bucket of water, coming back over and pouring it in the middle. We both follow her to the water, the warm liquid running over our feet as we step in a bit to grab the water. I carry both the pails as we run back and forth to our mountain, and at one point, I stop, and

Abigail looks over at me.

"What's wrong?" she asks, and I laugh.

"It looks like a pile of shit," I tell her, and she looks over at the mountain that is now half the size because of the water.

"It does, doesn't it?" She laughs. "But now comes step four. We start creating the castle."

"How?" Penelope asks.

"That is the fun part," she says, walking up to the mound and getting on her knees while she pats it down. "We play pancake until it's level."

Penelope walks up to her, and she talks quietly to her as I watch. She has always been good to Penelope. Even before I knew she was my daughter, it was Abigail sitting beside her bed, making sure she was never alone, out of the pureness of her heart. I walk over to them, getting beside Abigail as I watch her. My hands now mimic hers as we build the foundation of the castle. Our hands touch each other as we pat down the sand. My whole body fills with feeling from her little touch. I'm trying not to overthink it when I hear her say, "Now, how about we add some steps?" Penelope just nods as she shows her how to do a step. "Now your turn," she tells Penelope, who does her own step. "Now it's Dad's turn." She smiles at me.

I move over, making the longest step for the bottom. "Well, we have steps." She claps her hands. "Now, let's make a couple of towers." She gets up, and Penelope follows her as they make four corner towers.

I can't help but watch how effortlessly she is doing

this. Not caring that her bathing suit is getting dirty. Not caring she is spending all her time with my girl and me. Not caring about anything else, only focusing on making sure she finishes this castle. She gets up and grabs a pail of sand, and then turns it upside down on the foundation. We work side by side the whole time as we put in more towers. I lean down to grab the pail at the same time she does, and our hands touch again. "I've got it," I tell her, and she moves her hand away. "So are we on step five?"

She laughs at me. "That is the fun of this. We have already worked into step five," she tells me. "We just have to shape things."

"It's hot," Penelope complains, getting up and looking at the water. She walks over and I think she will rinse off her hands. After a minute, I look over and see Penelope is in the water with the other girls.

"Penelope!" I call her name. "Stay where I can see you."

"I've got her," Xavier assures, walking past me toward the water with Vivienne behind him. "You two can continue to play in the sand."

"Just watch my daughter while I build her a sandcastle," I huff, turning back and looking at Abigail. "It's okay. You can go and grab a drink or whatever, and I'll finish the rest."

"Um, not on my watch." She shakes her head. "Although, I will go and get us something to drink, but I'm invested now." She puts down her pail. "What do you want to drink?"

"Get me what you are having," I tell her, "and a bottle

of water."

"Got it." She brushes the sand off her hands as she turns and walks over to the tiki bar. Her ass is on fucking point, and my cock starts to rise. I look around to make sure no one is looking at me before I walk back into the water and beg my dick to go down. When I see her coming back holding two white drinks in her hands with umbrellas, I almost groan. Not only is her ass on point, but I'm pretty sure her tits can fit perfectly in my hands.

I think about walking out of the water, but my cock is still awake, and I can't do anything to shield him. "Tomorrow, I'm wearing bigger shorts," I mumble as Abigail stops by the sand castle. Opening her arm, I see a water bottle fall from her arm to the sand. She walks into the water toward me with the drink in her hand.

"Here you go." She hands me one of the drinks, and I look down at the slush inside the glass.

"What's this?" I ask before I take a sip from the straw.

"It's a double pina colada," she states, squatting down in the water in front of me as she takes her own sip. "Nothing says vacation quite like a coconut drink."

"I guess so," I agree, taking another sip.

"You don't like it?" she asks, and I just shrug. "It's an acquired taste. I can take it off your hands if you want."

"No way." I shake my head. "Not after you slaved away over a sandcastle and then went to get me something to drink." I hold up the glass to salute her. "To the best sandcastle forewoman I know."

She can't help but throw her head back and laugh, and if that doesn't make my cock even harder. *What the fuck is wrong with me?* my head screams as I take another sip of the drink, trying to finish it fast so I don't have to drink it anymore.

"This is so peaceful," she observes as she turns around in the water, "almost like the calm before the storm."

I walk a bit farther out into the water, hoping she follows me. "What are your plans after this?" I ask her, and she slowly moves toward me, drinking another sip of her drink.

"I start work one day after we get back," she informs me, and I just stare at her.

"Where?" I ask her, shocked that I had no idea where she will be working. I knew she had just graduated from nursing school, but no one mentioned where she would be working.

"I got a job in the pediatric unit at Mercy Hospital," she says, and I just look at her with my mouth hanging open.

"Holy shit, that's amazing. I knew you had moved to Dallas, but I had no idea where you would be going."

"There were a couple of places interested in me, but my heart was set on Mercy," she says, standing up and holding out her drink to me. "Can you hold this?" I reach out for her drink. "Don't drink any of it." She smirks at me as she takes the black elastic on her wrist and pins up her hair. I hand her back her drink when she reaches for it. "Thank you." She takes another sip. "What about you? What are your plans after this?"

"Go home," I say, looking over to make sure I see Penelope. She is with Xavier as he carries her on his shoulders into the deep water.

"So you are staying in Dallas?" she asks, and I shake my head.

"No, I meant go back home to Canada. I have a house in Muskoka, right on the lake. My parents don't live far from there so…" I tell her of the little lake cabin I have, and by little, it's a ten-bedroom house right on the lake. I love it so much. It's just so peaceful there.

"That sounds like so much fun." She smiles at me, and the need to kiss her is so much stronger than it's ever been before. The need to touch her and just be next to her is growing so much, it's only going to be a matter of time before I ruin it all by admitting to her how I feel. I could never take advantage of her like that. I could never cross that line with her because she means so much to me, and the thought of losing her is just unbearable.

"It really is. I have a trainer there who comes over every day. I train in the morning, and then in the afternoon, it's either hiking, or I take Penelope fishing." I smile, thinking about how much fun we have there. "It's a dream, and it's so peaceful." I look at her. "You should come up sometime." The minute the words come out of my mouth, I want to take them back. Why the hell would I say that? It's not that I don't want her there, but I don't know how I can last living in the same house as her. "I mean, if you are ever in the area."

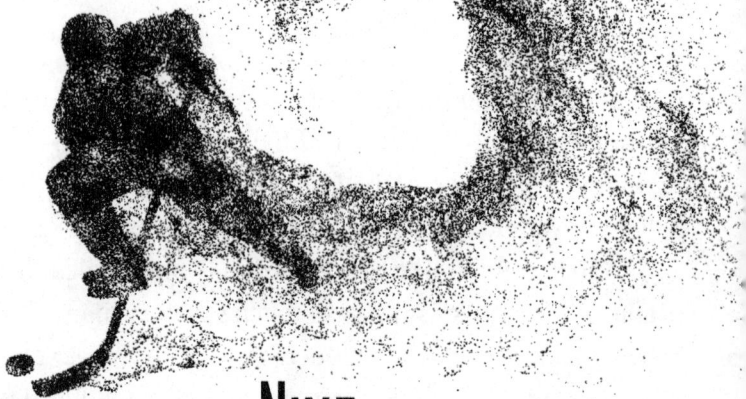

NINE

ABIGAIL

DID HE JUST invite me to go to his house in Canada? My brain screams at me as my mouth wants to ask, "When is a good day for you?" But instead, I take another small sip of my pina colada. "Your house sounds like a dream," I finally say, "and not going to lie, I might be a bit jealous of you missing the summer heat in Dallas."

He chuckles and takes a sip of his drink, and all I can do is wish I was a fucking plastic straw. This is insane. From the minute we started building the sandcastle together, my body has been on fire. I'm blaming the sun for it, but the truth is that it's all him. I want to climb him like a monkey climbs a tree, wrap my legs around him, and basically hump him to the ground. The thought of me humping him makes my head spin, and I stare into my drink to avoid him looking at me. If he knew what I was thinking right now he would be so grossed out.

"It'll be nice to get away from the heat," he confirms. "Not going to lie, we went back to Canada during the winter break, and I swear my blood has gotten thinner. I was frozen the whole time."

I can warm you up. The words almost slip out of my mouth, but I catch them just in time.

"Dad." I hear Penelope from behind me and look over at her. "Watch!" she yells as she stands up on Xavier's shoulders as he holds her ankles until she jumps off. Xavier takes two steps forward to make sure he can grab her. She smiles at Tristan and then swims over to us. "Did you see?"

"I did." He puts his hand out to grab her and pull her to him.

"Did I make a big splash?" she asks, and he lies to her.

"So big, I felt it here," he fibs, and then I just look at the two of them.

"I'm going to head out and take a nap. All this playing in the sun," I say, "it's rough."

"I'm not tired at all," Penelope declares to me, and I just laugh.

"The joys of being eight," I say and get up, walking out of the water and to one of the daybeds. I spot Gabriella sitting down with Erika, Franny, and Vivienne so I make my way over there.

"What did I miss?" I ask, grabbing a towel and wrapping it around my waist before looking around for a chair to drag over. I sit down in the shade, looking at Gabriella lounging on the daybed. Her camera is right next to her in her hand.

"I got a couple of candid shots of you guys building a sandcastle." She tells me, looking out toward the water. "I got a couple of good shots of Xavier tossing Penelope into the water also." She looks back at me as I lie down next to her. "We are having the welcome barbecue on the beach in two hours," Gabriella informs me.

"What time is it?" I ask them.

Erika presses the button on her phone before turning to me. "Five thirty."

"Oh my gosh, I just said I wanted to take a nap," I huff, knowing there isn't going to be enough time to nap.

"No rest for the wicked," Franny teases me as she looks over at Wilson, who is sitting on the sand with their daughter. "I need a snack." She gets up and puts her hand on her belly, which is starting to show. She announced at the beginning of the playoffs she couldn't drink because she was expecting.

"A food snack," Gabriella asks, "or his dick as a snack?"

"You are so crass," Franny chastises her, then turns. "Mom, can you watch the baby for me? I need Wilson to help me with something."

We burst out laughing as I get up and turn to Gabriella. "I'm going back to relax before dinner."

"Well, playing in the sand can make one tired," she taunts, and I just glare at her and then look at Erika, who rolls her lips.

"I know nothing. I see nothing." She puts up her hand.

"I remember a while back, a certain couple hooking

up on our family vacation one year." I point at her, and she laughs as she gets up.

"Best vacation of my life," she swears to me and then turns to call my cousin. "Cooper," he calls him, and he springs out of his chair, coming over to her. "Will you come in the water with me?"

"Anything for you," he says, grabbing her hand and walking with her into the water. I watch how he gets into the water, and she hugs him before placing her head on his shoulder. I take a second to look at Tristan, as I see him chatting with Xavier while Penelope plays close by. What I wouldn't give to have just one kiss from him. What I wouldn't give to have the love that any of my relatives have.

I turn away and walk back, rinsing my feet off as soon as I leave the beach. I walk into the room and head straight to the shower, washing off the sunscreen before I unpack my luggage. I walk out of my room, still wrapped in the towel, to grab a bottle of water and hear the shower coming from Gabriella's room.

I grab a white strapless bra with a white silky tank top that falls just under my boobs. I grab my long, blue flowy pants that fall straight to my ankles. The minute I walk, my legs poke out of the peekaboo slit that goes all the way up to the top of my thigh. I slip on a pair of black flip-flops before walking back into the bathroom to do something with my hair. I comb it and then shake it out, letting the air dry. I don't even bother putting on makeup because my face has a nice tan color.

Gabriella and I walk out of our rooms at the same

time and laugh because we are wearing the same thing. "I'm not changing." She laughs at me.

"It'll be fun. Think we can mess with people?" I tell her, "Take off the ring." I point at the gold and silver ring she wears on her index finger. "Fluff your hair a bit more." I walk over to her and touch up her hair a bit. We both raise our hands and touch each other's noses. "Boop," we say at the same time, turning and walking out of the door. The lights from the edge of the pathway make it very bright.

I take two steps when I turn and see Penelope coming out of her room with Tristan behind her. She wears pink shorts with a white shirt, and her hair is in a French braid. I smile as I watch Tristan walk behind her with his head down. He's wearing light orange shorts and a short-sleeved white button-down shirt. My stomach literally flips over as I see him run his hand through his hair. My mouth waters when I think of how it must feel to have his hair under my fingers. I wonder if it feels as silky as it looks. Gabriella stops walking as she looks over also. "Great timing," she mumbles, and Penelope looks up.

"Look." She turns around, showing us her back. "Dad did a French braid."

"Oh, jealous," Gabriella replies, and Tristan looks up at the same time that my eyes find his, and I quickly look back at Penelope.

"Hey, you two," Tristan greets us. "Nice outfits."

Gabriella laughs, and Penelope looks at her and then at me. "But can you tell us apart?" Gabriella asks, and he just smirks.

MADE FOR US

"You're Gabriella." He points at her. "And you're Abigail." We just look at him with our mouths hanging open.

"How in the H E double hockey sticks did you know?" I question him, and he just shrugs.

"It's easy," he just states. "What time is dinner?" He looks at his black Apple Watch on his wrist.

"Now," Gabriella says, turning to walk down the path while I walk next to Penelope, who slips her hand in mine.

No one really says anything. When we walk on the beach, picnic tables are set up everywhere, with about two hundred tiki lights all over the place, so it looks very bright. "Hey, you guys," my father says to us and looks at our outfits. "How are my girls?"

I whisper, "He doesn't know who is who." Tristan just looks over at me.

"I know who is who," my father defends, putting his hands on his hips, "but I'm not going to tell you. Go grab a plate and eat." He points at the long tables set up on the far right with silver platters on them and chefs standing behind them.

"Nice save, Daddy-o," I say, kissing his cheek. "Nice save."

"My dad knows who is who," Penelope tells him and then walks toward the tables with a chuckling Tristan behind her.

I just roll my lips as Gabriella folds her arms over her chest. "It wasn't even a question; he knew right away." She then looks at me. "I wonder how that could be."

79

"I'm getting food." I ignore her, trying not to even think about that question. Even though the whole time I was walking here I asked myself the same one. How did he know? How could he know?

I grab myself a plate of food. My head still going around in circles, I don't even notice when Penelope sits next to me, and Tristan sits next to her. I'm saved when Xavier and Vivienne join the table, so I don't really have to talk.

I look over as I see them setting up a bonfire in the middle of the beach off to the side. "What is that?" Penelope asks, and I look over and see the fire starting and they are preparing a small table beside it.

"Smores." I smile as I tell her and her eyes light up.

"Dad, can we get smores?" she asks, and he just nods at her. "Can we go?" She looks at me, asking me, and I get up and hold my hand out to her.

We make our way over as the kids all come running. I help a couple of the kids put their marshmallow on the long metal rods they provided. "Remember when we did this with sticks?" Dylan says from beside me, and we all laugh.

"One year, I think I ate a piece of stick," Michael remembers. "We didn't get the fancy stuff. We had to go grab a stick somewhere."

I can't help but laugh as Penelope comes running to me, and I see her marshmallow is still burning. "Help!" she shouts as Tristan walks over with his hands in his pockets. I blow out the marshmallow as she laughs, clapping her hands.

"Here you go," Tristan says as he holds a graham cracker with a piece of chocolate on it. I watch Penelope and Tristan do the smores, and she takes a bite of it, then turns to hand it to me so I can taste it.

I grab it from her and bite a piece, but the marshmallow strings out all around me. I move my hand to break the strings, but the wind blows, and I feel some fly onto my face. Penelope laughs at me, and Tristan just smiles at me as he leans in, raising his hand. I hold my breath as I watch his thumb come up and touch my cheek. "You've got a piece," he says, and my whole body lights up. My heart feels like it's going to explode in my chest. "Right here," he adds as he takes the marshmallow off my face, and then he puts his thumb into his mouth, licking off the piece on my face.

"Thanks," I mumble to him. "I'm going to go wash my hands." I make an excuse and walk away from him. My cheek feels on fire as I walk away from the beach and toward my villa. I close the door behind me and only then do I let out the deep breath I was holding. "What in the fuck was that?"

TEN

TRISTAN

WHAT DID YOU just do? I ask myself after I lick the marshmallow from my thumb and I watch her thank me. She quickly rushes off and I feel like I'm going to throw up as I watch her walk away, knowing it's because she got creeped out by my gesture. I sit on the sand trying to calm myself down.

"Are you ready for tomorrow?" Xavier sits next to me.

"What is going on tomorrow?" I look over at him as I watch Penelope go off with Parker to play hide-and-seek.

"Fishing trip," he informs me, and I just look at him, shocked. "Did you not read the itinerary?"

"There is an itinerary?" I ask, shaking my head. "I just thought it was a beach vacation."

"Have you met Max and Matthew?" He laughs. "Go

big or go home."

I sit on the beach, waiting for Abigail to come back, but thirty minutes later, I know I have to get Penelope into bed when she comes over and is rubbing her eyes. "Daddy," she whines, sitting in my lap as I wrap my arms around her and kiss her head. "I'm tired."

"Let's go to bed," I tell her, and she gets up, holding out her hand for me. I nod at Xavier as we walk back to our villa. I make Penelope wash off her feet, and by the time I tuck her in, she's already sleeping. I walk out of her bedroom and grab a bottle of water before I slide open the back door and walk out onto the back deck. I hear the water hitting the stairs as I walk over to the railing. I open the bottle and drink some before leaning on the railing with my arms. My eyes go to the side where I saw her this afternoon, wondering if she's in there, wondering if I should knock on the door and try to tell her… I stop right there. *What exactly do you want to tell her?* I ask myself. My head now mocking my questions with their own. *Do you want to tell her you're madly in love with her? Do you want to tell her that the past six years all you've thought about besides Penelope has been her? Do you want to tell her you dream of her at night? Do you want to tell her that all you want is one night with her, knowing it's a bald-faced lie.* I look over and see a soft light coming out of their villa. Pushing off the railing, I walk back inside and to my bed.

Falling fast asleep, I only wake when Penelope slides into bed with me. "Dad," she whispers, "it's eight o'clock, and I'm hungry."

I turn around and wrap my arm around her waist. "Snuggle with me," I mumble as I bury my face in her neck, her hair falling over my face. "Did you take out your braid?" I ask her, and she nods. "We are going fishing today," I inform her, and she shrugs

"You can make me a fishtail braid?" Penelope asks so effortlessly. When she turned five and started school, she asked me to braid her hair one day, and I had no idea how. She looked so sad it broke me, so I hired someone to come and teach me. She got me fake hair on a mannequin head, and every single night, I would practice, even on the road. While the guys were playing *Call Of Duty,* I was perfecting how to braid.

"Do you want to order some room service?" I ask her, and she just nods her head. "Pick up the phone and order me eggs and some bacon." I slip out of bed, keeping my back to her. There is only so much explaining I can do about my dick. When she was four and saw it, she thought it was an elephant. Then last year, she waited for me to get out of bed, and I did, but I still had my morning hard-on. She wanted to know if I brought a toy to bed. "Press zero."

"I know that," she huffs at me, pressing zero, and I hear her. "Good morning," she says. I laugh, closing the door. She sounds so grown-up sometimes. I slip on some basketball shorts before walking out and seeing her sitting on the bed on her iPad. "They said twenty minutes."

"Okay." I walk to the window and throw open the shades and see the sun in the sky. I walk over to my phone, finding there is a text from Matthew

Matthew: *Meeting in the lobby at 10 a.m. sharp.*

Me: *See you then.*

I walk out to the living room to the mini fridge, grabbing a bottle of water, when there is a knock on the door. I open it, and there are two carts. "What did you order?"

"The woman asked if I wanted one of everything," she explains, coming out of the bedroom, her iPad in her hand. "I said 'okay, but my dad wants bacon and eggs.'" I shake my head because how do I reason with that logic?

The man wheels in the first cart and then the second, taking off the domes, and I see there really is everything. There are two types of pancakes, regular and blueberry. There are scrambled eggs and an omelet. There is also bacon, ham, and even sausage. The huge platter of fruit will most likely be the first thing Penelope eats. I look at her when the man leaves. "Do you want me to make you a plate?"

"Nope." She walks over, just grabbing the platter of fruit and a fork. "I'm good. We can have a picnic." I laugh that she is using my words against me. She really needs to stop remembering everything I've said.

As we sit and eat, I turn on the television, flipping to the news as we finish up. Surprisingly there isn't much left after we finish. "Go change," I tell her, and she gets up and skips to her room while I clean up the plates and push the carts into the hallway. I'm in my bathroom when she comes back in and yells she's done. I open the door and see her there in her bathing suit. "You need a cover-up and bring me some sunscreen; I'll do it now before we get on the boat." It takes her less than a minute to come back into the room wearing a pair of shorts and a tank top with the sunscreen in one hand and her hairbrush in the other. I do her hair first as she looks in the mirror. "We are going fishing today," I remind her, and she lights up because she loves to fish. "How about we just stay the two of us today?" I focus on her hair. "Let everyone else relax." And by everyone, I mean Abigail. I don't say the words out loud, but I hope I don't have to.

"Okay," she agrees, and I wonder if she understands what I'm saying. I finish her fishtail braid, then apply sunscreen on her face and arms, and she does her own legs. I grab my backpack, throwing in more sunscreen, her iPad, and a change of clothes for her, just in case. When we walk out of the room, the carts are gone.

Penelope holds my hand, and when we get to the lobby, there are already two buses waiting for us and it looks like everyone is here. "Morning," I say to Matthew, who is standing beside Max each with a clipboard.

"Right on time," Max relays, writing something on the board in front of him before turning to Matthew. "Can you keep up with me, please?" He points at the board. "No wonder we are always late. You are supposed to check them off."

"What is going on?" I ask of them as they check off names.

"We are taking control of the people," Matthew states, "so we don't leave with anyone missing."

"I wish," Gabriella mumbles, walking past us. She

wears a huge straw hat, a black bikini top, a wraparound black skirt, and strappy high heels. "Gabriella is here." She walks to the bus and gets in.

"Ignore her." I hear Abigail from behind me. "Someone drank too much with Christopher and Matty on the beach."

"She's wearing heels," Matthew observes, and I roll my lips.

"We are going fishing," Max says, shaking his head.

"She put on a sequined dress this morning, so you are all welcome," Abigail shares, looking at Penelope. "Love your hair."

"Dad did it," she affirms. I wait for her to look at me, and when she does, it's like everything in me feels complete. She's wearing a white bikini top, a white wraparound skirt, and flip-flops. Her hair is piled on her head. "It's a fishtail braid."

"That's very cool." She smiles at her. "You are one step closer to becoming a mermaid." She winks at her before she looks at her uncles. "Abigail is present," she announces before walking into the bus Gabriella just walked onto. I grab Penelope's hand and go to the opposite bus, just to make sure that I give her space.

It doesn't take long before the buses leave and an even a shorter time before we get to the marina, where four catamarans are waiting for us. "Two are for fishing, and two are for swimming." I hear someone say and walk toward the boat that is fishing.

Five guys are waiting to help us set up. Penelope and I sit next to each other with the fishing poles in front of us. There is one seat left on our side, and before I can say anything, Penelope gasps, "Abigail, are you fishing?"

I close my eyes and curse everyone in the universe and even out of the universe. "Yes," she confirms, looking around, and even she is trying to get away from us.

"Come sit with us," Penelope invites, and I don't know if she is guilted into it, but she comes over and drops into the seat next to me. Cooper comes onto the boat with Emma, Mia, and Parker. "Dad, can I go say hi?" she asks, and I nod at her as she goes, leaving me and Abigail alone.

I rub my hands on my shorts because they are so sweaty with nerves. "So you fish?" I say.

"Yes," she confirms, "when we were younger, we used to go up to Canada where Uncle Max has a place, and we used to fish all the time."

"Sounds like fun," I reply, and as of right now, I would like the boat to tip over to shut me up. Neither of us says anything as we sit side by side so awkwardly.

"How good are you at fishing?" Abigail asks.

"I think I'm pretty decent, why?" I ask her and grab a water bottle from the cooler that is tucked in the corner.

"We are going to be on a team," she tells me. "Biggest fish wins."

"What team?" I ask her, looking around and see the seats are all set up in sections. "Really?"

"Have you just met my family? It's always about winning." She laughs out loud, and then Penelope comes back. It takes a bit more time before the boat leaves, and when we are far enough out, they come around and hand us some bait. The three of us stand, and I cast the pole for Penelope and then myself. Abigail does it perfectly, and I can only smile proudly at her. I don't know how long we are here. I keep applying the sunscreen on Penelope to make sure she doesn't burn when her pole tilts a bit. "Oh, you have one," Abigail says to her, and she squeals.

"Careful," I urge her, putting my pole in the holder to go stand behind Penelope. "Reel it in easy," I instruct her, and she starts to wind it in, but the pole gets pulled hard, and Abigail grabs it before it's ripped out of her hands. "Nice catch," I praise her as she holds on to the top of the handle and I hold on to the bottom. "Okay, start reeling."

"You've got a big one there," one of the workers on the boat tells us.

"I can't," Penelope says as she tries to reel it in again.

"Yes, you can," Abigail encourages her. She puts her hand on hers as they work together, reeling it in. "Let's do it together."

The three of us work to bring the fish in, and when it's close enough, Penelope squeals so loud that everyone turns around. We get it closer to the boat before the man leans over and picks it up. "Big grouper," he says, looking at us.

I wipe my brow with the back of my hand, my arms feeling like they are cramping from holding on to the pole so tight. "I caught a fish," Penelope declares, telling everyone who is looking our way.

"Look at how big that is," Abigail says, looking at the fish.

The man hands me the fish for me to hold. "The three of you get together for a picture," the man says, and I hand him my phone for him to take it with mine. "Can you hold it?" I ask Penelope, who isn't sure she can.

"We can all help," Abigail suggests, leaning forward to hold the front end of the fish and I follow her lead by holding the back end. The three of us squeeze in for the picture. The rest of the day is not as eventful, and when we dock, the kids look like they will fall asleep in a split second.

The day after is very low-key with everyone pretty much staying out on the beach or by the pool. Every day that passes by and I see Abigail, it makes me fall even more in love with her. If that was even possible. No matter what she is doing, if one of the kids asks to do something, she is up and doing it with them.

The days fly by faster than I can even imagine, and it's finally the last night here.

The big bonfire on the beach is bigger than I've ever seen. Penelope plays with Parker beside us, and the two have become stuck to each other. "Dad," Penelope starts when she comes over. "Can I sleep over at Parker's house?" she asks with Parker right beside her as the two of them hold hands.

Cooper now sits up from somewhere beside me. "It's more than okay with us," he says, and I just think about it for a second.

I mean, she's done a couple of sleepovers, but usually, it's at my parents' house in the summer. "Please, Daddy?" She puts her hands together, and I just smile at her and nod my head. "Yes!" she shouts as the two of them run away.

"If there is anything, call me," I tell him, and he just nods at me. Cooper gets up as he wrangles up all his kids as Penelope comes over to kiss me before running back to them.

I walk back to my room alone, already missing her. I walk into the room and see there is no light on. I head straight to the back, opening the door and walking out, something I do every night. Except tonight, it's different; when I lean onto the railing, I look over and see her standing there. Her head turns to look at me, and before I can even think twice, I ask her, "Want to have a drink with me?"

ELEVEN

ABIGAIL

I HEAR HIM walk outside into the darkness, and I think about turning around and hightailing it back inside, but like an idiot, all I can do is stand here and watch him. He walks to the railing, putting his hands on it. I can picture what he's wearing since I've spent the majority of the night looking at him. He is wearing pink shorts with a baby-blue linen button-down shirt, his sleeves rolled up to his elbows. The shirt made his eyes pop even more. I escaped the beach early so I didn't get dragged into going out with the gang. I just wanted to go back to my room and relax. I hold my breath as I see him turning his head and looking at me. I don't know if he's shocked or surprised to see me. "Want to have a drink with me?"

I want to have more than a drink with you, my head says. "Sure." I push off my own railing, my head screaming, *this is a bad idea*, as my vagina screams, *go and get me some*. I think about jumping onto his patio, but the linen skirt I'm wearing is tight on top with a long slit.

"I'll open the door," he says, turning and walking back inside his house. I walk into my own house and out the front door. When I walk over to his villa, he is waiting for me at the front door.

"Hi," I whisper when I see it's dark inside, afraid I'm going to wake Penelope. His musky smell fills the whole doorway

"Penelope is sleeping at Cooper's," he informs me, and I stop in front of him, my heart speeding up to the point I feel like it's going to come out of my chest. "What do you want to drink?"

"Whatever you are having is good," I reply, omitting the fact that I've never really drank anything. I've had some wine a time or two at the games, but I was just not drawn to it. Plus, it's not like I had time to party in college. I left that all to Gabriella, who did enough for both of us to last a lifetime.

"Go sit outside," he says, and just being in his space gives my whole body tingles. I nod at him as I walk out to the deck.

"You can do this." I try to give myself a pep talk. "It's going to be fine." I sit on the couch, and before I think about it, I see that it's the only seat up here. The couch seats two people. I'm about to get up when I see him walking out with two glasses in his hand.

It's also at this moment I realize there isn't that much

light here. A soft glow from the front makes its way into the back. He stops next to me, handing me the crystal glass with a ball ice cube inside. It clinks against the side of the glass as I reach up and grab it. Our fingers graze each other, and he looks at me for a second longer than I think he should, or I should. He sits next to me, and his leg brushes mine. I don't even wait before I take a gulp of the amber liquid. I try not to grimace when it burns all the way down to my stomach. "Smooth," I say, hissing a bit, making him laugh. My knees knock together with nerves. My palms are so sweaty that I'm praying I don't drop the glass onto the floor and make a fool of myself. I look down into my lap because I'm afraid he's going to see how nervous I am.

"It's whiskey," he says, holding his glass up. "To the end of the vacation."

"I already took a sip." I laugh nervously, looking at him. "Does it show I don't do this often?" I make a joke, and I hold up my own glass, clinking it with his.

He chuckles at me. "This is, hands down, one of my top vacations," he admits softly as he brings the glass to his lips. I don't bother answering him that I don't think I'll have another vacation quite like this one. Instead, I take another sip of the whiskey, and this time, it doesn't hurt as much when it goes down. I say a sip, but it's more like a gulp. I guess this is what they call liquid courage. I look into the glass, turning it in my hand nervously, watching the ball go round and round. "It's going to be a rough day two days from now when I have to get up and make my own breakfast," he states, making me laugh.

"Today, I didn't even know she ordered room service until I heard a knock."

I throw my head back and laugh, bringing the glass back to my lips and drinking the rest of the whiskey. From the side, I watch him lift the glass to his lips, wanting to be a crystal glass all of a sudden. Truth be told, I want to be anything he touches. "Tell me, Abigail." He says my name in almost a whisper. "What is it you are going to miss?"

Seeing you every day, I say in my head. "Spending time with everyone," I finally say, bringing the glass to my lips again, swallowing the little liquid that the ice gave off.

"Everyone," he emphasizes, almost as a joke.

"Christopher less than anyone." I lean in closer to him as we sit with our back to the couch. I hold my glass in my hand as I look over at him, a soft breeze blows my hair into my face, and I let out a little chuckle.

His hand comes up to my face as he takes a strand of hair and tucks it behind my ear. "I'm going to miss this," he says softly. I want to ask him what exactly he is going to miss, but I don't say a word because if I do, I'm afraid he will realize his head is getting closer and closer to mine. I'm afraid to do anything to stop what I think is going to happen.

His hand still on my cheek, his head closes the distance between us, and all I can see is his eyes on mine. My mouth goes suddenly dry as my tongue comes out and licks my bottom lip. "Abigail," he says breathlessly, right before his lips are on mine. My eyes stay open to make sure this is really happening and I'm not dreaming about it. I keep my eyes open until his tongue comes out and finds mine. My hand comes out to hold his cheek as his hand moves from the side of my face into my hair. He grips the base of my head, pulling me to him as his tongue goes around and around.

I feel like I'm having an out-of-body experience. My eyes flicker open again to make sure I'm not dreaming. I almost pinch myself to make sure I'm not asleep. He turns his head to the side, deepening the kiss, and just from this one kiss, I know I never want to kiss anyone else ever again. Just from this one kiss, I know that everything I thought was a kiss… wasn't. Just from this one kiss right now, I know I've been ruined for all men who will come after him.

He lets my lips go as his forehead presses into mine. Our chests rise and fall at the same time as his eyes search mine. "Abigail."

His hands fall out of my hair, and he moves away from me. My lips tingle from the kiss and also missing his. He shakes his head. "I'm so sorry." The three words come out of his mouth, and it sounds like he's in pain. "I am so, so sorry." He just looks at me.

I put the glass in my hand onto the couch next to me where he just got up from. His eyes watch my every move. I walk to him, taking the glass out of his hand. The whole time, I'm waiting for him to run away. The whole time, I'm telling myself if I have him for only one night, it might be just enough. The whole time, I'm telling myself there is no way I'm not taking a chance at it. He kissed me, but one kiss isn't enough. "Tristan." I say his name when I turn around and stand in front of him. The liquid courage of the whiskey is probably taking over, but I don't care. "I'm not sorry," I declare right before I lean in and lick his lips. "I'm not sorry, not one little bit," I reaffirm, crushing my lips on his. My hands don't go to his cheeks this time. Instead, they go into his hair. My body presses against him, and I swallow the moan that wants to escape him. His hands come up to my waist and then roam my back into my hair.

My chest is crushed to his, my tongue fighting with his. The first kiss was soft and tender, the way a first kiss should be. I haven't kissed many guys—in fact, I've only kissed two—but I know this kiss is different. It's full of need, the need to get even closer to him, which seems to be ridiculous because I'm literally plastered to him. His whole body feels like he's covering me, yet I want to get even closer. I don't ever want this kiss to end. I never want this moment to end. "Abigail." He finally lets my lips go, but I don't give him much time to talk, or maybe he doesn't give me much time to talk because our lips meet again.

Our heads move from right to left, following his lead. I don't know how long we spend outside kissing, but I feel his hands let go of my hair and then move down my back. I feel like I'm on fire when his fingertips touch the skin on my back. My stomach sinks in when he moves even lower to the base of my spine. My nipples feel like they are going to cut through my linen top. My body feels like it's on fire. I feel like every single time his fingertips touch my skin, I'm going to explode. I try to pull him closer to me by wrapping my arms around his neck. He lets go of my lips for a second so he can call out my name. It's almost as if he's pleading with me. "Abigail." Again, he doesn't give me a chance to answer him. Instead, he picks me up around my waist as he turns to walk inside his villa. I wish I could wrap my legs around his waist, but this linen skirt is giving nothing away. He stops walking, and I almost groan in disappointment. *This is it,* I think to myself. This is when he'll tell me it's all a mistake and we shouldn't be doing this. I look into his eyes, and I wish there were lights on so I could see what he's feeling. I wish there were lights on so he could see what I'm feeling. So I can tell him with my eyes that I'm his. His mouth comes to mine again as he walks through the living room and straight to his room.

The curtains are open, and the only light coming into the room is that of the moon. He finally puts me down in front of his bed. His mouth lets go of mine; his hands go to my hips. I can feel the heat from his hand through my pants. "Are you sure?"

I smile when it finally sinks in that he's not going to tell me it's a mistake. "Tristan," I say his name and I can't help the way my whole face lights up, "I'm more than sure." I lean in and take another kiss from him before letting his lips go. I cross my hands in front of me, grabbing my crop top, and in one full movement I pull it over my head. I toss the small top to the side as I stand there in front of him topless. My nipples pebbled and itching to be touched.

"Oh my God." His hands come up to cup my tits. "Fucking perfect," he utters right before his head leans down, and he sucks one into his mouth. My hand comes up to cup the back of his head as I watch him work from one nipple to the next. My head falls back as he bites down on one of my nipples while he rolls the other one with his fingers. My full C cup tits feel so full while he plays with them.

"Tristan," I moan his name, and he kisses his way down my stomach. My eyes flicker open as I watch him trail butterfly kisses all the way down as he lowers to his knees. He rubs his nose across my stomach, trailing even lower.

His hands grip my hips. "Is there a zipper on this?" He looks up at me, and I nod my head. My hands go to the base of my back to show him, but his hands are already there. The sound of us breathing heavily fills the room, but then it's as if we both stop breathing when he pulls the zipper down. I don't think I actually breathe as the dress falls from my hips, pooling around my feet, leaving me standing there in front of him with just my ivory-colored lace thong. There is nothing left to the imagination. His eyes never move from my pussy as he puts his hands on my hips and pulls. The lace panties never stood a chance against him.

"I need to taste you," he says, and my head is dizzy with need and desire. I don't even know if I understand what he's saying until he pushes me to sit down on the bed. "Open your legs for me, Abigail." I'm mesmerized by his words, my legs opening for his. "Intoxicating," he murmurs, right before he leans in, and I see his tongue come out as he licks up my slit. There has never been a more erotic moment in my life.

"Fuck," he hisses before he buries his face into me. His tongue licks me up to my clit as he flicks it with his tongue. My eyes are transfixed on him as he takes his two thumbs and opens me up. "Perfect." He leans in, sucking my clit. "Fucking perfect," he says again, and my hands go back as my nipples itch. I move my hands up to roll them between my fingers as his tongue slides inside me.

"Open wider," he urges me, and I open as wide as I can for him. "So wet." He takes his finger and rubs it up my slit toward my clit as he rolls it. My eyes feel hooded right now. I put my heels on the bed to be even more open for him as he slides two fingers inside me, and my breath hitches. "Fucking tight," he says, and I just watch as his fingers fuck me, his tongue flipping my clit back and forth. It takes me no time to come. I feel the tightness in my stomach as my hips want to move up and down on his tongue. It's animalistic the things I want to do to him. "Tristan." I say his name breathlessly, right before I come on his fingers. I have never come harder in my life, but then again, I'm the only one who has ever made myself come. "More," I say, not even sure what the means. "I want more."

"What more do you want?" he asks as he slides his fingers out of me, his fingers wet with my juices. He flicks my clit with them right before he puts them into his mouth and cleans them off.

"Stand up," I tell him, because I know if I tried to stand right now, I would probably fall. He stands, and I put my feet on the floor, my hands rising as I unbutton his shirt until it falls open. I lick my lips as my hands come up, and I touch the chest I've been thinking about this whole time. I lean in and kiss his stomach, just like he did mine, but I want more. I just hope to fuck I know what I'm doing. I also hope like fuck he doesn't figure out that I've never done any of this before. "Here goes nothing," I mumble to myself before my hand unbuttons his shorts.

TWELVE

TRISTAN

I STAND IN front of her, the taste of her pussy lingering on my tongue. I want to kiss her, but I don't want to share her taste with anyone, not even her. When she opened wide to me before, I thought I was going to cry out. She was so fucking beautiful. Nothing I can say will ever do her justice. She palms my cock, which I'm even ashamed to say is two seconds away from blowing a load in my shorts. She mumbles something, but the only thing I can hear is my heart thudding in my ears. I watch her fingers open the button of my shorts, my eyes never leaving her fingers.

The sound of my zipper fills the room as she pushes the shorts over my hips. "I knew it," she says as she looks up at me, and all the words are stuck in my throat. "Your cock is huge." I want to laugh out loud, but I can't because she just pulls my boxers down over my cock. Her hand comes out to fist me. "I can't even close my fingers," she observes as she inspects me.

"If you do that a couple more times," I say between clenched teeth, "I'm going to come on that pretty face."

She doesn't say anything to me, and I wonder if I went too far, but then she just moves her hands. "You can come on my face," she offers, "but I think I want you in my mouth." She licks the tip of my cock like she's licking a fucking ice cream cone. "Hmmm," she hums, and my cock becomes even more rock hard, twirling her tongue around my head. "I don't know if I can take the whole thing down my throat," she admits, sizing it up, "but I'm going to fucking try." She takes half of it in her mouth, gags, and then moves up again as she tries to take more into her mouth the second time. She then lets go of my cock as her tongue comes out, and she licks from my balls, up my shaft, and to the tip. "You taste good," she compliments, taking the head back into her mouth. Her hand grips the base of my cock as she works it with her hand and her mouth.

"Abigail." I think I say her name, but I'm not sure. Only when she looks up at me with her mouth full of my cock do I know that she heard me call her name. "I don't know how long I'm going to last," I tell her, my hands coming out and playing with her tits. I roll her nipples before I pinch them, and when I do, she lifts her hips off the bed.

"I'm going to come again," she declares, taking her mouth off my cock. "Do that again," she says, and while she sucks my cock, I play with her tits. I lean down a bit, my finger finding her pussy again. It slides in right away, but it's so tight it feels like she's strangling my finger.

My hips move on their own, fucking her face as I slide another finger into her. She moans around my cock, and it's just too much for my cock. "I'm going to come," I warn her, trying to get out of her mouth, but her hands go to my hips, holding me in place. Her eyes watch me as I come in her mouth with her name on my lips.

I thrust between her lips, and she swallows until the last drop. Even after I finish coming, she doesn't stop sucking my cock. "Want to do it again?" she asks, and I shake my head.

"I want my cock in you," I tell her, and her eyes watch me as I shrug the shirt over my shoulders and pull down my boxers completely, kicking them to the side with her skirt. "Get in the middle of the bed," I urge her, and she turns around and crawls. My cock that was going to half-mast is now rock-hard as she looks over her shoulder at me.

My hand finds my cock as I stroke it. "Now that is a sight," I tell her as she smiles at me. Opening her legs, I see her hand is hiding her pussy from me. "Let me see you," I tell her, and she drops her hand, leaving herself open to me. I get on the bed behind her, and I can't resist tasting her again.

My tongue slides right into her pussy, her moans fill the room. "Tristan," she calls my name, "I need more."

"On your back," I urge her, and she looks surprised I didn't fuck her from behind. "The first time I want to watch your eyes when I slide into you." She turns on her back and lies in the middle of my bed. I don't know how many times I pictured her right here, but I know that nothing is like the image I have of her. She opens her legs for me, and I crawl right to her. Neither of us says anything as her hand comes out to grab my cock. She guides my cock to her pussy, rubbing it up and down. "Put your legs back," I direct her as she bends her knees and pulls them back. "I want to get as deep as I can into you."

"Yes," she says, squirming on the bed, "fill me up."

I don't even know what the fuck is going on right now. It's been such a long time since I've done this. I'm afraid I'm going to fuck it up. I take my cock out of her hand, rubbing it up and down, stopping at her clit, slapping it with the head of my cock, before moving it down and sinking the head into her. The feeling of her pussy on me is ecstasy. I move my hips just a touch to let her get used to my size, and from the way she is strangling me, I'm guessing that it's been a while for her also. I look into her eyes, but all she can do is stare down at my cock in her pussy. "You like that?" I ask her as I slide in a little bit more. "Look at how your pussy takes me." I slide in a touch more, and it's like it's going to get stuck. "Look at us." I pull out again, pushing back in, and then get stuck again. "Baby." I look down at her, and she looks up at me.

"More," she urges me, lifting her hips, and I pull out, and this time, I slide all the way into her. She cries out, and I look down at her.

My cock feels like it's found its home and never wants to leave. I put my hands beside her shoulders as I stay buried balls deep into her. My cock feels like it's being strangled, and it finally dawns on me that this might be her first time. The blood drains from my whole body and in its place is this red-hot need to fucking claim her. She's fucking mine from this moment on. She just doesn't know it. "I'm going to move," I tell her, and she just nods her head, and I can see that she's holding her breath. "I'm going to go slow."

"Okay," she says in a whisper, and I can't help but bend my head to kiss her. I put my forehead on hers as I look into her eyes, feeling like I'm looking into her soul.

"I'm going to move, and you are going to help me," I tell her, and she just lets out a breath as I pull out halfway before pumping into her again. "Do you want to help me?" I pull out again, this time a little bit more than before. "I want you to pinch those perfect nipples," I instruct her as she moves her hands to her perfect fucking tits. "Roll them back and forth twice." My hips move slowly. "Then, on the third time, I want you to pinch them just a bit." She follows what I tell her, and I can tell right away how turned on she is because her pussy is wetter than before, making it easier for me to move. "That's it, baby," I praise her, and it's taking all of my energy not to ravish her. To not pound the shit out of her and make her call my name repeatedly. "Do it again. This time, pinch a bit harder." I slide my tongue into her mouth as she moans every time I pull out and push back in. "Move one of your hands and play with your clit."

She just stares at me, and I look down between us, seeing my cock planted into her pussy and her finger going back and forth. "Fuck, you're a goddess."

"Tristan," she says my name in a plea. "I need." She starts the words and then stops when I slam into her a little harder than I wanted to, but her eyes roll back in her head. "Like that," she says to me, "I need you to fuck me like that."

"I don't want to hurt you."

"But I need it," she almost cries.

"Your pussy," I tell her, pulling out and slamming back in, "was made for me."

"Yes," she says. "Harder."

"Fuck," I grit between clenched teeth.

"Show me," she baits me, "show me how hard you can fuck me." She arches her back. "I like it."

I couldn't stop myself. Even if I wanted to, my hips pull out and slam into her over and over again. This time the sound of skin slapping together is even louder than our moans. "Tomorrow, I want you to feel me inside you tomorrow when you walk." I fuck her harder than I did before. It's almost barbaric.

"If you want me to do that," she states, her hand now moving faster and faster between her legs, "you are going to have to fuck me a bit harder." I grit my teeth together as I slam into her. "I think you can do better than that." She pokes the bear, and everything I wanted to do before is thrown out the window. Wanting to handle her with care, knowing I should go slow, but I can't. I slam into her over and over again, her pussy getting tighter and tighter the harder I go. Until my mouth slams down onto her as I swallow her moaning out my name, I try to last longer, but with her pussy squeezing me, I can't help it I come right after her.

Her tongue rolls with mine as she lifts her hips up to meet my slow thrusting ones. "I want to ride your cock," she announces between kisses, pushing me to my back. "Can I?" she asks, straddling me. She reaches behind her to grab my cock, which is still wet with her juices. "I'm waiting."

"Abigail," I say with my back toward the headboard, "my body is yours." I watch her hover over my cock and then slowly slide down it.

"Hmm," she hums as she rises and then falls on my cock. My hand comes up to play with her tits.

"Fuck, I could stay buried in you forever." I pinch her nipples as she moans, her head rolling back as I lean forward to take a nipple in my mouth. "You like that?" I ask, and she doesn't say anything because she's too busy grinding down on my cock. "What do you want?" I ask her, going to the other nipple.

"To come again." She doesn't even back away from it. "I need to."

I lick my thumb as she puts her hands on my shoulders for leverage, and I've never ever wanted to please someone like I want to please her. I finger her clit with my thumb, moving it from side to side. "Tristan," she moans my name, and I know she's close but needs more.

I grab her around her waist and buck up into her, her hands wrapping around my shoulders, and I fuck her until she comes again and again. I follow her two seconds later, and the both of us collapse on each other. Our bodies are covered with a sheen of sweat. I'm still in her, and I can't wait to get back into her again. I kiss her shoulder as I turn her on her side. She buries her face into my neck and the both of us finally start to breath normally. "That was," I start to say and I slip out of her, "was…"

She looks up at me. "Was it okay?"

I lean back so I can see her. "Are you joking right now?" I ask her, and she shakes her head.

"Were you not in the room?" I ask her, and she smirks.

"I came three times." I hold up my fingers. "In a matter of thirty minutes."

"So that's good, right?" she asks, and I put my head back.

"It's better than good," I inform her, and she laughs as I roll away from her. "You would win gold if this was the Olympics."

I laugh as I walk into the bathroom, turning on the water while I grab a cloth. I wet one and wash my dick, seeing that it's pink. I look over into the room as I wet a cloth for her and walk into the room. "Abigail," I say her name, "was this your first time?" I ask her. She looks at me, and right before she is going to answer, there's a knock on the door. The both of us jump and look at each other. I look at the door, wondering if maybe I heard it wrong, but then there it is again. I move to grab my boxers before walking to the door, taking one second to look over my shoulder at her.

I close my bedroom door as I take a deep inhale. When I open the door, Cooper standing there with Penelope in his arms. "I'm really sorry," he says, "but she had a bad dream."

I hold out my hands for her, and she flies into them as she lays her head on my shoulder. "What's the matter?" I rub her back. "Are you okay?" I ask her and then look at Cooper. "Sorry about that."

"Hey, it's the joy of parenting," he reminds me as he smiles and turns to walk away.

"Are you okay?" I ask her as I walk her to her bedroom, putting her down on her bed and tucking her in. "Do you want water?"

"No," she says softly as she closes her eyes.

I wait a second before I walk out of her room and go back to mine. I turn the door handle, opening it and expecting to find Abigail where I left her. Instead, the bed is empty, and the door to the patio is open. I look at the bed and then down to where my clothes are, confirming she's gone.

My heart sinks as I think about texting her when I hear Penelope, who stands there rubbing her eyes. "Daddy, can I sleep with you tonight?" she asks and I look at her.

"Um," I say, looking at her and then back to the bed where I just left my heart. "How about I come sleep with you?" I suggest as I walk out of my bedroom, not even bothering to close the door, hoping somehow, she comes back tonight for me.

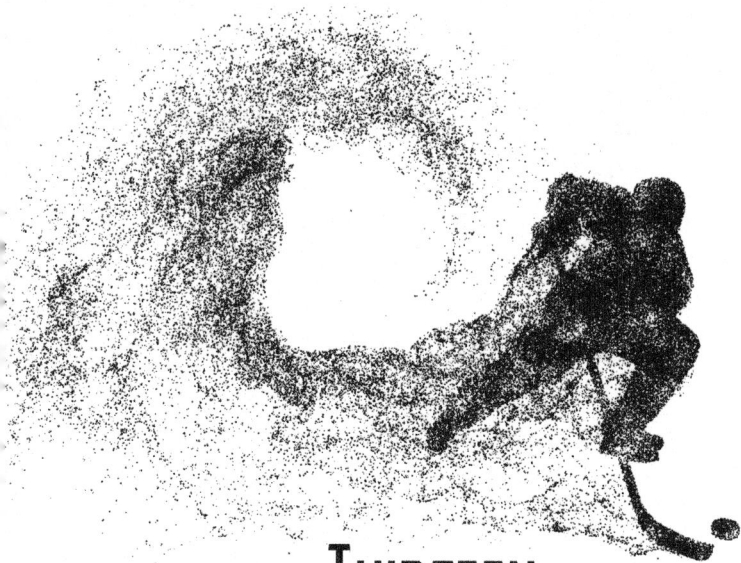

THIRTEEN

ABIGAIL

I SLIP INTO my room in the darkness, trying not to wake Gabriella. I tiptoe from the living room until my bedroom door closes behind me. I put my head back against the cold door as I wipe away the tear escaping. I put my hand to my chest, and the beating of my heart is racing out of control.

I take a deep breath in and out, trying to get my breathing under control before I push off the door and walk into the bathroom. I don't bother turning on the lights before I walk to the bathtub and start the water. My body feels like it's on autopilot. I pull my shirt that I quickly threw back on when he walked out of the room and went to the door.

I had no idea who it could be, but I also didn't want to be caught in his bedroom naked. At least if I was wearing clothes, I could have said we were just talking. Although, I don't think anyone would have believed we were talking in his bedroom in the dark. I was putting my pants on when I heard Cooper's voice. It literally felt like you took a bucket of ice water and threw it on me. I got my skirt on, grabbed the remainder of my panties, and slipped out his door. I felt like I was James Bond as I tried to sneak back into my house without anyone seeing me. I held my breath the whole way as I jumped from his patio to mine. The only thing I could think was what if I fell and broke my face? Even when I made it over, I was like a cat burglar, walking with my back pressed against the side of the house until I finally reached the villa.

I slip my skirt off my hips, put one foot into the tub, and then another, sitting down and wincing. I lean back onto the rear of the tub as I replay the last hour over and over in my head. It was everything I thought it would be and more, but I'm sure it was only because of Tristan. When he pushed himself into me, I tried not to wince in pain, and after a couple of seconds, the burning left, and I felt so full. I had no idea if he knew or not. I thought for sure he did at the beginning but then when he continued, I was like, *phew, dodged that bullet*. I even stupidly asked him if it was okay. I mean, it was better than okay for me. It was everything Gabriella said it would be and so much more. I was lying in bed feeling like a rock star until he came out of the bathroom and looked at me, confused. I can still hear his question clear as day. "Abigail, was this your first time?" I felt the heat run up my neck at the same time that my mouth went suddenly dry. I was trying to think of anything to say, pretend that it was my period. It was probably the most embarrassing moment of my life to pretend I got my period in the middle of sex, but it definitely was better than the real reason. Anything, and I mean anything, but all the words got stuck in my throat until the knock on the door saved me.

"If anything, I owe Cooper a huge thank you," I say, getting up from the bath and pulling up the latch to let the water drain out. I step out, grabbing the plush white robe. Slipping my arms into it, I tie the sash in a knot. I walk over and turn on the soft light before I walk back over and look at myself in the mirror. I look into my eyes to see if I look different, but nothing is there. I touch my face, and I can't help but snort out that I thought for sure it would be written on my face I had sex. I thought for sure you would be able to tell. I turn off the light as I walk out and slide into bed.

My head hits the pillow, and all I can do is turn to look out the window. The soft light from the moon comes into my room as I stare ahead, the night now on repeat in my head. The way he kissed me. The way I kissed him back. The way he buried his face between my legs. The way he looked over me. The way his blue eyes got dark right before he came in me. The way he said my name over and over again. I don't even feel the tear that escapes my eye until I'm lying on a soaked pillowcase.

I hear the front door open and close. Looking at my door, I see Gabriella poke her head in. "I'm back," she whispers, and instead of answering, I just pretend I'm sleeping. She quietly closes the door shut. I feel like I'm hungover when I close my eyes and then when I open them again, I stare again into the darkness. Finally, when I see the sky turn from a black to a dusty gray, I fall asleep.

Only when I feel the heat on my face do my eyes flutter open. They feel extra heavy today and I can only imagine how horrible I look. I don't have a chance to check when the door opens and Gabriella stands there in a long dress. "Are you not coming to our last breakfast?"

"No," I reply, sitting up and avoiding her eyes.

"You look like shit." She folds her arms over her chest. "Are you sick?"

Pretend you're sick, my head screams at me. "I don't think so," I answer and then fake sniffle. "Maybe I caught a cold with the hot and cold." Even though it's a total myth and the only way you can actually catch a cold is from a virus.

"So then why aren't you coming to breakfast?" she pushes me.

"I'm going to start packing," I tell her, walking into the bathroom and away from her eyes.

"Do you want me to bring you back something?" she shouts from my bedroom, and I take one look at myself in the mirror and shriek.

"No, I'll order room service," I yell over my shoulder and hear the door slam behind her a couple of seconds later.

Turning the water on in the sink, I stick both hands under the faucet until they are full before splashing the water on my face a couple of times, then grabbing a white hand towel and dabbing the water on my face. I take another look at myself in the mirror and laugh out loud before walking over to the phone.

I sit on the bed before picking up the tan phone from the bedside table. I press zero for room service. The woman answers right away. "Good morning, Ms. Stone."

"Good morning," I reply to her. "Can I have a pot of coffee and also a glass of ice cubes."

"Would you like anything to eat with that?" she asks.

"Actually, can you send me a fruit plate as well."

"Sure thing," the woman confirms, "that will be there within ten minutes."

"Thank you," I reply before I hang up the phone. Walking to the closet, I grab my suitcase.

I place it on the bed, unzipping it and letting it flop open. "I'm not avoiding him," I tell myself as I walk over and start to grab my stuff, hanging up and bringing it back to the bed. I fold the clothes, trying not to think about the man who is probably next door doing the same thing.

I'm halfway done after five minutes and there is a knock on the door. I walk over, and when I pull open the door, I'm disappointed it's a man with a room service cart instead of Tristan. "Good morning," the man says smiling at me, "where would you like this?"

"I can take it from here," I tell him, taking the cart from him and rolling it to me. "Thank you." He nods at me before turning and walking away.

Pouring myself a cup of coffee before I grab an ice cube in my hand, I walk back into my bedroom. Sitting on the edge of the bed, I take a sip of the coffee while I ice under my eyes. I move the ice cube from one eye to the other until it's numb and the ice has melted.

The door opens and Gabriella comes back in and looks into my bedroom from the living room. "Aren't you done yet?"

"Almost," I tell her and she turns to walk to her own bedroom. I hear slamming coming from her room, along with some swearing.

"Why did I pack so many fucking clothes?" she asksself and I just laugh as I finish packing. I'm zipping the piece of luggage closed at the same time Gabriella yells that she's done.

"Did you even fold anything?" I laugh as I pull the suitcase off the bed and roll it to the front door. Getting the Dior purse from my bed, I walk into Gabriella's room.

Her two suitcases are at her door, and she rushes out of the bathroom with her toiletry bag. "Almost forgot this," she says, tossing the bag into her carry-on bag.

"Ready?" I ask her as she wheels her luggage to the door, and we walk out. We roll the suitcases down the path toward the lobby. I can hear the commotion already, and I'm not even there yet. "One of these days." I look over at Gabriella. "I'm going to opt-out of traveling with the family and find my own way home."

"Girl, same," she agrees, and I look over at her, laughing, not paying attention to where I'm going when I crash into someone. My eyes look at the man in front of me, who looks over his shoulder at me. The blue eyes that have haunted me all freaking morning long. "I'm so sorry," I tell him, and he just smiles at me. "I wasn't watching where I was going."

"All good," he says to me. I thought I was ready to face him this morning, but when I finally lay eyes on him, I can confirm that I am not. "How are you doing?"

His question makes my cheeks turn pink from the embarrassment of the question. I avoid even looking into his eyes. "I'm fine," I answer curtly. "I should get my luggage into the bus." I just walk past him, trying not to show how unsteady my legs are. He must think I'm such a loser for still being a virgin at my age.

I breathe out through my mouth and inhale through my nose to stop the tears that are threatening to come. "Here is my bag," I say to the man loading the bus.

I turn and walk up the steps of the bus and spot Tristan, of course, in the front with Penelope. I don't spend more than a second on the bus before I turn around and bump into Gabriella, who huffs. "What the heck are you doing?" she says to me. Now all eyes are on me, and if I could secretly push her off the bus, I would.

"I forgot to get a water bottle," I tell her, walking around her and down the steps. I pretend I'm walking back into the lobby but duck into the other bus instead. I don't say anything to anyone as I take the first seat. The man packing the bags hits the side of the bus, telling him he's all done. The driver leans over and closes the bus door, and the sound of a hiss starts right before he takes off. I watch as we drive out of the resort, and my eyes fixate on the room that was his. The room where I gave him everything in me. The words replay in my head, "What are you going to miss, Abigail?"

My heart screams out, *"You!"*

Fourteen

I'M TRYING TO calm down and tell myself it is all in my head when I hear the commotion coming from the front of the bus. "What the heck are you doing?" Gabriella shrieks, and I see Abigail glaring at her.

"I forgot to get a water bottle," she mumbles and gets off the bus. My stomach sinks even more than it did when she walked away from me not too long ago. I peer out the window to see she isn't going to get water. Instead, she's going to get on the other bus.

My stomach lurches and then rises to my throat as my hands start to shake. God, what have I done? I should never have kissed her. I have ruined everything for what? The best night of my life. I didn't sleep a fucking wink last night. I kept telling myself I should go to her. I lay awake in Penelope's bed and wondered if I should go over and talk to her. The only problem was I didn't know what room she was sleeping in. Having Gabriella come to the window because I knocked on hers was not something I wanted to do.

When I saw her this morning after she bumped into me, it was as if my world was complete, which is so dumb to say. It felt like all the pieces of my heart were together, and I just wanted to wrap my arms around her and tell her I missed her. But she avoided even looking me in the eyes; it was as if someone reached into my chest and ripped my heart out. Now she runs away from even being on the same bus as me. The banging on the side of the bus makes me look up as I see the bus in front of us, the bus I know she is on, start to move.

I put my head back on the headrest, and I watch out the window as the resort fades away in the distance. Every second we get farther and farther away, my chest gets tighter and tighter. It's the strangest thing and something I don't even know how to explain.

The bus drives through the stainless-steel chain-link fence toward a plane that waits on the tarmac. We slowly make it off the bus as I hold Penelope's hand. My head is not paying attention to anything. Instead, I'm replaying last night over and over again. I can still taste her kiss on my lips. When we walk up the steps, my eyes roam the plane looking for her. She sits in a seat near the window with Gabriella next to her. She has her head against the side of the plane with her eyes closed.

"Let's sit here." I point at a seat on the opposite side of the plane, farthest from her. "Do you want the window seat?" I ask Penelope. She nods as she walks in and takes off her backpack before sitting in the seat. I do the same thing, tucking my backpack under the seat in front of me.

I look over and see she is already getting her iPad out of her bag and yawning at the same time. "Someone partied hard." I look over and see Justin sit down in the row next to me.

I laugh nervously as I put my hands on my stomach, linking my fingers together to stop them from shaking next to him. "Yeah, I don't think she's going to last the whole trip." I swallow down the way my heart is beating in my chest. I can't even imagine what he would do to me if he knew I took advantage of his daughter last night. What the whole plane would do to me. I feel sick with the thought that I took advantage of their generosity and what I did do. I slept with Abigail.

"When the girls were younger…" He starts to tell me a story, and I listen as I always do when it's about Abigail. "They packed their bag full of their favorite things." He smiles. "Got on the plane and forgot the bags at home."

I open my mouth, not even imagining how that would have been. "Back then, there wasn't a lot to keep them entertained. So we all had to whip out our iPhones."

"That sounds like a vacation gone wrong," I say as the plane fills up and people start getting their seats. I lay my head back and close my eyes, but they are haunted by her eyes. It's the longest plane ride of my life. The number of times I had to stop myself from turning back to look at her were too many to count. Even when Penelope had to go to the bathroom, I got up to let her pass and looked around but never in her direction. I am a chickenshit, and I'm not afraid to admit it. I don't think I can handle seeing the regret in her eyes, especially not when the only thing I regret is not going after her after she left.

The plane touches down, and we make it out, my hand in Penelope's as we grab our bags. It's only when I'm loading my car with the luggage do I look around for her. I don't even know what I would say to her. Actually, I do know what I would say to her. "Come home with me," I say. I look around as I see everyone lugging their stuff to their cars.

I scan the crowd looking for her, but I can't find her anywhere. "Dad, are we leaving?" Penelope asks from the back. "I'm tired."

"I know you are," I say, taking a deep breath in before pulling out of the parking spot. My eyes even look at the rearview mirror to see if I can find her, and she is nowhere to be seen.

When we get home, I press the button for the garage door, driving right in. I pop the trunk, grab our bags, and make my way into the house. Penelope is already inside, opening the fridge. "It's empty." She looks over at me, shocked.

I just laugh at her. "It's empty because we are leaving tomorrow," I remind her, and she huffs.

"I'm starving," she exaggerates just a touch. She ate less than an hour and a half ago on the plane.

"Why don't we order some food and then start doing our laundry?" I suggest and she comes over and grabs my phone, opening up the Uber Eats app.

"What do you want to eat?" she asks, but it's the same answer I tell her all the time.

"Choose something, and then I'll pick." I take her bags to the laundry room.

"Okay, I ordered you a cheeseburger with bacon and a side salad," she tells me, coming back into the room, "and a side of fries so you don't take mine."

I laugh at her as I separate my clothes, my hands touching the shirt she unbuttoned yesterday. I put it aside as I throw a load into the machine. "We have to pack."

"Why can't we just bring what is already packed?" she asks, or better yet, she groans. The tiredness of the week at the beach and doing everything she could do is coming out.

"We can't bring the same things because these are beach clothes and we need lake clothes," I explain to her, and she puts her head back and slaps her hand on her face. "Life is rough at eight," I mumble to her. "Good news. I already packed your bag before we left." She smirks at me. "Go lie down on the couch." She is already halfway out of the room. "It's going to be an early night tonight."

"Okay, Daddy," she says so sweetly and I just snort. I grab the shirt I put aside and walk up the steps to my room. Entering into my walk-in closet, I grab a hanger, getting ready to hang the shirt up when I bring it to my nose and smell. I can smell her faintly and my cock goes hard thinking she's nearby. I hang the shirt up behind my suits and I let my head hang. I wish this feeling would go away. I wish I knew that it wasn't a mistake. I wish I knew I haven't ruined our friendship by kissing her.

I'm busy fixing everything for us to leave tomorrow and when I tell Penelope it's bedtime, she doesn't even fight me on it or ask me for five more minutes. Instead, she walks upstairs and heads straight to her room. I peek my head in after ten minutes, seeing her coming out of her bathroom with her robe on. I swear, sometimes she looks like she's eight going on twenty. "Did you brush your teeth?" I ask her.

"I did in the shower," she confirms, and I have to laugh. She found that shortcut last year when she told me that conditioner has to sit in the hair for two minutes so she brushed her teeth while waiting.

She crawls into bed and huffs, "There is no place like home." I can't help but chuckle.

Walking over to her, I sit on her bed next to her, leaning down and kissing her forehead. "I love you, baby girl," I tell her, and she smiles at me.

"Love you too, Daddy," she replies before she turns over to face the wall. I don't close the door behind me when I walk out.

I throw my T-shirt into the laundry basket before taking my shorts off and tossing those in also. This is something I had to learn to do. Before, I would just toss my shit everywhere, and Penelope was doing it also. When I told her to pick up her things, she asked me why I didn't pick up mine. She was one-hundred-percent right, and then I had to change my ways.

I head into my walk-in shower, putting one hand on the marble wall and the other on the glass wall before I hang my head down and let the hot water run over my neck. I put on my boxers once I dry myself off and slide into bed, grabbing the remotes next to my bed.

Grabbing my cell phone also, I pull up her name. I'm just going to text her and ask her to call me.

Me: *Can you call me?*

I don't press send. Instead, I delete it and type something else.

Me: *I just want you to know that I'm sorry.*

I don't press send on this one either, deleting it right away.

Me: *Do you want to come over?*

"Don't be an idiot," I chide myself, deleting the text and tossing my phone to the side. "If she wanted to talk to you, she would have said something to you today. But she didn't. Instead, she ran away from you." I turn the television off and roll on my side, very much like Penelope. "If she wanted you, she would have said so," is the last thing I say before I fall asleep. The next day I get on a plane with her still on my mind.

FIFTEEN

ABIGAIL

Six Weeks Later

"HOW MANY MINUTES left to go?" Sarah, my co-worker, asks when she walks out of her patient's room.

"Forty-seven minutes and counting," I declare as I write down my notes in one of my patients' files. I'm finishing my fifth night shift in a row, and then I'm off for five days, and I'm planning on sleeping for three straight days. This week has been the longest week in my life, or at least it seems like that. I'm just so tired. Today, I opted out of eating my dinner and instead took a one-hour nap, which only made it worse.

"Any exciting plans for the days off?" she asks as she sits next to me at the nurses' station. The desk is in the middle of the floor, and there are twenty rooms all around us, with four nurses on shift every day. Even though we have our own five patients to look after, we have a whiteboard right at the front of our desk, where we also write down our notes.

"Sleep, sleep, and more sleep," I say, shutting the file and putting it away before I grab another one. I always read over my notes right before I clock out to make sure I wrote everything down. Sometimes it gets crazy, and you don't have the time, but surprisingly tonight has been one of the calmer days out of the five, even with the full moon.

I finish my files up and then do a quick checkup on everyone to make sure everything is okay. I almost bow down to Everly when she walks through the double doors. "You are the sexiest thing I've ever seen in my life," I tease her as she laughs, putting her cup of coffee on the desk.

"I figured you would be eager to leave," she says, and I just smile at her.

"What gave you that idea?" I ask her, leaning onto the nurses' desk as she sits down.

"Sarah sent me a picture of you sleeping on the desk." She rolls her lips as I gasp. Ever since I started the job five weeks ago, it's been even better than what I could have imagined. The women I work with are so helpful and kind. It makes coming to work that much better.

"I was not sleeping. I was resting my eyes," I inform her, and she just laughs. "My mind was alive."

"Well, either way," she says, grabbing the file on top and opening it, "you can go."

I clap my hands quietly since it's only six o'clock. "Thank you." I turn and walk into the nurses' lounge, where I take off my stethoscope from around my neck. Opening my locker, I grab my bag and toss it inside before I make my way outside.

I feel like I'm literally dragging my feet by the time I unlock the front door. I hear the television coming from the living room, so I know Gabriella is up. I dump my bag at the door, kick off my black Nike sneakers, and then peel my socks off. "That feels good." I sigh as I walk into the kitchen and see Gabriella standing in a robe and her hair wrapped up in a towel. "Morning," I greet as she pours a cup of coffee.

"I'm assuming you don't want a cup?" She chuckles as I slide onto a stool at the island. I fold my arms in front of me and put my head down.

"I need a shower and to sleep for twenty-four hours," I declare, looking at her, but having no strength to even get up, "thirty-six if I'm lucky."

"I've never seen you this tired before." She pours some milk in her coffee before taking a sip.

"I don't think I've ever been this tired before," I admit to her. "Not even after staying up for a three-day stretch to study for my test."

"Maybe you are getting your period." She shrugs before she grabs the milk, walking to the fridge and putting it back in.

The minute she says that, I sit back up. "I don't really get my period," I share with her, and she just looks at me. "I skip the sugar pills, continuously taking the pill."

"Is that good for you?" she asks, but I don't listen to the question. Instead, I jump off the stool and run to the front door, grabbing my bag.

I squat down, my hands shaking, as I unzip it to grab my phone. Heat now climbing up my neck and rushing to my head as I open the period app. "No-no-no-no-no," I chant over again and again, seeing I was ovulating while I was on vacation and we didn't use protection.

"What's the matter?" Gabriella stands there in the hallway.

"I think I'm late," I tell her, turning back to my phone and checking to see if I'm actually doing it right.

"Well, maybe with the vacation and then coming back home and starting to work, it messed with your schedule." She shrugs her shoulders, not even realizing what I'm saying.

"Oh my God." I close my eyes. "Oh my God." I sit down because my legs can't hold me up as my stomach sinks and then rises. A burning sensation forms at the top of my stomach. "Oh my God." My heart picks up even more speed, and I suddenly have trouble breathing as my head screams at me.

Gabriella just laughs, and I open my eyes to look at her, or better yet, glare at her. "What is your problem?" she asks, cocking her hip to the side and putting her fist on it. "It's not like you had sex." She throws her head back and laughs.

All I can do is close my eyes and chant, "Fuck-fuck-fuck-fuck-fuck-fuck."

My chanting has Gabriella's laugh come to a halt. Her

eyes open wide as she looks at me. "You had sex?" she shrieks at me.

"Um," I start to say, thinking there isn't going to be any way I can deny it now. "Maybe."

"Maybe?" She throws her hands up in the air. "Maybe. Obviously, you weren't doing it right if you don't know if you had sex." I put my hand to my stomach, making her freak out more. "What the fuck?" she yells. "When the hell did you have sex?"

"Six weeks ago," I answer quietly. *Almost one thousand and ten hours ago*, my head chimes in. It's been six weeks since I've seen him. Six weeks of thinking of nothing else but him. Six weeks of memories. Six weeks of nightmares of me seeing him, but him turning around when he sees me. Six weeks of me wishing I could go back to the day. Six weeks of emptiness.

"Six weeks ago?" Her voice goes even louder. "With who?" I think about making a name up. I think about saying anyone but him, but she knows me better than that. If I didn't have sex in college or university with the guys I casually dated, there could only be one answer. "Who?"

"Fine." I give up, standing. "Tristan," I admit finally, and I'm sad the moment that was just ours now has Gabriella in it.

"Tristan!" she yells out even louder. "Tristan, Tristan?" she repeats his name twice as if she didn't hear me right.

"How many other Tristans do you know?" I ask her.

"Tristan," she says, her face in shock. "The Tristan you're in love with?"

"Oh my God." I roll my eyes at her. "I'm not in love with him." She folds her arms over her chest. "I'm in lust with him. There is a difference."

"Wow, pregnancy has made you a liar," she snaps out. "When the hell did you have time to have sex with him on family vacation?"

"The night before we left," I tell her as my mouth becomes dry and my tongue feels like it's getting thicker. "I went back to the room and went outside to just look at the stars."

"And his dick fell into you?" she jokes with me.

"He asked me to have a drink with him, and then he kissed me." I walk past her and to the fridge to grab a water bottle. Opening the stainless door, I grab a water bottle, hoping maybe she will give me space, but obviously, she doesn't. In her defense, if the roles were reversed, there is no way I would leave her alone either.

"He kissed you?" she quizzes me softly, and I unscrew the white bottle cap and bring it to my lips, nodding instead of answering. "And then you had sex?" All I do is nod. I don't tell her the next day I avoided him. I also don't tell her he probably regrets doing it.

After swallowing half the bottle, I put it down, but my mouth still feels dry. "I need to take a test," I announce. "Do you have one?"

"Yeah, sure." She rolls her eyes at me. "I stock up on them with my deodorant." She shakes her head. "I practice safe sex."

"I'm on the pill," I remind her, "and it just happened."

"Ugh," she grouses, walking up the stairs. "Let me

go get dressed, and we'll go out and get a test." I lean back on the counter and hang my head, bringing both my hands up to rub my face.

"You aren't pregnant," I comfort myself. "It's all in your head."

It takes her less than three minutes to come back down wearing a pair of shorts and a top. I follow her out and get into the car and we make our way over to the pharmacy. Gabriella opted to drive, and it's a good thing because I'm in a daze.

When she stops the car, I open the door and walk into the pharmacy with her right beside me, "What aisle has pregnancy tests?" I ask her, and she side-eyes me.

"Probably where they stock the condoms you should have worn." She rolls her lips. I walk down two aisles before I come to the shelf with pregnancy tests. "Wow, there are so many choices," she states, picking up a box that says First Response. "This one will tell you six days sooner." She puts it back on the shelf, grabbing another one and the only thing I can do is watch her. My hands feel like they are filled with concrete. "This one is straightforward." She holds it up to me. "Yes or no."

"We should take one of each," I suggest, and her eyebrows pinch together, "in case one is defective."

"Good idea," she agrees, grabbing about six boxes of tests. "We'll have a backup for your backup."

I nod at her as we walk to the counter to pay and then back to the car. Grabbing the plastic bag in my hand, I walk to the bathroom as soon as I walk into the house.

Opening two boxes up, I pour the contents onto the counter. Each comes with a long white foil-covered stick. I tear open both and then look down at them. One has a blue tip the other has a bright pink tip. I pull the tips off each before I sit down on the toilet and start to pee on the first stick. Holding my pee for a second, I grab the other one and look down between my legs, just like I did with the other one, to make sure I'm in my stream.

I look over at Gabriella, who is leaning against the doorjamb. "I can't be pregnant," I tell her, the tears coming on full force now. I swallow down the sob as I grab the tips, covering up the top of each test.

I press the round button on my Apple Watch. "Set timer for three minutes," I direct Siri, putting the sticks down on the counter before getting up and pulling up my scrub pants.

I can hear the ticks of the seconds go by. The sound gets louder and louder as the seconds go on. Gabriella doesn't say anything to me. Instead, she comes to stand next to me as I look down at both tests. The one with the blue cap has a screen that looks like it's flashing, while the other one is showing the liquid is filling it as the white center answer turns a bit blue. I put my head back, trying to calm myself down. Gabriella puts her hand on mine when the timer goes off on my watch.

"Are you ready?" she asks. I open my eyes, and nothing could prepare me for what's coming. Nothing and no one could prepare me.

On the blue test, the word Pregnant is written in big bold black letters, while the other test has two lines down the middle. "I'm no doctor," Gabriella declares, "but I think you're pregnant."

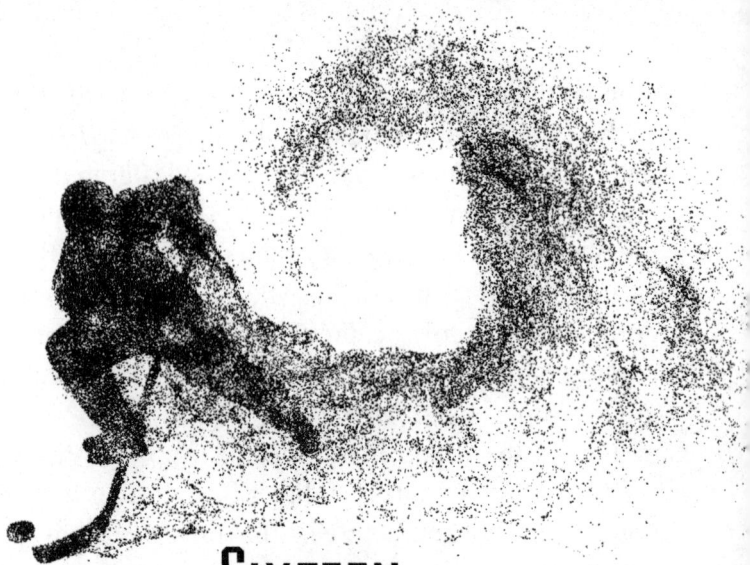

SIXTEEN

TRISTAN

One Month Later

THE ALARM RINGS, and my hand slides out of the covers to smack it off, but the phone falls on the floor. "Fuck," I mutter, leaning off the bed and grabbing the phone that is still going off.

"I'm up!" I hear Penelope yell from down the hall.

"Okay," I yell back at her. "Good morning."

"Morning," she shouts back, and I can't help but laugh as I throw the covers off me and get up to go to the bathroom. I close the bathroom door behind me as I walk over and go to the bathroom.

I slip on a pair of basketball shorts before walking downstairs and starting breakfast. "Pancakes or eggs?" I ask her when I get to the bottom step.

"Surprise me," she replies, and I laugh, shaking my head. We returned two days ago because we had to get ready for the first day of school. It's also my first day back on the ice with the team.

I walk into the family room first, turning on the television before walking to the kitchen. I press the coffee maker before walking to the fridge and grabbing the carton of eggs and pack of turkey bacon. I open the cabinet, retrieving a glass bowl and breaking six eggs into it. Walking over, I snag two frying pans, putting them both on the stove and turning the red knobs to low. Then I put a bit of butter in the pan before adding the eggs to one pan and four slices of turkey bacon to the other. Before Penelope came along, I usually just ate at the rink, and then I would have a chef prepare me meals that all I had to do was warm up.

I mean, I do that also now, but I cook a lot more than I did before. All her breakfasts I make, and I pack her snacks for school. Luckily, they have a full cafeteria, so I don't have to pack her anything for lunch. I grab a plastic spoon from the jar beside the stove and start scrambling the eggs a bit before bending into the lazy Susan in the corner and taking out the toaster. "I'm ready." I hear over my shoulder when I put two pieces of toast in the toaster.

I turn around, seeing her dressed in her school uniform of a white, button-down, short-sleeved cotton shirt, and a plaid pleated accordion skirt. It's just like everyone else's, except I made them sew in tight shorts under her skirt. I bought five of them with five pairs of tight yoga shorts and took them to a woman who sewed them in.

There was no way she was going to go and not have shorts under there. "You look so pretty," I tell her, and she does. She has little pieces of her mom in her, but she is all me, from her eyes to her hair and her chin. "Just like me."

"Ew, Dad," she whines, walking to the fridge, where she grabs the orange juice. She puts it on the counter as she grabs a plastic cup. "Guys are hot, not pretty." I side-eye her while I stir the eggs in the pan.

"Who told you that?" I ask her, and she just shrugs. "No guys are ever hot." I point the spoon at her. "Actually, we are all gross." She laughs at me and rolls her eyes, and I swear I want her to stop growing. I want to stop time right now and have her still skipping into the room with the pigtails around her face. "And we all have smelly feet and fart." I try to think of more disgusting things to throw her off the guy trail.

"Okay, Dad," she says, pouring herself a glass of orange juice and then walking over to the toaster when it pops up. She opens the cabinet and gets on her tippy-toes to grab two plates, just last year her fingers barely touched the plates, and I had to get them for her. She puts the plates down in front of her, grabs a butter knife, and puts two pieces of toast on one plate and two on the other. Side by side, we work as a team, and I can't help but lean over and kiss her head after I plate her eggs. She leans her head into me before she walks over and grabs two slices of turkey bacon, then makes her way over to the island.

We sit side by side, neither of us saying a thing. She

finishes at the same time I do. "Can you do me a half braid?" she asks, and I just nod my head.

"I'll clean up the kitchen"—I drink the rest of my coffee—"then I'll do your hair."

"Cool beans." I shake my head at how even her voice is changing.

I put everything in the dishwasher before running upstairs to brush my teeth and get dressed in my Dallas gear. I put on black shorts with the Dallas logo on the bottom corner of them and a matching T-shirt with my number on the sleeve. I wet my hands and then run them through my hair when I hear a knock on the door. That also changed this summer, I walked into her room while she was changing, and she hid her boobs from me. Also, there are no boobs, but we now have to knock when entering each other's room. "Come in."

She comes in with her brush and stands next to me. I go behind her as I brush her hair. "Do I have hockey tonight?" she asks, and I nod my head.

"You have skating from five to six," I tell her, and she smiles. When she was younger, I put her in ice-skating lessons. She liked it, but then she came on the ice with me, and she had a much better time, so two years ago, I finally caved and signed her up for hockey. She's usually the only girl on the all-boy team, but she doesn't care, and to be honest, she's even better than most of them.

I bring the sides of her hair up in a ponytail and then braid it. "Go get your bag. I'll meet you downstairs."

She jumps and kisses my cheek before walking out of the room. Grabbing a sweater from the closet, my eyes go to the shirt I hung up and never washed. My chest constricts when I think about her, just like every day since. I wish I could tell you I got over it. I wish I could tell you I didn't dream of her every night, except this time she's happy to be with me. I wish I could tell you I didn't wish she would reach out to me. I wish I could tell you I'm over it. But if I did, I would be a liar, and I'll never lie.

I turn off the light and walk out of the room, going downstairs and seeing her waiting for me with her backpack in her hand. "Let's go, baby girl."

"Dad," she moans as we get into the car in the garage, "I'm not a baby."

She gets into the back seat as I get in the front. Looking into the rearview mirror, I watch her put on her seat belt. "You'll always be my baby," I remind her. She rolls her eyes at me, and all I can do is laugh at her.

I pull out of the driveway and see we are exactly three minutes early. When I pull into the parking lot of the school, I see all the parents parking to drop off their kids. I pull up in an empty parking spot before turning the car off and getting out. I meet her on her side of the car, making sure she is okay. She slides her hand in mine as we walk toward the gated playground. "I'll be here to pick you up when you are done."

"Okay," she says, and someone calls her name. She looks up and smiles at me as she takes her hand out of mine to wave. "Bye, Dad." She turns and starts to run.

"Hey," I call her, and she turns back. "A hug?" She groans as she comes over and hugs me. I kiss her head as she wraps her arms around my waist, her head pressing on my chest. "Have a good day at school."

"Bye," she repeats, running off into the schoolyard. I watch her until the bell rings and she lines up to go inside, making sure she walks all the way into the school.

I take a deep breath as I walk back to my car. Getting in, I make my way to the rink. I pull up and see that most of the cars are already here. I even spot some news crew people here getting ready to snap pictures. I get out and walk to the door as they call my name. I smile and hold up a hand to say hello before walking into the rink.

There seem to be people everywhere. I walk down the hallway toward the locker room, stopping when I see some of the trainers. I shake their hands, and we welcome each other back. It's almost as if this is my back-to-school day also. I walk into the locker room and spot a couple of people there getting ready.

"Hey," I greet everyone who just looks up.

"Jesus, what happened to you?" Wilson says when he looks up. "Someone stopped jerking off and started lifting weights."

I can't help but laugh at that comment because, if anything I've jerked off more than I ever have. But I have also started lifting heavier weights, which has made me leaner and bigger if that makes any sense. I reach out my hand to him as he grabs it, getting up and giving me a hug. "How was the summer?"

"Short," he replies, sitting back down as he finishes his protein shake.

"Isn't that the truth." I sit at my spot.

"Hey," Michael says, coming into the room wearing pretty much the same thing I'm wearing, just with a baseball hat.

"About time you showed up," Xavier pipes up, coming into the room from the gym, his chest heaving up and down. "You said you were coming straight here."

"I had to drop the kids off," Dylan explains, entering the room and giving me a chin up when he sees me.

Xavier comes and sits next to me, slapping my knee. "You look good. Been working out, I see."

I laugh. "A bit," I say, looking around, seeing everyone sitting down and not wanting to move much.

"How was everyone's summer?" I ask, and Xavier puts his head back and groans.

"Don't ask," Michael states, sitting down next to Dylan, who just glares at him. "It's been eventful."

"I don't know what the big deal is," Wilson says as he gets up to get a water bottle from the fridge.

"It's a huge deal," Dylan retorts, and I look over at Xavier, hoping he can fill me in on what everyone is talking about. "She's like a baby."

"She's not a baby," Xavier cuts in. "She's an adult."

"What is going on?" I finally ask, and Michael just looks at me, shaking his head, almost as in a don't do it way.

"What's going on?" Dylan repeats, his voice going louder. "My sister is having a baby!"

I just look at him, my heart starting to speed up in my chest. "Gabriella?" I ask him, and there is nothing, and I mean nothing, that could have prepared me for what was going to come next.

There in the middle of the locker room, the little bit of my heart that wasn't broken shattered. "Not Gabriella. Abigail is the one who is pregnant." All hope I had that we would get together is now gone, knowing she is having a baby with someone else.

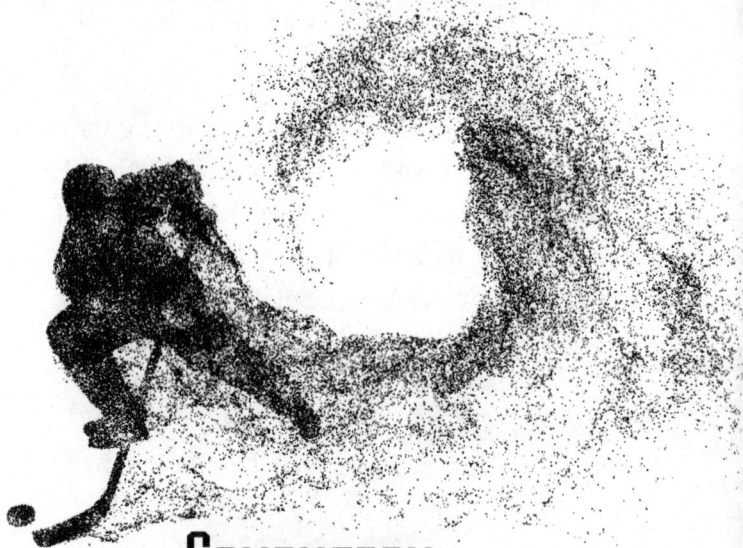

SEVENTEEN

ABIGAIL

One Month Later

"ABIGAIL STONE," THE nurse calls me, and I get up from the waiting room and walk back to the examining room. "This must feel strange to you," the nurse says when she sees me in my scrubs.

"Definitely on the other side of things now," I tell her as she points at the exam table.

"Have a seat while I ask you some questions."

I sit down on the black bed covered with the white paper that crinkles when you sit down while she looks at the computer. "So it says your last period was May." I nod.

"Yes, I was on Linessa," I tell her of the birth control, "and I get my period usually every two to three months, depending. I was on Zithromax before I went on vacation, and when they say it takes one time." I hold up my hand with my finger pointed up. "They were not kidding." I try to calm my heartbeat down so when she takes my blood pressure it won't be high. I blink away the tears that are stinging my eyes

"It says the date of conception was July seventh." I nod, the nerves from my stomach now moving to my throat. "No allergies."

"None that I'm aware of," I tell her, and she smiles at me.

"Your due date is going to be…" she starts telling me, and I can't help but smile.

"March thirtieth," I declare.

"You are fifteen weeks," she informs me, and my hand goes on my little baby bump. She stands up, looking at me. "The doctor will be right in."

"Thank you," I tell her as I sit on the exam table. I take a deep breath in as I try not to shed a tear. The last month has been a roller coaster of emotions for not only me but the family. After getting not two but a total of twenty-seven positive tests, I finally called someone who got me into the doctor. I had my blood drawn, and they confirmed I was pregnant. I wish I could say it was an easy time, but it was not.

I have never felt more alone in my whole life, even though I had Gabriella beside me throughout the whole thing. I felt like I was missing the biggest piece, and that was Tristan. I must have picked up the phone seven times a day to call him and tell him. I must have pulled up his number to text him over a thousand times, but each time, I chickened out. I couldn't do this to him. He already regretted the night we spent together. The last thing I wanted him to do was resent the baby we created. I don't think my heart could have survived if he told me that he didn't want me to have it. I wanted to remember our night as the best night I've ever had and this was a gift. So I took the coward's way out and kept it my secret.

Breaking it to my family, well, that was another adventure. My parents handled it well or as well as you could think they would. Dylan, on the other hand, was planning the wedding until I told him that I didn't know who the father was. Of course, I don't think anyone believed me. I said he was a random hookup, and we never exchanged names. My uncle Matthew came to see me with my uncle Max. I should have known them coming to see me was a clue that something was coming.

They showed up with a man who was holding a leather briefcase. I sat down next to them as they explained this man was going to draw a picture of the man I spent the night with, and then we'd put it up on social media. Like a wanted photo. They even thought about doing a billboard in Times Square and running an ad in the local papers. What surprised me even more was that Michael and Dylan thought it was the best idea ever invented.

The door opens, and my doctor comes in smiling. "Hello, you."

"Hi, Dr. Emmy." I greet her as she comes over and kisses me on both cheeks. We've worked together a couple of times.

"You look fabulous," she compliments me, going over and sitting down on the small chair. "How are we feeling?"

"Um," I start to say, "so far, so good. I feel less tired, which is great. I only need to take one nap during my night shift." I hold up my hands in celebration. "Nausea isn't too bad as long as I snack. During meals, that's another thing, so I always have a snack around me." I smile. "The staff has even started to add to my basket that I keep under the nurses' desk." She laughs, clapping her hands. "I'm also super emotional." I blink away the tears. "Especially this past month." I don't tell her that it's probably because I know he's back in town. I see him every time I turn on the television. Okay, fine, I only turn the television on when the pre-games are on, but still.

"It's normal," she tells me. "Lie back."

I turn and lie back on the table, pulling up the top of my scrubs. "This is my favorite time," I tell her, and she just smiles at me. I've had one ultrasound before this one, and that was at ten weeks when I first saw her. Usually, they wait until you are twelve weeks to see you, but I saw her when she came to follow up with a patient and heard the news I was expecting. She dragged me down to her office, which was two floors down, and showed me my little nugget.

"This time, we don't have to do it internally," she explains, walking over and shutting off the lights and then coming back to me. "Lower the top of your pants." I untie the string of my scrubs and lower it under the little baby bump that has just started to show. She squeezes the gel on my belly, and then the magic happens. I look over at the screen, and I see my baby, who actually looks like a baby now. Before, it looked like a blob with four limbs. The baby looks like it's doing summersaults, yet I don't feel anything. She clicks a couple of things. "We have an active one," she tells me, and all I can do is smile as the tear escapes the corner of my eye, my hand coming up to wipe it away. "Big baby," she states, and I just look at her, my eyes going wide, "I think I can see what sex it is. Do you still not want to know?"

"No." I shake my head, "I don't really care as long as there is only one and the one is healthy." She laughs as she wipes my stomach off before turning on the lights.

"There is only one, and they are perfect," she confirms, and I get up smiling as she hands me four pictures from the machine. "Baby book material."

"Thank you," I say, looking down at my baby and getting up. "I'll make an appointment later for next month."

"Just text me, and I'll get you in," she tells me, and I nod at her. "See you later," she says before she walks out, leaving me alone.

I take out my phone and take a picture of the baby, sending it to the family group chat.

Me: *Baby nugget is growing.*

I press send, and my phone clicks right away.

Christopher: *They have your big old head.*

Gabriella: *Did you rip Mom's vagina with your head?*

Christopher: *Can you never put me and Mom's vagina in the same sentence again in my life?*

Gabriella: *Why do you take things so sexual?*

Alex: *I'm in love already, but why do you guys keep adding me to this chat?*

I can't help but laugh, and I'm about to answer her when my phone rings, and I see it's Dylan. I answer right away. "Hey, big brother." I walk out of the office and head toward the stairs.

"How is my nephew?" he asks, and I laugh and roll my eyes at the same time.

"It could be a girl," I remind him, just like I do every time he says it's a boy. I really hope it's a girl just so I can say I told you so, but I think it's a boy also.

"Nah," he says, "you're pretty."

"What the hell does that mean?" I retort as I walk up the stairs to my floor.

"Apparently, if you are having a girl, you turn less pretty," he explains, and I put my head back and hold my nose, shaking my head. "Because she is taking the beauty from you."

"Who told you that?" I gasp.

"Uncle—" I stop him midsentence.

"Never ever repeat anything that either of them says. You know this," I scold as I pull the door open to my floor. "Actually, can you tell that to Mom when you see her next?" He laughs. "Or better yet, Alex. I think you should tell Alex."

"Are you out of your mind? I don't want to die," he huffs, and I can't help but chuckle. "Anyway, you coming to the game tomorrow?" I stop mid-step.

"I don't know. I'm just getting off shift."

"You have to come. It's season opener," he says. I know eventually, I'm going to have to go to the game, or they will ask more questions, and I don't want to answer any of them.

"Yeah, I'll come with Gabriella," I confirm, "try not to fuck up."

"I love your child. I don't like you," he teases as he hangs up on me. I grab my bag from my locker. That night, all I do is lie on the couch and eat.

"How do I look?" I ask Gabriella when I step out of my bedroom in jeans and a Dallas sweater. Apart from my little baby bump, my tits have grown more than anything. I mean, I can't complain. They are great.

"Like you fucked Tristan and are pregnant with his child," she fires back, smirking at me and walking toward the door because our ride is here.

"I do not look like that at all," I huff as I grab my phone and put it in my back pocket. I grab my crossbody purse and walk out to the waiting car. We get to the arena and make our way up to the family lodges. Every second I'm in the building, my heart beat echoes in my ears louder and louder.

I pretend I'm okay as I kiss everyone hello, and they ask me how I'm doing. I pretend I'm okay, but I'm not. I feel like my skin is going to fall off me. I'm going to stay a bit, take a picture or two to have evidence I was here, and then I'm ducking the fuck out of here. I'm about to tell Gabriella of my plan when I hear my name being called. "Abigail."

I turn and spot Penelope walking into the box with Erika behind her. She comes to me and hugs me around my waist, and I can't help but smile and hug her. "Did you grow?" I ask her as I kiss her head and put my cheek on the top of her head. "You got so big."

She lets go of me. "Will you come to the glass with me?" she asks when she hears cheering, and we know the guys are on the ice. I try to make an excuse, but she puts her hand in mine as we walk down toward the boards where the other kids are. All the kids are wearing their fathers' jerseys. Penelope wears Tristan's as she stands by the boards with the other kids, slapping the glass.

I have been training for the past two months for this moment, right here. I told myself I would pretend I was okay. I told myself I would treat him just as I had been before that night. I told myself all these things, but everything is out the window when I see him skating toward the glass. He slams into the glass and smiles at the kids as they yell, and then it happens. It's like I'm standing in the middle of the train track with the train coming full force at me, and I'm not moving. His eyes find mine, and it's like he's in shock when he sees me. It lasts one second, or maybe it's even less, before he skates off.

I swallow down the lump and turn to see Erika. "Can you take Penelope back up?" She looks at me, worried.

"Are you okay?" she asks, and I blink the tears, but one escapes.

"Yeah, just too much seeing the kids with their dads." I play it off, and she gives me a hug. "I'm going to head out. Can you tell them?" She nods her head at me as I turn and walk out of the arena, leaving my whole heart behind.

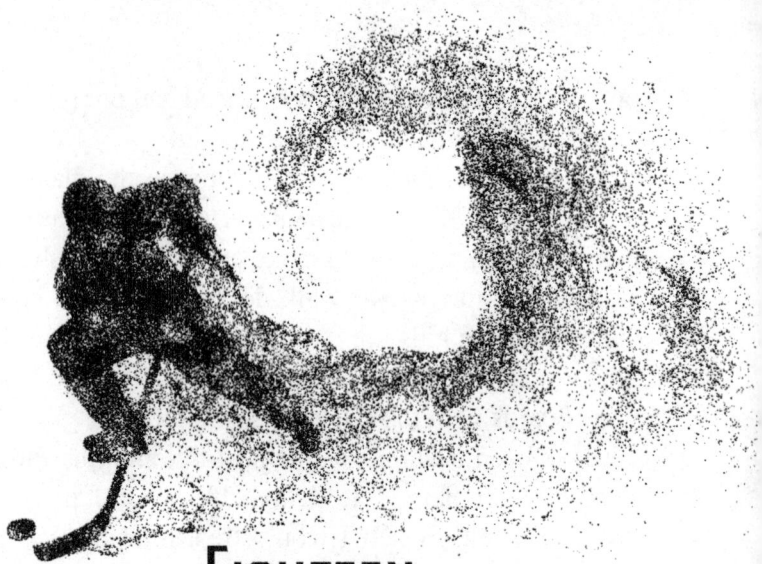

EIGHTEEN

TRISTAN

I KNEW THIS moment would be coming. I was bracing for it. I have been preparing for this moment like a soldier prepares for going to battle in the war. But I'm sure, like most soldiers, I was not ready. Looking up and seeing her there shocked me. I couldn't look at her long without my chest feeling like an elephant decided it would be a nice spot to sit. I quickly turned around and skated off the ice. My heart in my throat, beating so erratically, I almost went to Chase and told him I was probably having a heart attack.

But instead, I just went to sit in my spot in the locker room, my head hanging forward as I replayed that conversation I had with Dylan a month ago when he told me she was pregnant. I tried not to show how affected I was.

"What do you mean she's pregnant?" I blurted out. My mouth had gone so dry it was as if fifteen cotton balls were stuck there.

"I think it's self-explanatory. She is with child." Michael laughed at my questions, and it made everyone chuckle.

"We don't even know the guy," Dylan hissed, and I think at that point, I had raised my hand to massage my chest. I can't explain how my heart shattered in my chest. All I know is I looked down and expected to see my shirt soaked with blood. It was at this point I got up and walked out of the room, not sure I wanted to hear what else was said.

"Hey," Xavier says, coming back into the room huffing as he takes off his gloves and grabs a bottle of water. "Penelope was looking for you."

"Yeah, had to use the bathroom," I tell him, and he just nods as the rest of the guys start filling in the room.

It's the season opener, which means the home crowd is usually the loudest. There are all sorts of activities outside and even inside. "Okay, we have to line up," Cooper says, getting up. "Let's make the crowd happy tonight."

We all get up, making our way out to the hallway and down to where we are going to walk out. The team is going to be announced to everyone by number. I line up, and I know that whatever I have going on inside now has to be shut off. I have to get in the zone. I focus my eyes forward as the coaching staff is announced. I bounce on one foot and then another as the team is announced.

Slowly, we make our way down the line until I'm standing at the door. The arena is in the darkness, only the spotlight following whoever is being announced from the door to the middle of the ice. The crowd goes nuts with every single person. I hear the announcer say my number, and I know they are playing some highlights of me from last year on the Jumbotron.

When he says my name, I walk down toward the entrance and slide onto the ice, holding up my hand to say hello to twenty thousand people. The sound of cheering and clapping is almost deafening as I stop in the middle of the ice, making sure to turn around to greet everyone before I skate back to the bench.

I sit on the bench until the rest of the team is announced. The minute the national anthem has been sung, I close off my mind. It's the only time I do, and for these two hours, I focus on one thing and one thing only. Making sure we don't lose our season opener because nothing sucks more in life than losing at home, especially big games.

We squeak out a win by the skin of our teeth, and when I finally walk back to the locker room, there is a huge after-party celebration, but I've opted out of going. Instead, I dress back into my suit, omitting the tie, as I walk up to the lodges where I know Penelope waits for me.

I open the door of the lodge, and my heart now speeds up tenfold, knowing she might be here, knowing I can't keep avoiding her. I have to make peace that we will only have that one night. The sound of adults chattering fills the room as I look around and see Penelope sitting on the couch with her iPad in her lap. Usually, I get the babysitter to bring her to the game, but Erika volunteered to bring her tonight since she was coming with all the kids.

"Hey," I greet, and Penelope sees me and gets up, running to me, wrapping her arms around my waist. I bend down and kiss her head, and she looks up at me. She literally makes everything better for me.

"You did good," she praises me, making me laugh as I nod. "Uncle Matthew said you could have scored at least four times if you shot the puck." From when I introduced her to him, he always called himself Uncle Matthew, so she's always called him that. Everyone else was jealous that he was Uncle Matthew, so they started throwing Uncle in front of their names too. They really have taken both of us in and have always treated us like family.

"Really?" I say, looking up at Matthew, who now throws his head back and laughs.

"I don't think I said that exactly." He walks over and holds out his hand to shake mine. "You played a good game." I chuckle. "How's the leg?" In the third period, with two minutes to go, the other team pulled their goalie, making it six on five. They were all over us, and we had a one-goal lead when their defensemen got the puck and shot a one-timer. I deflected the shot off my leg.

"Probably going to have a big bruise," I tell him, omitting the fact it hurt like a motherfucker. "Ready to go home?" I look back at Penelope, who just nods her head before going to get her backpack.

She comes back and goes to hug Matthew. "Bye, Uncle Matthew." She gives him a side hug.

"We'll see you tomorrow at lunch?" he says, and the word no gets lodged in my throat.

"Yes," Penelope says, and I don't say anything. I just smile, not wanting to get into anything here. Besides, I'm fucking beat.

We walk out of the lodge and back down to the car. We get in, and when I drive out, the streets are still busy with people.

"Did you have fun tonight?" I ask her, looking into the rearview mirror to see her.

"Yeah," she says, "Uncle Dylan threw me a puck to add to my collection." She started collecting all the pucks she catches at the games and then makes whoever throws it to her sign it.

"Did you see Abigail?" The words are out of my mouth before I can stop them. But I'm jealous my daughter got to see her, and I didn't. How crazy is that?

"Yeah, only for a bit," she replies.

"Was she with her boyfriend?" I want to bite my tongue. When the talk about Abigail comes up in the room, I always get up and walk away. There is only so much I can take. Actually, there is only so much my heart can take.

"No," she says. "We have to study for my spelling test tomorrow." She changes the subject, and all I do is nod at her.

When we get home, she's already half asleep by the time she walks up the steps. I go into my bedroom to undress, taking off my suit and tossing it in the dry-cleaning pile before slipping on shorts. When I make it back to Penelope's room, she is already in bed and sleeping. I lean down and kiss her head. "Night, baby girl." She doesn't even grumble.

I usually go and have something to eat after the games, but I'm just not up to it, so instead, I slide into bed. Lying here in the dark, my head goes around and around as I try not to think of the one person I want to think about. I expected it to be hard to see her, but I wasn't expecting to feel physical pain.

I turn on my side, and before I know it, I'm asleep. I wake when I hear plates clinking from downstairs. Turning over and grabbing the phone, I see it's almost ten. Tossing the covers back, I go to the bathroom before I walk downstairs, where I find her in the kitchen making something to eat.

"Morning," I say, and she looks over at me. I move to her and bend to kiss her head.

"I'm making a bagel," she states, and I turn to the coffee machine, putting a pod in before starting it. She makes herself her breakfast, stopping at the fridge and grabbing some fruit from the shelf before sitting on one of the stools. She takes a bite of her bagel before she pushes back from the island and walks out of the room. I make my coffee, looking back when I hear something slapping the island. "We can study while I eat," she states, and I can't help but smile. She must get that from her mom because there was no way when I was her age. I even thought about studying. I don't have many regrets in my life, but not knowing her mother is going to be one of the biggest ones. I wish I knew her even a little.

I sit on the stool next to her, grabbing her book, "What lesson?" I ask as I open the book and start flipping pages. We spend the next hour going over her spelling words and then her math to make sure she understands it. I wish I could say I understood it, but the way they are teaching math today is just to fucking complicated.

"What time are we leaving," Penelope asks when she puts her plate in the dishwasher, "to go to lunch?"

"You really want to go to lunch?" I ask her. "You just ate."

"That was breakfast. I'm going to go get dressed."

"We can go catch a movie." I try to make her change her mind, but she just pulls her eyebrows together and shakes her head. She leaves me alone in the kitchen as she goes to get dressed.

I put my own cup in the sink before I go upstairs and get in the shower. I literally take the longest time getting dressed. So long that Penelope comes into my room twice to ask me what I'm doing. I put on jeans and a baby-blue polo shirt and a pair of white sneakers. Penelope is dressed in jeans and a pullover.

I make my way over to Matthew's place, and like always, cars are everywhere. I park on the street as far away from the cars as possible so I can get out easily when we leave. Last time, Cooper was stuck in the driveway for forty-five minutes, waiting for people to move their cars.

Penelope puts her hand in mine as we walk up the

driveway to the front door. I don't bother ringing because I did that the first time, and then they asked me what the fuck was wrong with me. The minute Penelope opens the door, I hear the chaos coming from the back of the house.

I don't even see Penelope as she walks in and hugs a couple of the adults before she makes her way over to the kids, who yell her name when she gets there. I can't help but smile when I see her run to them but then turn around and come back to me. I'm kissing Parker on the cheek when Penelope finds me. "Dad, can you get my backpack so Dylan can sign my puck?"

"Sure thing," I say, hugging Cooper, OG I call him. Actually, everyone is calling him OG lately. The kids are even calling him Grandpa OG. "I'll be right back," I tell Matthew when he finds me walking toward the front door. "Penelope forgot her bag in the car."

I take five steps to the front door when everything stops. I literally stop mid-step when I see her walking in. She is so fucking beautiful I stop even breathing. Her eyes go big when she sees me but then she is pushed inside the door by Gabriella behind her. "Can you move any slower?" she huffs before she is pushed aside by Michael, who comes in with Jillian and their kids, followed by Dylan and Alex. There are about ten people now standing in the entryway, but my eyes are only on her. Always on her.

NINETEEN

ABIGAIL

I PUSH OPEN the door, breathing through my nose and out my mouth. The queasiness has never been this strong. The only thing I'm trying to control is not barfing all over the place. My hand is still on the door handle when I take a step in and see him coming to me. My eyes go big when I see him. I don't even have a chance to do or say anything when I'm pushed inside the door by Gabriella behind me. "Can you move any slower?" she huffs out at me.

I feel like I'm having an out-of-body experience. My breathing is coming out in puffs right now. My ears feel like they are ringing, and all I can hear is the thumping of my heart. My mouth goes so dry it feels like paste in my mouth. I don't even have a chance to do anything before Gabriella is pushed aside by Michael, who comes in with

Jillian and their kids. "What are you guys doing blocking the door?" He is then pushed to the side by Dylan.

"Is this a meeting that I didn't know about?" Alex asks everyone standing by the front door.

I can feel his eyes on me, but I'm afraid to even look over at him. My stomach lurches when Michael comes to stand next to me, pushing me closer toward Tristan. I tuck my hair behind my ear when I look at him. It's almost as if everything is standing still. My head goes up slowly, and our eyes meet.

"Hi," he says to me, my body now feeling clammy as I try to wipe my hands on my yoga pants. I tried to wear my jeans today, but the zipper stopped halfway, so the yoga pants won out yet again. The past couple of weeks all I've been wearing has been yoga pants and sweaters.

"Hi," I say nervously, wanting to get the fuck away from him as soon as I can.

"Congratulations," he says, his smile forced on his face, "on the baby." I can't stop the vomit that comes out of my mouth. In the middle of the entryway, I vomit all over Tristan, including his shoes.

"Oh my God," Alex shouts, jumping in to help me while Michael and Dylan rush the kids away from me.

Jillian and Gabriella both rush to get me some water and all I can do is run away from him and go to the bathroom; not sure I'm not going to vomit on him again. I shut the door, putting my forehead on it. I turn around and walk over to the sink, turning on the cold water, putting my hand under the stream, and rinsing out my mouth. I grab a small hand towel out of the basket on the counter, wetting it and then wringing it out before putting it on my face. "Well," I say, putting the towel on the counter, "that couldn't have gone any worse." My stomach rises and then falls to let me know that maybe, just maybe, it could have been worse. I was almost afraid to ask if he would be here today. I thought he might be, but then he hadn't been here in a while, so I thought I might have been saved. But, apparently, I've dodged this bullet for as long as I could.

I wait in the bathroom until I can walk without feeling like I'm going to barf, opening the door and slowly walking out. There doesn't sound like there's any noise coming from the front. All the noise I hear sounds to be coming from the back of the house.

I literally take a second to think about ducking out when I round the corner and come face-to-face with Tristan as he's walking down the steps from upstairs. He is now wearing shorts and a new shirt. "I'm so sorry," I apologize as he walks down the last step and stands in front of me.

"Not the first time I've been vomited on." He tries to make me feel better. "Don't think it'll be the last time." We stare at each other, and it feels so awkward between us, unlike all the other times.

"There you are," Vivienne declares, walking into the room with a bottle of water in her hand. "Gabriella said you were in the bathroom." She looks at me and then at Tristan. "How are you feeling?"

"Better," I reply, avoiding looking at Tristan. "Less queasy, but I think it's because I skipped breakfast."

"Well, you should get some food in you," Vivienne suggests, handing me the bottle of water. "The food just came out."

"Sounds good," I say as the three of us turn and walk into the kitchen. I'm saved again when my aunt Allison spots me and comes over to me. I veer toward her as I feel Tristan move away from me and go toward the food and the men.

"How are you feeling?" she asks with a look of worry on her face. "Do you want some ginger ale?"

"I think I'm good. I just need to eat something," I tell her as she puts her hand around me and takes me over to get a plate of food. I grab a plate and fill it up with a little bit of food, not wanting to overdo it. I put some pasta on the plate and then also add a little bit of grilled chicken and of course some french fries. I've been craving those the past couple of days with loads of ketchup.

I walk out into the backyard, where white tables are set up. I spot Gabriella sitting at the table with Erika, Alex, Vivienne, Jillian, and Julia. I sit down in the empty chair, grabbing a bottle of water from the middle of the table.

"You just threw up, and you think eating pasta is a good idea?" Gabriella asks as she cuts her grilled chicken and pops a piece into her mouth.

"I'm fine. I got sick because I didn't eat breakfast." I glare at her.

"Why are you giving me that look?" she asks. "I'm not the one who slept until five minutes before we had to leave."

"I told you yesterday to wake me at eight." I point my fork at her, then stab two pieces of pasta.

"Do you think I was up at eight?" She laughs. "I got home at four o'clock."

"I'm actually surprised she's even here." Erika chimes in. "When we left her at the bar, she was yelling tequila!"

"You left me alone at the bar." Gabriella shakes her head. "What happened to leave no one behind?"

"You are so dramatic," Alex declares. "We were there the whole time." She shakes her head. "Who do you think brought you home?"

"Wait." She holds her fork up. "That was you guys?"

"Who did you think it was?" Alex shrieks.

"Um," Gabriella says, "I thought it was Chase and Julia."

"Why the hell would you think it was Chase and Julia?" Alex asks.

"Well, for one, you guys stopped at McDonald's for me," Gabriella states. "Dylan is never that nice."

"Yes, I am." I turn and see Dylan coming to the table with his plate in his hand. Alex just laughs at him, and then when he turns to glare at her, she just rolls her lips.

"I'm sure it had nothing to do with Gabriella saying that Chase was nicer than you," Alex points out as Dylan grabs a chair from the other table and brings it over to ours while Alex moves over to give him a place for him to sit.

"It did not," Dylan denies, sitting down and grabbing a french fry from Alex's plate.

"I think what she said was, 'You suck. Why can't you

be more like Chase?'" Alex reminds him, and he just glares at her.

"Oh, I remember that now," Gabriella says, making us laugh. "I think I even chanted it."

"You did," Alex confirms when she picks up her own bottle of water. "Sucky Stone was what you were saying."

"Then I just said, 'You suck, Stone,'" Gabriella recalls as I see Chase start coming over, followed by Xavier and Michael behind him.

"So basically, you bullied him into going to McDonald's for you?" Julia clarifies.

"This is also an answer to why I found a trail of fries from the driveway into the house," I observe as I cut my own piece of chicken, making everyone laugh. "So the moral of the story is that Dylan isn't very nice until you bully him." I look at Dylan, who looks like he's going to flip me the bird. "And Chase is still the nicest cousin ever."

"I have no idea what we're talking about," Chase joins in, grabbing a chair and putting it next to Julia, "but I agree with it."

"Don't you have some yoga class to go to?" Dylan leans back in his chair.

"He does Pilates," Michael corrects him as he too tries to squeeze into the table.

"Laugh all you want," Chase says, "but when I can go four hours in bed, I'm the one who is laughing."

"That is so not true," Julia retorts. "I'm also laughing." Chase smirks at her, leaning in and kissing her neck.

"Can you guys be more gross?" Jillian whines from beside her as she pretends to vomit.

I grab another piece of pasta as I listen to the talk going on around the table when I hear Xavier call over Tristan.

I swallow down hard when I see him walking over to our table. "There are about fifteen tables in the yard. Why do we always gather around one?" Erika says, and I want to give her a high five.

"Why don't we just grab another table and connect it?" Michael suggests, getting up.

"Or," Alex says, "women can stay at one table and men sit at another."

"But then who will steal all my food?" Dylan asks, and she smiles at him sweetly before raising her hand and flipping him the bird. Out of everyone's relationship, the one I am always envious of is Dylan and Alex's. They are the best of friends, and they know exactly how to push each other, but then you also know no one loves each other more than they do.

Michael and Dylan get up while Chase, Vivienne, Erika, and Jillian move their chairs so we can put the two tables together. I breathe a sigh of relief when Chase sits beside me so I know Tristan has to sit on the other side of the table. When he sits down right in front of me, I suddenly wish I was sitting at the other end.

"Where did your clothes end up?" Michael asks Tristan, and I look down at my plate instead of at him. I cut a piece of chicken even though I know my stomach is going wishy-washy.

"Your aunt said she's going to have them cleaned," Tristan replies, "I told her to throw them away."

I feel so bad when he says this that I look up at him. "I'm so sorry," I finally say out loud and all the chatter from the table suddenly stops, or maybe it was stopped beforehand, but I just noticed now that I wish there was noise around me.

"Like I said, no worries." He cuts his own piece of chicken. "Penelope throws up on me at least once every six months." He chews his piece of chicken. "Hopefully, your baby is better." He laughs at me, and I can tell he's not sure what else to say. "How are you feeling?"

"Actually, this is probably only the third time I've ever thrown up," I admit to him honestly.

"Morning sickness will do that to you," Erika cuts into the conversation.

"But that usually lasts the first trimester," Chase butts in, and I want to tell him to shut up, but he's literally just minding his business as he eats his food. "After twelve weeks, it usually subsides."

"It can last longer," Alex adds. "I think I was sick for nine months when I was pregnant."

"I remember with Parker, I was sick in my second trimester and not in the first," Erika shares. All I can do is nod, hoping they find something else to talk about.

"How far along are you?" Tristan asks, and I feel Gabriella put her hand on my leg. I don't know how I thought I would be able to hide this from him. I don't even know why I even convinced myself that it was better this way. At this moment, staring into his eyes, I wish I could go back to when I found out, but we all make choices in life. Some we regret, and some we don't.

I take a deep inhale as I look at him and answer his question, "I'm fifteen weeks."

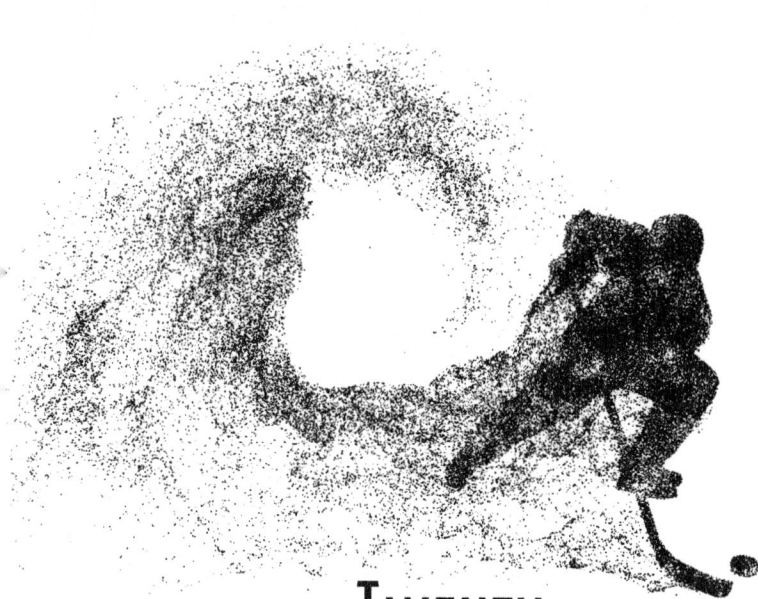

TWENTY

TRISTAN

I'M SITTING AT the table listening to her family talk about when they were pregnant, and all I can do is try to look down at my food. Coming face-to-face with her at the front door was a shock. Technically, I knew she might be here, and it would have been a lot easier if I just watched her from across the room instead of having no choice but to come face-to-face with her. I don't think anyone was expecting her to throw up on me. She ran away from me, and I didn't even have a chance to go after her because Matthew came running to the front door to make sure she was okay. He took one look at me and pointed at the stairs. I followed him up the stairs as he took me into the spare bedroom, showing me shorts and shirts that were still brand new. I walked into the bathroom and undressed before putting the new clothes on. I washed off my hands and made sure I was better before walking out with the dirty clothes in my hands. Allison met me at the bottom of the stairs and took my clothes. I was actually just going to toss them out.

"But that usually lasts the first trimester," Chase cuts in, chewing on a piece of his chicken. "After twelve weeks, it usually subsides."

"It can last longer," Alex adds. "I think I was sick for nine months when I was pregnant."

"I remember with Parker, I was sick in my second trimester and not in the first," Erika shares. My stomach gets sick when I think about if she was dating this guy before the vacation. But she was a virgin when we had sex. Did she come back and go straight to his bed?

"How far along are you?" I ask, though I really wish my mouth and my head would get the memo about minding my fucking business. I put down my fork because I think this time, I'm the one that is going to be sick when she tells me.

"I'm fifteen weeks," she says, and I just sit here not sure I understood what she said. All I can do is blink at her as I play her words over and over in my head.

Did she say fifteen weeks? It's impossible, I think to myself. There is no way. I mean, there is a way since we didn't even use protection. Something that made me feel like an asshole, but I was so caught up in the moment. We both were. The fork in my hand is playing with the food on my plate.

"I can't believe you are almost four months along," Vivienne says, and all I can do is look down at my plate. Everything inside me goes cold. I sit here, my head spinning around and around as I try to go back in weeks in my head. The chatter keeps going on around me, but the only thing I can do is think about the weeks since. I don't say anything to her as she gets up to use the bathroom. I watch her walk inside, wondering if she will take off.

I bide my time at the table for a couple of seconds longer before I get up. "I'm going to check on Penelope," I tell everyone at the table, pulling the phone out of my pocket and opening the calendar as I walk across the yard to where the kids are. "Hey," I say when I'm close enough for her to hear me. "Are you okay?"

"Yeah, I'm fine," she replies, confused, before she turns around and goes back to playing. Instead of returning to the table, I walk inside and go to the bathroom. The door is still closed, giving me the time to pull up the calendar and start counting down the weeks. The blood rushes to my head as I count the weeks from July when we were on vacation to today.

"Could this be?" I ask myself as I hear the water turn on in the bathroom and then the door opens.

She jumps back, shocked to see me there. "Oh, you scared me," she says, putting her hand to her chest.

I look around for a second before I walk to her. "I think we should talk," I state as calmly as I can. My insides feel like a hurricane and a tornado are coming together, if that is even possible.

"Yeah, sure," she says. "What's up?"

"I don't think we should talk here," I suggest and turn

my head toward the hallway entrance when I hear voices. "I think we should do it privately."

"Um, I don't really think we need to," she replies as she moves her hand from her chest to her stomach. I can't even see a bump because of the baggy sweater.

"Did you drive here?" I ask, afraid for a whole different reason. What if the baby isn't mine? Then what? The need to just ask her if it's my baby is so strong, but I know this conversation can't be done here. Even if it's not mine, I want her to know what our night meant to me.

"No, Michael picked me up," she says, and I nod.

"I have to go drop off Penelope and see if I can get a sitter, and then I can come to you," I tell her so she knows that we are definitely having this conversation.

"We really don't have to do this today," she says softly.

"It's not up for debate," I state. "I'm going to try to get a sitter, and then I'll call you."

"Okay," she agrees right before she puts her head down and walks away from me, leaving me alone in the hallway.

I lean my head back and look up at the ceiling, the tears stinging my eyes. *This isn't happening to me again,* is all I can think. The guilt inside me comes to the surface, and I can't even catch it in time to push it away.

I live my life with the guilt I missed Penelope's first everything. The guilt goes straight to my stomach as it starts to eat at it. I walk back into the yard and search for Penelope, finding her sitting in the grass, looking up at the sky, talking about the shape of the clouds. "Hey," I interrupt, and she looks over. "Time to go."

"Okay," she says, getting up. "Can Parker sleep over next weekend?"

"I have to see the travel schedule," I inform her because right now, I don't even know what day it is. The only thing going through my mind is fifteen weeks.

"Okay," Penelope chirps. She's always been good at getting ready when I tell her it's time. I often see kids ask their parents for five minutes more, but she's never done it.

I don't bother going back to the table because, for one, I don't trust myself to not just ask her in front of everyone the question that has been eating at me since she told me she was fifteen weeks, since I counting the weeks on my phone calendar. I do stop and thank Matthew for inviting me and, of course, kiss Allison goodbye, even though Matthew always pushes me away from her.

I grab a pair of flip-flops out of the basket at the door because after Abigail threw up on my sneakers, I tossed them in the trash. We walk outside, and the only thing I can think of is calling Roxanne and asking her to come over.

When we make it home, Penelope walks up the stairs. "I'm going to go read," she says. "Then after, do you want to watch a movie with me?"

"Yeah, I might have to go out for a bit later."

"Can I come?" she asks, and I just shake my head.

"Not this time," I say, and she turns and walks up the stairs. "Movie in twenty minutes?"

"Okay," she says, rushing up the steps. I pull out my

phone and call Roxanne, who answers after two rings.

"Hello," she answers, and I can hear cars honking in the distance.

"Hey, Roxanne," I greet, "it's Tristan. Sorry to bother you on a Sunday, but I was wondering if you were free?"

"I'm in New York," she replies, and I close my eyes, remembering she went to visit her sister for the weekend and will be back on Tuesday.

"I'm so sorry," I apologize, sitting on the couch. "I totally forgot." I put my head back. "Have a great trip, and I'll see you when you get back."

I hang up the phone and close my eyes. Besides Roxanne, I don't have another sitter, only because, if I'm not traveling, I'm home with her. I lost two years with her, so I promised her she would never be without me unless I was working. I think about maybe calling Xavier and Vivienne, but then I'd feel like a dick for lying to them.

I close my eyes when the pounding starts in my head as I pull up my calendar and start counting down again to make sure I didn't fuck up, and each and every time, it lands on fifteen weeks.

Penelope comes back down and over to the couch, sitting with me. "Ready?" she asks as she grabs the remote and lies down on her side. "I love this movie."

I take my phone and put it on my stomach, waiting for it to ring, knowing that if it doesn't ring by the time Penelope goes to bed, I'll be making my own call. It's time for a one-on-one that has been a long time coming.

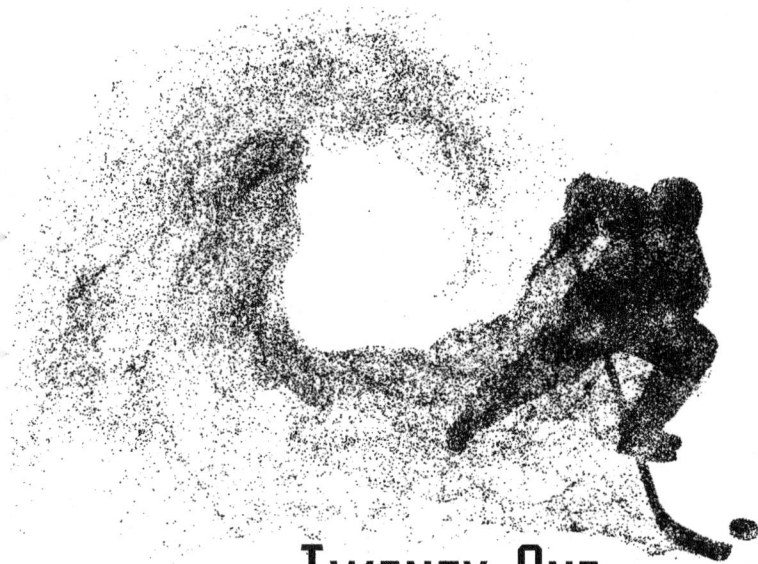

TWENTY-ONE

ABIGAIL

I WALK BACK to the table after leaving him in the hallway, the whole time expecting my legs to give out on me. I knew that the minute I said how far along I was, he would have questions. I just didn't expect him to have questions at that moment. Arriving at the table, I sit down and grab the water bottle.

I listen to the chatter and wait for him to come back, but he doesn't. "Okay," Franny announces, getting up, "time to get going."

Wilson follows her. "I'll get the baby." He turns to walk away and go to the little play area where the kids are.

"I guess I'll go too," Gabriella states, getting up. "I think I need a nap."

"I miss napping," Franny sighs. "It used to be my all-time favorite thing to do."

"I thought sex was your all-time favorite thing to do?" Vivienne teases.

"It's a close tie." She laughs. "Definitely a nap after sex." I can't help but laugh at her as she comes over to kiss me goodbye and touch my little bump.

"We should head out also," Vivienne declares, looking at Xavier.

"Can you guys drop me off?" I ask, and they both nod at me.

"I'm coming too." Gabriella gets up, and we start the process of leaving.

At this point, it takes an extra thirty minutes before you get through hugging everyone. I take a look around for Tristan when I'm saying goodbye, but I don't see him or Penelope.

The drive takes them no less than five minutes, and I laugh as I see the trail of french fries still there. I kick off my sneakers at the door and walk over to the fridge, grabbing the bottle of water, wishing it was something stronger. Gabriella walks in and looks at me, leaning against the counter, and instead of coming to me, she walks over to the cabinet and takes out the Patrón.

I watch her like a hawk as she grabs a shot glass from the other cabinet and then goes to the island stool. She places the tequila on the island and then pulls out her stool. "What…?" I start to ask, and she holds up her hand to tell me to wait a second. She pours a shot of tequila and then takes it. She hisses and then looks at me.

"The things I do for you." She wipes her mouth.

"Now, you can talk."

"Talk about?" I just stare at her, and she gives me a *come on* look. "Let's talk about why you moved to Dallas?" She just looks at me knowing I'm deflecting off myself and onto her, "Shall we talk about the fact that you are brokenhearted but pretend everything is okay?"

"There is nothing to talk about."

She avoids looking at me and takes another shot of tequila, "But we can talk about the fact Tristan asked you how far along you were?" She taps her finger on the counter. "And are we going to discuss that he followed you to where you went and never came back?"

"I think he knows," I finally admit, and I have to put my hand on my knees because I think I'm going to have a full-on panic attack.

"Shocking," she deadpans as she pours herself another shot of tequila and laughs.

"It's not funny." I look up at her, blowing the hair out of my face.

"I'm not laughing," she says, leaning back in the chair her voice as calm as can be. Right now, she knows that she has to be the calm one because she knows I'm freaking the fuck out.

"He asked me how far along I was," I tell her as if she wasn't sitting at the table with me. As if she wasn't the one holding my hand.

"Why didn't you just lie?" she asks what I've been asking myself the whole time.

"Because I was in front of everyone." I throw my hands in the air. "What the hell was I supposed to say, 'oh just a couple of months'? Then knowing our family, they would all sit down and be like, 'wait, didn't you tell me.'" Then they were going to sit down and start doing math."

She just shrugs. "Well, now you get to tell him the truth."

I roll my eyes, but the pain in my chest kicks in, along with the stinging of tears, one escaping down my cheek as I use my index finger to wipe it away. "What if he doesn't want me to have the baby?"

Her eyes go into slits. "Then we cut his balls off and call Uncle Matthew and Uncle Max."

"This isn't funny," I hiss at her.

She shakes her head. "You already decided you didn't care if he wants to be involved or not." She reminds me of the conversation we had when I found out I was pregnant. "You sat down and we went over this. You were like, 'It doesn't matter if he is involved or not,

I don't care.'"

"I don't." I put my hand on my stomach. "I'm willing to do this by myself."

"Never by yourself." She smiles at me. "I mean, it's almost as if it's my child since we are twins."

"Almost." I smile at her, the sound of my phone ringing from the front door has my whole body going cold and stiff.

"My Spidey-Senses tell me that it's the baby daddy," she teases, pushing off from the island. "I need a shower." She looks over her shoulder at me. "Everything will be okay." She takes a couple of steps up, stopping. "And if not, I'll dust off my black clothes."

"For what?" I ask her, the sound of ringing now stopping, giving me a couple of minutes to get my nerve up.

"Well, if we are going to kidnap him and kill him, I'm not going to wear flashy clothes," she huffs. "You would think after all the *Dateline* that our family has made us watch, you would know this already." She shakes her head going up the steps, and only when I hear the water come on in her room do I push off from the counter and walk over to my purse.

"What are the chances that it's not him?" I ask myself as I grab my purse and search out my phone. "Like fifty-fifty?" I ask the walls, but my head screams out it's one-hundred-percent him.

I turn the phone over, and sure enough, his name is there with a missed call notification. "What if I don't call him back?" I look at my phone. "Like, what if I didn't get this call?" I try to convince myself. "It's technology. Sometimes things go into the cloud, and this could be one of them."

I look down at the phone, and it starts to ring again, this time in my hand. "Well, now you're just showing off." I look up to the universe, and I press the green button to accept the call.

"Hello," I answer, walking over and sitting on the bottom step.

"Hey, it's me," he says, and a smile just fills my face, "I have a bit of a problem." I sit up, worried that something is wrong. "I called Roxanne and she's in New

York. So I can't come to you. Do you think you can come over here?"

"Now?" I ask him, putting my hand on my forehead to see if maybe I'm getting a fever, and then I won't have to see him.

"Whenever you can. I just put Penelope to bed."

I take a deep breath in. "Might as well get this over with," I mumble. "I can leave now."

"I'll send you my address," he tells me

"I have it," I confirm to him and close my eyes. "Roxanne came to the game once, and you guys took off for the away game right after. Well, her car didn't start so I drove her home." I quickly add, "Not that I'm like stalking you or anything."

"I'll see you soon," he says and hangs up the phone.

"Could you be more of an idiot?" I ask myself.

"Yes," Gabriella yells from her bedroom and then walks out, wrapped in her robe with a towel around her hair.

"Who asked you?" I look at her while getting up.

"Well, I felt sorry for you talking to yourself so I figured I would help you out." She folds her arms over her chest. "You're welcome. Now go declare your love to him."

"I don't know why I tell you anything," I grumble, grabbing my bag.

"I would tell you to be safe." She snickers. "But it's way too late for that."

"Don't think I forgot about our fight. You will have to tell me what happened in LA one of these days." I don't wait for her to answer. Instead, I just slam the door shut. Pulling open the car door, I sit inside and press the red button. I turn the air-conditioning on right away before I buckle myself in. "It's going to be fine," I reassure myself. "It's going to be like, 'am I the baby daddy'? I'm going to say yes, and then it'll be over."

I take my time driving over there, even making sure I go under the speed limit. When I pull up to his house, I park on the street. "This is a good idea." I look at the light at the front door. "This way, I can leave whenever I want." I grab my bag, getting out of the car and closing the door.

I don't think I could be more nervous, and the more I keep pretending I'm not, the sicker I feel. I walk up the driveway, making sure I don't trip over my feet. Stepping up the one step, I reach the door. I lift my hand, and I'm about to ring when I remember he told me that Penelope was sleeping. Instead of ringing, I bring my hand up and softly knock on the black door. My stomach lurches up and then down again, as if it is doing the wave, and my neck starts to get warm with nerves. I listen to hear if maybe I'll hear footsteps, but I don't hear anything. "I can just say I came, and he wasn't home," I mumble to myself.

I'm about to turn around and do just that when the door opens, and he stands there wearing shorts and a T-shirt. His hair looks like it's wet from the shower. "Sorry I didn't hear you ring." His tone is different than I've ever heard before. It's curt and tight, making my nerves kick up even more.

My stomach now fills with flutters. All the words are stuck in my throat as I just stare at him. I clear my throat. "I didn't ring," I say softly, "I was afraid to wake Penelope."

He moves aside. "Come in." His hand is still on the door. I take a step up into his house, the smell of him floating all around me. "Where do you want to do this?"

In your bed? On the couch? Against the door? "Wherever you like," I finally say. "If it's not too much trouble, can I have some water?" I ask him, and all he does is nod at me and everything inside me shifts.

Twenty-Two

TRISTAN

"WHEREVER YOU LIKE," she finally says, and I can see her gripping the purse in her hand so tight that her knuckles are white. "If it's not too much trouble, can I have some water?" All I can do is nod at her. I'm so afraid I'm going to snap. The whole time I've been trying to calm myself down, telling myself that it's not what I think. But then the only thing that kept going over and over in my head is she didn't tell me.

"We can talk in the family room," I suggest to her as we walk from the front room, past the stairs, and into the family room attached to the kitchen. "Have a seat, I'll get you water." I walk to the kitchen and turn around mid-step. "Do you want juice instead?"

She looks over at me, and fuck, if she doesn't always take my breath away. "No, I'm good with just water."

She stands there in the middle of the room, she doesn't move. I want to tell her to make herself at home, but the anger in me stops me.

I grab the bottle of water from the fridge and then walk to her, handing it to her. I make sure I don't touch her because I know that one touch will change everything. She'll touch me and I'll forget it all. Instead, I walk to the couch and, sure enough, she follows me.

I sit on one side of the couch that faces the other side and she sits down at the corner of the seat. This is so much different than how I thought it would be. I somehow always pictured her here with me, but the situation was different. "Should we start?" I ask as she takes a sip of water, and I can see her hands shake. She's a nervous fucking wreck, and if I had my head on straight, I would keep that in mind, but I'm just as fucking nervous.

"Sure," she finally says, taking a sip of her water . I don't even know how to start this conversation. "We should start." She laughs nervously, and I love the sound of it. It literally gives me butterflies. "Well, I'm pregnant."

I nod at her. "So I've heard," I say tightly, and I have to squeeze my hands together when I ask her this next question.

"Am I the father?" I figure might as well just get it out of the way. If she says no then my heart is broken for a whole other reason. If she says yes, then my heart also breaks.

"Of course, you're the father," she mumbles. "I can't even believe you are asking me this."

"Well, how was I supposed to actually know," I answer back to her question and then my head hangs down and the tears come to me. "Why didn't you tell me?" I ask as she looks at me with her own tears in her eyes. She opens her mouth to say something but nothing comes out. "How could you keep this from me?"

She shakes her head furiously. "I wasn't keeping it from you," she denies.

"But you were," I point out to her. "You didn't come to me." I get up now, the anger almost ripping through me.

She just looks at me. "It really wasn't like that," she says softly

"Really?" I put my hands on my hips. "So me finding out through the grapevine is not you keeping it from me?" I run my hands through my hair, and I want to pull it out. How can she do this to me? I just can't understand how she could do it.

"I just didn't know how to…" she finally says, and she uses her index finger to wipe away the tears that have escaped her beautiful eyes.

"Here is a thought? How about you pick up the phone and call me?" I pretend to put the phone to my ear. I put my head back and close my eyes. "When did you find out?"

"I was six weeks," she says softly, and my heart sinks hearing it. I was really hoping she would tell me she just found out.

"Wow," I can't help but snap at her.

"And nowhere in the nine weeks after did you

think that maybe I deserved to know?" She tries to say something, but everything I'm feeling is just raw. It's a guilt I never thought I would feel again. "Nowhere did you think maybe I wanted to know?" The tightness in my chest is so strong that it's making it so hard to breathe. "That's my child." I point at her.

"It's our child," she corrects me.

"Technically, it's just your child." I sit down, but then my legs start to shake again, so I get up and start to pace the room. "You know, since you didn't think I deserved to be included." I'm so hurt by this. Hurt I'm in the situation again. Hurt I wasn't there again. Hurt she didn't think better of me. "Did you for one second think about how I would feel? Think, hey, maybe I should call Tristan and tell him he's having another child?" My voice cracks when I ask her the question, and all she can do is roll her lips as the tears continue to pour down her face. "You, out of everyone, know what I went through with Penelope." The tears now pour down my face. My whole body is shaking with pain and anger. "I missed everything, all the firsts."

"Tristan," she says my name in a plea, or maybe to shut me up, but she has to know how much this means to me. "You can be as involved as you want to be," she assures me and I glare at her now.

"How involved I want to be?" I ask her the question, hoping I didn't hear it right.

"Yes. This must be a shock to you."

"A shock to me?" I look at her. "A shock. It's so much more than that." I swallow down the rage that wants to come up. "I can't even put into words what I'm feeling right now," I tell her, and tears come out of my eyes. I don't even bother wiping them off at this point. "You have no idea the guilt I carry." The sob wants to escape, but I push it down. "The guilt that I try to make up for every day." I shake my head. "I missed all the firsts," I say, the guilt coming to the surface. "The guilt that eats away at me every time I sit down, and my mind wonders about her, hopefully feeling like I didn't desert her. Or that she thought I didn't fucking care." The thought guts me. "First heartbeat, first picture, first breath. First cry, first smile." I'm gutted again. "First time she crawled. The first time she took a step. The first time she fell and got hurt, I wasn't there for her. I missed it all. It was ripped away from me." I can't help the broken way my voice is. "And I vowed to myself that the next time it happened. The next time I had a child, it would be different. I was not going to miss anything."

"I'm never going to keep you away," she says, her voice cracking too.

"You did, though, by not telling me." I point at her. "By not giving me the chance to do things right." I shake my head. "By not coming to me and telling me that we are having a baby. By pretending I'm not the father. By making me find out from everyone else instead of you."

"I didn't know how you would react." She gets up now. "I didn't know if you even wanted to have more kids."

I look at her, confused. "What are you talking about? Of course, I want to have more kids. I just thought this time it would be different. I would know I'm doing it."

"Did you not know you were doing it when we were together?" She glares at me. "I mean, we did the main thing you need to do in order to get pregnant."

"Don't you dare, Abigail." I say her name at the same time my heart squeezes. "Don't you dare turn this around on me."

"I'm not turning it around on anyone," she refutes, her voice going higher and then she looks up the stairs to make sure she isn't waking Penelope, which just makes me love her even fucking more. "I'm sorry I didn't tell you," she apologizes softly. "Do you think I didn't want to tell you?"

"I have no idea," I tell her the truth. The anger is less now that I told her why what she did was wrong.

"The only person I wanted to tell was you." She is the one who doesn't give me a chance to say anything now. "But I was a chicken, okay?" She swallows, and I can see her hands shaking. "I was so fucking afraid I would tell you, and you would tell me you didn't want the baby. I was so scared you would tell me to get rid of it, and then I would end up hating you."

"How can you think so little of me?" Her words cut right through me. "How can you think I wouldn't want a child?"

"I have no idea what to think because we didn't exactly talk about it." She gets up. "We went from being really awkward with each other…" She puts her hand on the side of her head. "Maybe I was the awkward one, but whatever, we went from that to jumping each other like lions in the forest." Her voice now goes a touch lower. "I am sorry I never put myself in your shoes. I am sorry I didn't come to you when I found out. I can never erase that mistake." She grabs her purse in her hand. "I hope in time you can forgive me." She puts the straps over her shoulder. "I hope, even though you now hate me, we can put aside the difference for the baby." She turns and starts to walk out of the room, my heart going to my throat.

"I don't hate you," I say to her. *I can never hate you*, I don't say. "But just so you know, this changes everything."

Twenty-Three

ABIGAIL

"I HAVE NO idea what to think because we didn't exactly talk about it." I get up, no longer able not to say anything. "We went from being really awkward with each other…" I put my hands on the side of my head. "Maybe I was the awkward one, but whatever it is, we went from that to jumping each other like lions in the forest." My breathing comes in pants as I lower my voice. "I am sorry I never put myself in your shoes. I am sorry I didn't come to you when I found out. I can never erase that mistake." I grab the purse in my hand, knowing I have to get out of here before I crumble. "I hope in time you can forgive me." I put the straps over my shoulder. "I hope, even though you hate me, we can put aside the difference for the baby." I turn, getting ready to walk out of the room without letting him know that him hating me is what I was trying to avoid. I start to walk out of the room without letting him know I love him, regardless of how he feels for me.

"I don't hate you." His words make me stop in my tracks, but I'm afraid to look over at him. I'm teetering on the edge. "But just so you know, this changes everything."

My head tells me not to look at him, but my heart, my heart tells me I need one more look at him. So I turn back and look at him standing there with tears streaming down his face. The anguish, the guilt, everything there for me to see. Something I never saw before, something he hid really well. All I can do is nod at him before I turn and walk out of the room toward the front door. My own tears stream down my face one after another, so many I don't bother wiping them away as I step out into the warm air. I take a deep inhale but the sob rips through me and all I can do is put my hand in front of my mouth. I rush away from his door to the car, getting in and driving away as fast as I can.

My head is spinning, my body feels numb, and when I walk into the house, Gabriella is waiting in the living room for me. "How did it go?" She looks over at me, seeing my face, and she sits up a little bit more.

"So much worse than I thought it would go." I walk toward the stairs. "I need a shower. I'll tell you everything tomorrow." She just smiles at me sadly

"I'm here if you need me," she reminds me, knowing I need to be alone.

I don't even bother switching on the lights as I step

in my bathroom and turn on the shower. I place my hand in the stream of the water, turning it just right before I undress and step in. Only when the water is washing over my face do I let the sob that I was holding in escape me. My body shakes as I put a hand in the middle of my chest, right over my heart. The same heart that

literally shattered in my chest. Listening to him tell me all the guilt he had, all I wanted to do was get up and go to him. All I wanted to do was tell him he was the best dad I've ever seen. All I wanted to do was take that pain away from him. All I wanted to do was go back to the beginning to when I found out. All I wanted to do was hold his face in my hands as I told him I was sorry, so fucking sorry. All I wanted was to take the pain away from him. To shoulder it, to fight with him and tell him that it's not his fault—none of it was his fault—not before and not now.

I let the water wash away the tears, if I'm honest, the tears blend into the water. Getting out, my body feels like it's run a marathon. I slip a shirt on and a pair of panties before getting into bed. Turning on my side and looking out the window, the shade is still open, showing me the soft twinkling of the stars.

I close my eyes and all I see is his face. All I hear are his words. "*First heartbeat, first picture, first breath. first cry, first smile, first time she crawled. First time she took a step. First time she fell and got hurt, I wasn't there for her. I missed it all. It was ripped away from me, and I vowed to myself that the next time it happened. The next time I had a child, it would be different. I was not going to miss anything."*

I can't help the tears that still come, to know I made him feel this guilt again. Knowing I am the reason is just too much for me to bear. I have to make it up to him, I have to do what I can for him to never feel that way about our child.

I sleep on and off all night long, and when I wake up in the morning, I know what I have to do. Grabbing my phone while I make my breakfast, I send a text out.

Me: *I need a favor.*

I have no idea if she will answer or if she is on call. I'll give her an hour, and if she doesn't answer me back, I'll go to my plan B.

I pop a bagel in the toaster, getting the cream cheese, when my phone pings. I walk over and grab my phone, seeing it's from her.

Emmy: *For you anything.*

Me: *Can you squeeze me in today?*

I don't have a chance to even put the phone down before it is ringing in my hand and I see it's her. "Hello, Dr. Emmy," I greet softly.

"Abigail," she says my name and I can hear that she's walking. "What's the matter?" she asks, her voice filled with worry.

"Nothing," I tell her and take a deep breath. "Everything is good, it's just." I stop talking for a second not sure how to say what I need to say. "I'd like to have another ultrasound."

"I can see you today at two." She doesn't even ask me another question. "Unless you want it now."

"I think two will work," I reply, looking at the clock and seeing it's just after eight. "If anything doesn't, I'll text you back."

"See you at two," she states and hangs up the phone. I take a deep breath before I call the next number.

At this point, I don't even know if he will answer me. My stomach hurls at the thought. He answers after four rings, "Hello."

"Hi," I say quickly and nervously, "it's Abigail." I swallow down the lump that is forming in my throat.

"Hi." His voice goes soft, and I want to know if he had a good night. I want to know how he's feeling. "Is everything okay?"

"Yeah," I confirm, blinking away the tears. "I was wondering if you're busy today at two?"

"I have practice this morning," he says, "but I am free." The pressure releases a bit from my chest.

"Do you think you can meet me?" I ask him, waiting for him to say no.

"Yes," he replies softly. "Where?"

"I'll send you the address."

"Okay, see you later."

"See you later," I repeat back to him and put the phone down, taking a deep breath in and out, "At least he's still talking to me," I tell the baby as I put one hand on my stomach while I text him the address to meet me at.

"You're up early," Gabriella observes, coming down the stairs dressed in a skirt and a blouse.

"Couldn't sleep," I admit, and she walks over to the coffee machine, making herself a cup. She leans against the counter and looks at me.

"Your eyes are puffy," she tells me, and I put my palm on them.

"I can imagine," I reply and take a bite of my bagel.

"Everything okay?" she asks. I know this is her way of giving me space, but she's internally freaking out.

"Not really. But the good news is he wants the baby." I shrug, avoiding her eyes. "So that's a win."

"Did he say anything to hurt you?" she asks softly, and I look up at her.

"No," I defend him, "he was sad I didn't tell him."

"Did you tell him why?" She folds her arms over her chest in defense mode.

"Not really," I admit, "maybe some other time."

"I think you should tell him why you didn't tell him." She pours herself a coffee in a silver thermos. "He deserves to know."

I only nod at her. "I'll see. Where are you going?"

"Work," she groans as she grabs her camera bag. "I'll text you later."

"Have fun," I say to her retreating back and all she does is flip me the finger.

I finish my bagel while I watch television. I wish I knew what the heck I am watching, but the truth be told, all I can think about is Tristan. Dr. Emmy calls me back an hour later to ask me questions, and I explain to her what I would like to do. I can hear her smile on the phone when she tells me she'll see me later.

Grabbing a pair of yoga pants and a tank top, I try my best to cover up my swollen eyes. I slip into a button-down linen top on my way out, leaving the buttons open, my little baby bump showing a touch. I make my way to Dr. Emmy's clinic office, which is different from the hospital one.

When I walk in, the woman behind the desk asks for my name and tells me to sit down. I'm not sitting for more than a minute when the door opens, and he walks in. The smile fills my face when I see him wearing black jeans and a white polo shirt, with a black tracksuit jacket with the team logo on it. A Dallas Oilers baseball cap is on his head as he looks around the room and finds me.

He walks over to me as he tries to take in the office. "Hey, sorry I'm late."

"You're not late," I assure him as he sits next to me and his arm touches mine. His smell makes my body become alive, and I can picture me in his arms. "I just got here."

He looks around before looking at me. "What are we doing here?"

I take a deep breath in, thinking maybe this wasn't the greatest idea I've had, and maybe, just maybe, I should have asked him before just bringing him here. "I'm trying to make it right."

"What do you mean?" he asks, his face filled with questions. I'm about to say something when the nurse comes out and calls my name.

I get up, walking toward the cream door, and I can feel him following me. I look over my shoulder and see him checking out everything. The nurse opens the door to the exam room, and Dr. Emmy is in there waiting already. She is sitting on the stool, reading something on the computer screen in front of her. "Abigail," she says my name with a smile.

"Tristan." I look over at him as he walks into the room. "This is Dr. Emmy." His face drains of all color when I say this.

"Is everything…" He stops talking to swallow. "Is everything okay?" He looks from me to the doctor and then back to me. "Is something wrong?"

I take a step forward, slipping my hand in his, and maybe because he's worried about me, he lets me. 'Everything is fine," I assure him softly. "This is me showing you, our baby." His eyes find mine and I really hope he can see the love I feel for him and our child in them. "I want you to know that I have no idea what we are having." I walk over to the table and sit down. "I also want you to know that this is the third time I've done this." I lean back on the table, putting my feet up before lifting my shirt a bit and then lowering my pants.

"Do you want to go and stand by Abigail?" Dr. Emmy asks and he doesn't answer her because his feet are moving on their own. He stands by the table, watching Dr. Emmy turn off the lights. "Here we go," she says cheerfully as she grabs the white bottle of gel and squeezes some on my stomach. I feel one of his hands hold the top of the table while the other one slips into mine.

"Does that hurt?" he asks, and I just shake my head.

"It's just a gel," I tell him, and his eyes are on Dr. Emmy. He watches her take the transducer and place it on my stomach.

"Now in here, you are going to be able to see your baby." Dr. Emmy points at the black screen.

"Will that hurt it?" he asks when he sees her pushing down on my stomach to get a picture.

"Nothing I do will hurt the baby," she reassures him and then smiles. "Tristan, meet your baby," she says, pointing at the screen where you can see the baby just chilling.

"Oh my God," he says, putting the hand on top of my head over his mouth. Dr. Emmy presses something on the machine and the sound of horses galloping fills the room. My eyes focus on him, watching him the whole time. My tears roll down my cheeks as I see the awe in his eyes. His whole face fills in a smile as he watches our child moving away in there.

"You hear that?" Dr. Emmy says looking at Tristan. "That is the sound of your baby's heartbeat."

TWENTY-FOUR

TRISTAN

"YOU HEAR THAT?" Dr. Emmy says, looking at me as what sounds like horses running through the field fill the room. "That is the sound of your baby's heartbeat." I can't help the tears that pour out of me. I can't explain how love works. I can't explain how a parent feels once they have a child. I can't explain the sense of unwavering love I feel for this child. The same love I feel for Penelope, it was instant. I pick up my hand, holding Abigail's, bringing it to my lips, secretly thanking her for giving me a child.

I watch the screen as my child does summersaults. "You have an active one," Dr. Emmy says, and all I can do is stare at the screen. When she called me this morning, I was shocked. After she walked out of the house last night, I didn't think I would hear from her.

I laid a lot on her. I bared my soul to her, things I had never told anyone before. Things I kept just for myself. Things I was afraid to share, but she had to know why I was so angry. "Look at his feet," I say and then look at Abigail, "or her. Either way, I'm good."

"Do you want to find out what you're having?" Dr. Emmy asks. "I know you said you didn't want to know." She looks at Abigail, who is wiping away her own tears.

"I didn't want to know because you weren't here," she tells me. "Secretly, I didn't think it was right to find out without you here."

"Thank you," I say because all the fucking words are stuck in my throat. She thought about me while she was going through this.

"So we got a good shot," Dr. Emmy states. "Do we want to know?"

"Whatever you want," Abigail tells me, and I just shake my head.

"I don't care as long as the baby is healthy. That is all that matters," I admit to her.

"The baby is very healthy," Dr. Emmy confirms.

"Okay," Abigail says, "what are we having?"

I don't even know, I'm holding my breath when Dr. Emmy starts to talk, "You are a having a very healthy baby boy." Abigail gasps and all I can do is stand there with my mouth hanging open. A son. I'm having a son.

"Shit," Abigail says, and I look at her, wondering if she's disappointed it's not a girl. "I hate when Dylan is right."

"Okay, Tristan," Dr. Emmy says. "Let's show you

your son." She goes step by step as she shows me both legs and arms. At one point, I can swear he waves his hand at me. I don't know how long we are in there, but I wish it could be longer.

Dr. Emmy grabs a white towel and cleans Abigail's stomach off before cleaning the transducer in her hand. Abigail slips her hand out of mine as she pulls up her pants over her little baby bump. A baby bump I didn't even know she had since she was wearing a sweater the last two times I've seen her.

Dr. Emmy presses a couple of buttons, and something shoots out from the machine. She gets up and hands me the long slip of white paper. "Here is a picture of your son."

My hand comes up to grab the paper from her, and I look down at it. You see the side view of the baby in black and white. My finger rubs his little cheek as all I can do is stare at it. I don't even hear Abigail get off the table until she clears her throat, and I look up at her. She looks beautiful as always, but her eyes are puffy and look tired.

"Thank you so much, Dr. Emmy," Abigail says to her. "I owe you."

"Let's just say this was the highlight of my day." She puts her hands in her pockets. "Tristan, it was great meeting you."

"Likewise." I nod at her. "Thank you for this."

"See you two in a month," she says, turning and walking out of the room.

I turn back to Abigail and smile at her shyly. "Thank

you for giving me this."

"I'm sorry," she says, two words she said yesterday also. "I know this doesn't cancel what I did, but I thought it would be a good time for you to have your first ultrasound."

I smile at her. "It was everything," I declare, my chest bursting with all the emotions in the world. "I think we need to talk."

"I think that is a good idea," she agrees softly. "There are some things you should know." She folds her hands together now, and I know she's nervous.

"I have to get Penelope," I say when the alarm on my phone rings. "Do you want to come with me?"

"I don't want to intrude," she tells me, and I just chuckle.

"You are never intruding," I tell her the truth. "We can go and get her, and then why don't we have dinner together?"

"Okay," she agrees, and I can hear the nervousness in her voice.

We walk out of the office together, and I look over at her. "Do you have your car here?"

"Yes," she admits, "but I can come and get it later."

"No." I shake my head. "Why don't you follow me to my house, and we can go get Penelope."

"Or," she counters, "how about I meet you at your house for dinner?"

"I'd really like to be with you right now," I admit to her, not ready for her to be out of my sight.

She smiles shyly as her head falls forward, and she

tucks the hair behind her ear. "Okay."

"I'll drive you back to get your car later," I tell her, *or tomorrow*, my head screams out.

We walk over to my SUV, and I open the door for her. "Thank you," she mumbles, getting in.

I walk around the SUV to the driver's side, get inside, and start the car. I can't help but look over at her. "We are having a boy." I shake my head in disbelief. "A boy."

"Apparently, the old wives' tale is true," she says, and I just look over at her. "Dylan said I was having a boy because I was still pretty." She laughs. "Apparently, if you are pregnant with a girl, you are less pretty because she is taking all the beauty from her mother."

"What the fuck?" I snort in shock.

"Yeah, that's what I said." She laughs, putting her purse on her lap.

"That's a bullshit superstition," I tell her, pulling out of the parking lot. "I've known you for six years and you've been beautiful every single one of those days." I don't bother looking over at her. "You've been especially beautiful the last couple of times I've seen you."

"You're just saying that." She tries to ignore my words. I let it be, knowing this isn't the time and place to let her know how I feel about her. There is a lot to talk about it and having this conversation five minutes before I get Penelope isn't enough time.

She gets out of the car with me when we get into the parking lot. I want to hold her hand but there will be so many questions, and I don't even have the answers. When Penelope sees me, she smiles and then looks over and sees Abigail, and her smile becomes even brighter. "Abigail!" She runs over to us going straight for Abigail, hugging her. I watch the girl who owns a part of my heart hug the other woman who owns a part, and all I can do is feel like I'm complete. Abigail kisses Penelope's head. "What are you doing here?"

"Well," she starts, looking down at my daughter with the same love in her eyes that I have for her. "I missed you and asked your dad if I could come over and visit."

Penelope's eyes go even bigger. "Are you staying for dinner?"

"If that's okay?" she asks, and all Penelope can do is nod her head.

"Do I get a hug?" I laugh at her, and she comes over and gives me a side hug. "How was your day?"

"Okay, I have to ask you something later," she says, putting her hand in mine. "But first, what are we having for dinner?"

"Well, Abigail is the guest, so she gets to decide," I throw to Abigail as we walk back to the SUV.

"Absolutely not." She shakes her head, laughing as Penelope holds her hand also.

"Okay, fine," I huff. "How about some chicken parm and some spaghetti?" I look at both of them, who share a look and agree. I take my phone out and order the food to be delivered to my house.

When we get home, Abigail sort of stays in the back, not knowing where to go or what to do, "Do you want something to drink?" I ask her softly when I walk into the kitchen, going to the fridge.

"I'll have some water," she says, and her stomach makes a huge gurgle noise, "and I think a snack might be a good thing." She puts her hand on her stomach, and I want to feel what she feels. My hand itches to touch her stomach, but Penelope takes her and pulls her into the pantry, where they decide on peanut butter and apples for a snack.

They sit at the island. Abigail cuts the apple for the both of them while Penelope gets a spoon for the peanut butter. *I could get used to this,* I think to myself. I watch the two of them talking like if I'm not even here. Abigail even asks about her homework as Penelope empties her school bag.

"What did you want to talk to me about?" I finally ask, leaning against the counter and drinking my own bottle of water.

"Oh yeah," Penelope says. "Do you think I should start wearing a bra?"

I choke on my water, and I have to rush to the sink to spit out whatever is left in my mouth. I cough as I try to get my breathing back to normal. "I'm sorry, what?" I ask her ask I cough.

"Well, Adriana said she went bra shopping so I was thinking maybe it's time for me to wear a bra."

"Um," I hum, not sure what else to say.

"You know," Abigail starts to say, "I started wearing a bra in the seventh grade." Abigail looks at her shocked. "But what I did do." She grabs a piece of apple. "Is wear a little sports bra."

Abigail looks at her. "Can I get a sports bra?" she

asks. "I think your boobs really start to grow when you get your period."

I almost choke for a second time in less than five minutes. "What the hell are they teaching you at this school?" Abigail just looks at me, rolling her lips. I don't have the time to ask her anything else because the doorbell rings with the food.

"Are you going to be okay?" Abigail asks when I come back in with the three bags of food.

"Who knows?" I shake my head. "Where is Penelope?"

"I sent her to wash her hands," Abigail replies. "Can I help?"

We work side by side preparing the table. The three of us sit down, and, thankfully, there isn't any more talk about bras or periods. When it's time for Penelope to go to bed, she gives Abigail a hug and then walks up the stairs. "I'll be right back." She nods. "Then we can talk."

I walk away from her without kissing her like I want to. I tuck Penelope in bed. By the time I go back down to Abigail, I find her on the couch, lying down on her side, sleeping with her hand on her stomach. I try not to make noise as I grab a throw blanket from the big basket in the corner, covering her. I sit down near her feet, watching her. Today has been a fucking dream come true in more ways than one.

Putting my head back, I close my eyes for a minute, and the next thing you know, I'm blinking them open. I turn my head and see Abigail just watching me. "What time is it?"

"A little after three," she tells me, and I sit up, shocked

that I just slept six hours.

"Are you hungry?" I ask her, running my hand through my hair as she shakes her head.

"We didn't have our talk."

"We did not," I reply, getting up and holding out my hand for her. "Let's get you in bed, and we can talk tomorrow."

"I don't know about that," she hesitates, and I want to kick myself in the ass.

"You can stay in the guest room," I offer, letting her know this isn't why I want her to stay with me. I am not ready to let her go yet. "It's too late to drive you to your car." My hand still hangs there, waiting for her. "Besides, I'd have to wake Penelope."

"Wow." She throws the cover off herself, grabbing my hand to get up. "Using Penelope." She shakes her head. "What a low blow."

"Whatever it takes," I tell her as she slides her fingers in mine, and I walk her upstairs to the guest bedroom instead of mine, where I really want her.

TWENTY-FIVE

ABIGAIL

"WOW," I TOSS the throw cover off, grabbing his hand and helping myself up. "Using Penelope." I shake my head. "What a low blow."

"Whatever it takes," he says, trying to hide his smirk. My fingers slide in his as he walks up the steps very slowly. The warm hand holding mine gives me butterflies in my stomach. I walk as slowly as I can to make sure it lasts as long as possible. "There is a bathroom adjoined to the bedroom," he explains when he stops in front of an open room. "Call me if you need anything," he says, and I can still see the sleep in his eyes.

"Go to sleep," I urge him, wanting to touch his face. Instead, I release his hand, turn, and walk into the room. "I'll be fine." He stands there for a minute longer before he walks away. I sit on the bed in the darkness. I should go straight home, but instead, I'm slipping into his guest bed. When I woke up on the couch, it was just after two o'clock, so I didn't move for fear of waking him up. I watched him sleep for about twenty minutes before my bladder told me that if I didn't get up, I'd literally pee all over the couch. I thought for sure he would be up when I got back, but he was still sleeping, and the last thing I wanted was to wake him up. I turn on my side and close my eyes for what I think is a second until I hear a soft knock on the open door.

My eyes flicker open as I look toward the door and see him standing there in the hallway wearing shorts and a T-shirt, a backward baseball cap on his head. "Morning." He walks in, holding a white Starbucks cup in his hand. "I got you a decaf coffee." He holds it up.

"You left?" I sit up in bed, blinking the sleep away from my eyes. "When did you leave?"

"I had to drive Penelope to school," he explains, walking in just a touch more. "I left a note on the counter in case you got up."

He hands me the white cup of coffee, and my hand comes up to grab it. "Thank you," I mumble to him.

"And this was going off every ten seconds." He holds up my phone that I must have left on the couch. I grab it and see texts from Gabriella. "We should have that talk now," he says nervously, and I just nod my head.

"We should," I agree with him, taking a sip of my coffee. "I'm going to go to the bathroom and meet you downstairs."

"I'm going to go and get you some breakfast started,"

he tells me, and I just look at him, my stomach fluttering.

"Okay, I'll be right down."

"Take your time," he says, turning and walking out of the room. I put the coffee down on the side table before opening the phone.

Gabriella: *Where the fuck are you?*

Gabriella: *Are you at baby daddy's house?*

Gabriella: *Did you want me to call Dylan?*

Gabriella: *Wow, harsh*

Gabriella: *I hope you get heartburn and have no Tums*

Gabriella*: I'm not talking to you.*

Gabriella: *Bring me my niece or nephew, and then you can leave.*

I laugh at the last message because she sent another one right after.

Gabriella: *Wait until I get pregnant and ignore you.*

I shake my head, typing out.

Me: *I'm fine, fell asleep on the couch, sorry.*

Gabriella*: Is that code for you fell on his dick?*

Me: *Absolutely not. Got to go. He's making me breakfast.*

Gabriella: *It's like you're married with kids.*

Gabriella: *If you need help, send out the Bat Signal.*

Walking to the bathroom, I wash my face and pee and then head downstairs, where I find him in the kitchen, going back and forth from the fridge to the stove. The counter is filled with the egg carton, sliced bread, bagels, waffle mix, pancake mix, and orange juice.

My stomach flutters again, watching. He must sense

I'm here because he looks back at me. "I don't know what you like to eat for breakfast." He puts his hands on his hips before taking off the baseball hat, tossing it like a Frisbee to the living room, before he runs his hand through his hair.

"I can't eat eggs," I inform him, walking to the stool and pulling it out sitting on it. "I mean, usually I can, but ever since I got pregnant, I just can't eat them."

He looks at me with a sad look before turning and putting the eggs back in the fridge. "So waffles or pancakes?" His voice is softer, and you can hear the sadness in it that he didn't know.

"I love toast," I share with him cheerfully, hoping it cheers him up, "with peanut butter and jam."

"I have that." He walks away and puts two pieces of bread in the toaster. "Is there anything else you can't eat since you got pregnant?"

"Not really." I put my hand on the counter. "I mean, I crave burgers more." He just nods at me while the toast pops up. He places both on a plate before walking over, putting it in front of me, and then walking off to get the peanut butter and jam.

"Thank you," I say as he hands me both before getting me two knives. He pulls out a stool beside me and sits down." Are you not eating?"

"I ate with Penelope," he says before taking a huge inhale. "We need to tell your parents." I look over at him, not sure what he means. "That I'm the father."

"Oh, that," I say, looking down at the toast on the plate in front of me and suddenly not feeling hungry. Instead, my stomach fills with nerves.

"Yeah, that," he reaffirms. "That I'm going to take care of you and the baby. That I'm not an asshole who just knocked you up and didn't care. That I'm in it for, well… ever." I try to process his words.

"We can either fly down for dinner tonight, or we can go tomorrow morning," he says, and I can feel him staring at me. "Or we FaceTime him right now, and I speak with him."

My finger starts to tap the counter as I try not to panic. It's one thing for him to know, but it's a totally different thing to tell everyone. "Why the rush?" I look at him, and I know the minute the words come out of my mouth, he gets angry.

He pushes away from the counter, going over to the fridge and grabbing a bottle of water. "Why the secrecy?" His tone is tight, and I know he's angry.

"It's not a secret. It's just…" I try to think of the words to say when he just stares at me, and I can't look away, even if I wanted to.

"I'm not supposed to be happy I'm having a baby with you?" he asks, and I want to kick myself.

"It's not that," I say softly. All the words feel like they are jumbled up in my head.

"The best thing I've ever done in my whole life, up to three days ago, was Penelope." He puts the unopened bottle of water on the counter. "I didn't get to celebrate it. I didn't get to tell people about it." He just stares at me. "I didn't get anything, and now I feel like I'm doing it again." He shrugs now. "Well, I guess I have no choice… again." He shakes his head. "I have to get ready for practice." He slowly walks away from me and goes to the stairs.

"It's not that," I say as my heart breaks for him, and I watch him walk up the steps with his head down. I can't even fathom what he is feeling. What if the roles were reversed? What if he didn't want to tell people right away?

"It is what it is," he says before walking to his bedroom and closing the door softly behind him. My stomach sinks even lower than before, knowing how hurt it would make me feel. I push away from the counter and walk up the steps to the door he just closed.

I take a huge, deep breath before I hold up my fist and knock on the door a lot softer than I intend to. I wonder if it's because I'm scared of what he will say next. I'm also scared I will hurt his feelings again. My hand knocks on the door before I can tell it to walk away.

This time it's louder than it was before. The door swings open, and he's standing in front of me wearing nothing but his black Calvin Klein boxer briefs, and I swear my mouth waters.

"Um," I start nervously, and I think I even stutter as I avoid looking at him. "Um." All the water that flew to my mouth before when I looked at him is now gone. Now my mouth is dry, and all I can say to him is, "Can you put on a shirt?" I look around him, to each wall around him. I look at anything but him.

"You've seen me naked," he reminds me, and I can see from my peripheral vision that his hands are now on his hips. Hips I wrapped my legs around, hips I want to wrap my legs around again. Hips I want to squeeze with my thighs while he eats me.

I roll my eyes, pretending I'm not affected by it. I fold my arms over my chest so he can't see how my nipples are peaked, wanting him to play with them. Fuck, being pregnant has made me a horny schoolgirl. "In the dark." I turn back and only look into his eyes. I make sure I don't let my eyes linger anywhere else.

"Do you want me to show you in the light?" He rolls his lips, and all I can do is glare at him,

"Would you like me to get naked in the light?" I ask him, and the smirk turns into a full-blown smile.

"Yes." He nods his head. "Yes, I would, but we don't have time for that," he replies, shocking me. "Did you need something?"

I'm completely thrown for a loop since he answered that way. My head feels like it's spinning.

"We can tell my parents whenever you are free," I mumble, trying to think of anything but him and me being naked. Or better yet, us being naked and having sex literally anywhere in his house.

"Okay," he replies.

"I'll let you get dressed," is the only thing I say before I turn and walk away from him. I don't even turn to look over my shoulder because I feel like my face is on fire. When I finally make it downstairs, I walk over to the kitchen sink. Turning the water on cold, I wet my hand and then put it on my cheek to calm it down. I feel like my face is on fire. Scratch that, my whole body feels like it's on fire, and the only thing I can think of is he's the only one who can put it out.

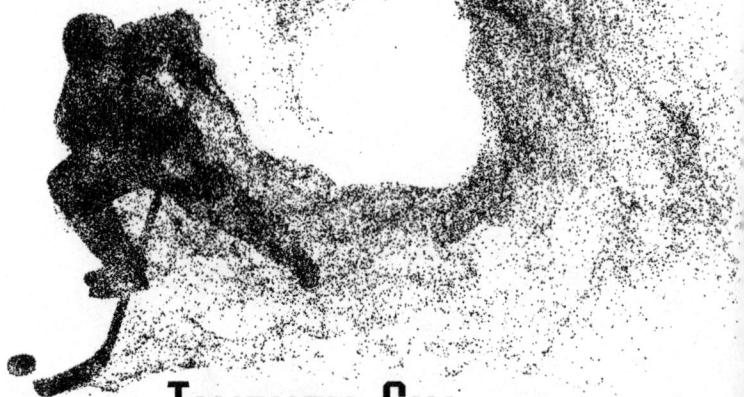

TWENTY-SIX

TRISTAN

I WATCH HER walk down the stairs and then hear the sink turn on before I close the door behind myself. My cock has never been harder in my life. It almost feels like it's stone.

Seeing her standing in front of me, getting all flustered, all I wanted to do was kiss the shit out of her and then place her on my bed and slide into her. The thought makes me even harder, if that is possible. I walk over to grab a pair of pants and a T-shirt before turning around and walking downstairs.

My cock is still hard, and even though I've tried thinking of things to deflate it, nothing is working. It's like my body knows she's here and wants her. I walk into the kitchen and see her bite a piece of toast as she cleans up all the stuff I left on the counter. My heart literally fills up to I don't even know what degree, all I know is I love that she is here. I love she slept here. I love I got to wake up with her, even though it wasn't in my bed. I love walking downstairs and seeing her here. I basically love everything about her. She goes back to the plate and takes a bite of her toast again before walking and putting the plate in the dishwasher. She looks up at me and smiles. "How long were you standing there?" she asks as she walks back to the sink and washes her hands.

"Not long. Are you ready?"

She grabs the towel to dry off her hands, walking around the counter and putting her hand on her stomach. I ache to touch her. "I am."

"Do you feel anything?" I ask her, and she just shakes her head.

"Sometimes I feel some flutters, but other than that, nothing so far." She rubs her hand over her stomach. "Would you like to?" She holds up her hands, and I can't stop myself from walking to her.

Both my hands go to her stomach. I look down, seeing my hands on her, which does nothing for my cock. I step even closer to her, wanting to lean down and kiss her stomach, but instead, I look up and see her watching me. The tears in her eyes evident. "Thank you," I murmur before I lower my head and my lips touch hers ever so softly. "For taking such good care of our son."

"You're welcome," she whispers, smiling at me. My hands fall from her stomach, and I wish I could put them back.

"Okay, so I have to go into work today for a couple of

hours," I tell her as we walk to the front door. "I can be done at noon."

She nods at me. "Then we are off tomorrow. We leave the day after for the West Coast. What is your schedule?" I stop at the front door.

"I am off for the next three days, and then I do four night shifts," she replies to me as she grabs her bag and puts it over her shoulder.

"Okay, so we have two options," I tell her, taking a deep inhale. "We can get on a plane this afternoon and arrive at dinnertime."

"If we leave here at noon, we arrive at around four thirty local time." She grabs her phone and pulls up something. "New York is not playing tonight, and they have a home game tomorrow, so I don't think he's traveling." I see her fingers moving over the keyboard. "Just texted my mother to ask."

"We can spend the night in New York if it's too late and you're tired," I tell her, "or we leave tomorrow morning and get back for dinner."

"What about Penelope?" she asks, and I just look at her, falling more and more into her.

"I can call the sitter," I respond, and she just nods. "After we tell your parents, I would like to tell her."

She gasps, "Of course." She makes me sound like I'm crazy. "She is a part of this just as much as we are." Yup, if I didn't love her before, I definitely love her now.

"Okay, so you tell me what you want to do, and I'll get the plane," I tell her as I walk out of the front door, locking it. I want to reach for her hand while we walk to the car, but I don't. Instead, I open the passenger door for her and wait for her to get in.

When I make my way around to the driver's side, she looks at me. "I think we should go tonight so you can rest tomorrow for your trip." She grabs the seat belt. "It'll be a quick trip, but we can be back. If we get there by five their time, we can head out at ten. It won't be that bad, and we can use tomorrow to recoup."

"Then today it is," I declare, starting the car to go to drop her off at her car we left at the doctor's office yesterday. "So how about I text you if I get out early, and we can head down?"

"That sounds good to me." She opens the passenger door. "I'll wait for your text." She lingers in the car for a couple of seconds, her hand on the handle of the door. "I'll wait until we are in the air to text my parents that I'm stopping by."

"Whatever you think is best," I say, wanting to lean over and kiss her goodbye, but she just smiles at me and gets out of the car. I wait for her to get into her own car and drive away before I pull out of the parking lot, calling the sitter and organizing for her to pick up Penelope and bring her home.

When I get to the arena, I look around, seeing not many cars are here. It is an optional day, but I told Xavier I would come and work out with him. I pull open the door and step onto the blue carpet, walking toward the locker room. There are some new pictures of Xavier and me from the Stanley Cup game on the wall as I walk down the hall.

Xavier is sitting at his spot on the bench, drinking a pre-workout drink as I walk in. "Hey." I walk beside him to my spot, putting my keys and phone on the shelf.

"Talk about getting here on time." He laughs at me when I take off my shirt.

"Sorry I'm late," I apologize to him. "Also, I have to be out of here at ten fifty-five."

He looks at me for a second, and I avoid his eyes. "Is everything okay?"

"Not really," I admit to him, sitting down. The pressure of not telling him weighs heavy on me. In the last year, he's been like a brother to me and vice versa.

He looks at me with concern on his face. "Is everything okay?" he repeats, his voice low. Then he gets up and walks over to the shower area to see who is in there and then over to the door, sticking his head out before closing the door behind him. "Is it Penelope?"

I shake my head. "No." My heart speeds up in my chest so fast and hard it feels like it's going to jump out of my chest. I rub my hands on my legs, trying to wipe the sweat off them. "This has nothing to do with her." My heart lurches up and then down like a wave in the ocean.

"What is it?" He cocks his head to the side.

"You have to promise me that you won't tell a soul." He nods his head. "Not even Vivienne." I take a second. "Or Beatrice." Beatrice is his support dog, who is also kind of his therapist.

"I would never betray your trust like that," he assures me, and I one-thousand-percent believe him.

"Okay." I take a deep exhale. "I don't know how to say this, so I think I'm just going to come right out and say it." He just waits for me. "I'm the father of Abigail's baby," I say the words out loud and watch his face. It goes from worry to confusion and then to shock, followed by a loud gasp.

His hand flies to the top of his head before he jumps up. "Why would you tell me this?" he shrieks. "Oh my God, how could you tell me this?"

"You asked," I point out to him as he starts pacing in front of me.

"Oh my God," he chants over and over again. "You." He points at me. "You were the one who left her."

I hold up my hands. "I did not leave her. I didn't even know. I found out she was pregnant when I got back. It killed me. I thought she was dating a doctor or someone. Then I found out on Sunday she was fifteen weeks, and I put two and two together."

"You had sex with Abigail?" he asks, and I nod my head. His mouth opens now as something else dawns on him. "On the family vacation?" I nod again. "Unreal."

"Does Dylan know this?" he asks, turning around to make sure we're still alone.

"That is why I'm leaving at eleven. We are flying to tell Justin this afternoon," I admit to him, and then my shoulders slump. "I don't know how he'll take it, but it is what it is."

"This is…" He puts his hands on his hips. "You swore me to secrecy over the biggest secret."

"You need to leave now and go and bare your truth so

I can bear mine." He grabs the shirt I just took off and tosses it to me. "Like right now." He then grabs my keys and phone and holds them out for me. "The sooner, the better."

"Are you serious?" I ask, putting on the shirt.

"I have never been more serious in my life," he assures me, his chest rising and falling. "It's ten o'clock." He looks at his Apple Watch. "Get on the plane in an hour, that's eleven, get to New York in, what… three hours, if you tell the pilot to gun it." I roll my lips. "So sitting down with Justin at four his time. I can tell Vivienne at three thirty our time." He puts his hand on his head. "This is huge."

"It's not that huge." I try to calm myself down and his eyebrows just pinch together. "You aren't helping with nerves."

"You know what would have helped?" He puts his hands again on his hips. "Not having sex with Abigail."

I just laugh as I grab my things. "I'll never take that one night back."

"It was one night?" He throws his hands up in the air. "Go play the lottery while you're at it."

I shake my head, and the door opens, so both of us stop talking when Chase comes in, "Everything okay in here?" he asks, and I just nod, pretending everything is okay.

"Why wouldn't it be okay?" Xavier asks, trying to act cool and failing miserably. "Of course it's cool." He picks up his drink. "I'm going to work out."

"I have a family emergency," I finally say to him.

"Got to go," I say before walking out of the room. "Here goes nothing," I mumble to myself.

Twenty-Seven

Tristan

I LOOK OUT the plane window for a second before turning and looking over at Abigail. "Did you tell your dad anything?" I ask, the nerves in my body are on a whole different level.

"I spoke with my mother today," she says, looking at me, "and she knows I'm coming down, but I'm going to call my dad when we arrive so he isn't freaking out with worry."

"You told your mom?" I can't stop my fingers from tapping the airplane seat. From the minute I walked out of the arena, I've been on an adrenaline rush. The first person I called was the airplane scheduler, and they gave me a window of forty-five minutes. I rushed home to change into an outfit that said," I'm the father of the baby and will take good care of him," but all I could focus on was the linen shirt I wore when we slept together. So I put on my dark-blue pants with the shirt. The second call was to Abigail, who was already ready for me to collect her. She was wearing a one-piece baby-blue dress that showed off her baby bump with white sneakers. She looked absolutely stunning, and when she got in the car, I awkwardly leaned over and kissed her cheek. Her smell sent me in a downward spiral, and I had to calm my cock down the whole way to the airport. "You told your mom you were coming with me?"

"That, I did not," she says, grabbing a piece of strawberry from the fruit tray they put in the middle of the table between us. "I just said I was coming by to talk to them."

"She didn't ask any questions?" I really wish I could kiss the shit out of her.

"She did, and I told her I was coming to tell her something." She smirks. "She put two and two together, but she doesn't know you are the dad."

"On a scale of one to five, how shocked do you think your parents will be?" I ask, grabbing the glass of sparkling water Abigail ordered for me while I was in the bathroom.

"One hundred and fifty-seven." She laughs, and it hits me right in the chest.

"Good to know," I reply, looking back out the window and seeing we are almost there. The flight attendant comes and takes away the fruit and the water. The plane touches down with a jolt, and I see the black SUV waiting for us. I get up and hold out my hand for Abigail.

She slides her hand into mine, grabbing her bag on the way out. The cool air hits me right away. "This is nice," I state, looking around and seeing her pull a jean jacket from her bag. She struggles to put it on, so I take it out of her hand and help her into it.

"Thank you," she says as she pulls the hair out of the back of the jacket. The man is standing there holding the back SUV door open, waiting for Abigail to enter. I watch her get in, and then, instead of sitting there, she scoots over so I can get in next to her. I nod to the driver as I get in beside her. She is fishing her phone out of her bag by the time the guy closes my door.

"Here we go," she mumbles as she presses the dial button, putting the phone to her ear. The driver gets in the front seat at the same time Abigail starts to talk. "Hey, Dad," she greets him, and I can hear Justin calling her beautiful girl. "I was wondering if I could pop in and have dinner with you?" I can hear him shriek, and I laugh. "Yeah, I have something to tell you and figured it should be done face-to-face." She rolls her lips and looks over at me. "No, it's not worse than me being pregnant and alone." I shake my head, hating she was alone. "I'll be there as soon as I can." She hangs up. "Well, this is going to be fun."

"For you." I shake my head. "I'm the one who left you pregnant and alone."

She reaches out and puts her hand on mine. "That is my fault, and I'll bear that." I turn my hand over to link our fingers together.

"There are a lot of things I think we should get on

the table," I tell her as we make our way to her parents' house. This is not the time to bring up that I want her to move in with us. This is also not the time to tell her I'm in love with her.

The SUV comes to a stop in front of the big house, and I don't have time to look outside before the door is opened by the driver. "Thank you," I say, getting out and again holding out my hand for her. She slips her hand in mine as she gets out, and this time, she keeps it in mine.

"Whatever happens," she starts to say, "it'll be okay." I'm about to say something to her when the front door swings open, and I see her mother there.

"Oh my," she says, putting her hand to her mouth when her eyes go to Abigail and then to me, followed by her looking at our hands together. "Hi," she greets us with a smile on her face, trying not to be shocked but failing miserably.

"Hi, Mom," Abigail replies as she lets go of my hand and hugs her mom. "So good to see you."

"Hello, Caroline," I say, walking to her and kissing her cheek like I always do when I see her.

"Your father is in the family room trying not to freak out," Caroline shares, moving away from the doorway to let us walk in. "I think the phone call to give him a heads-up was not the best plan we had."

"Is she here?" I hear Justin say from somewhere in the house, his footsteps coming closer and closer to us. My stomach literally feels like it's on fire when I finally see him round the corner. "She is here," he says, smiling at her and then looking at me. "Did you give her a ride?"

"Sort of," I reply, my mouth suddenly so dry it feels like my tongue is fifty times bigger than it should be.

"Come and sit," Caroline invites nervously, knowing her husband has not put two and two together yet. I take a step forward, and the front door swings open. "Here we go," she mumbles as I look over my shoulder to see Max and Matthew saunter in. "What are you guys doing here?"

"There is a family meeting," Matthew explains, looking at her. "Justin called me."

"And you?" She points at Max.

"I was with him, so I decided to tag along." Max shrugs. "Why, am I not invited?" He puts his hand on his chest and pretends to be hurt.

"Listen, you two," Caroline warns, her voice tight. "I want no dramatics when my daughter talks, do you get me?" Her voice is stern.

"Dramatics?" Matthew defends. "We aren't dramatic." I roll my lips to keep from laughing out loud.

"Yeah, right," Max blurts out. "At least I'm not dramatic."

"Did you not go Donkey Kong on Dylan?" Matthew points at him.

"Didn't you go Donkey Kong on everyone?" Max points at him.

"This is what I'm talking about," Caroline declares and glares at Justin. "You couldn't shut your mouth, could you?"

"I didn't say anything. I just said she's coming to town to tell us something," Justin tries to plead his case.

"What the hell are you doing here?" Max finally looks at me, confused, and I'm about to answer him when the front door swings open again.

We all look over and see Xavier running in, panting as if he ran here from Dallas. "Oh good, we didn't miss anything." He is followed by Chase, who just walks in with his hair blowing like he's on the catwalk.

"This better be good," Dylan grumbles, walking in after Chase, followed by Michael, of course.

"Hey," Max says to Michael, walking to him and hugging him. "Did you bring the kids?"

"I'm here for three hours," he huffs. "I didn't even want to come, but this guy"—he points at Xavier—"was like it's a life and death phone call.

"It wasn't that dramatic," Xavier says finally. "I just needed to get a plane fast."

"What's going on?" Abigail says. "How is everyone here?" She looks at me, and I avoid looking at her.

"I sort of told Xavier," I lean in and whisper in her ear.

"Why don't we do this in the living room?" Caroline suggests. "But if any of you make a scene"—she points at Max, Matthew, and then Dylan, who gasps and points at himself—"you will be thrown out."

"By who?" Dylan puts his hands on his hips.

"Chase," she replies, and Chase puffs his chest out more.

"It will be my honor." Chase walks to her and puts his hand around her shoulders. "Anything for you, Auntie Caroline."

"Wow, can you suck up even more?" Dylan accuses.

"She's my mother."

"She's my aunt and my mother-in-law," Michael says, and we all laugh; this might not be so bad after all.

They walk into the family room, and I wait back for Xavier. "What the hell are you doing here?"

"I thought you could use some backup," he says. "I also told Vivienne." I just stare at him. "It was a big secret, and I had to explain why I was flying to New York for three hours." He puts his hands on his hips. "She wasn't even that surprised."

"What is taking you two so long?" Justin questions when he comes to get us. "We are waiting for you two."

I nod at him and walk into the room, seeing Abigail sitting on the couch next to her mother. She moves over so I can sit next to her, and she smiles at me. "I don't even know what to say or how to start, so I'll just lead with…" Abigail says. The room is so quiet you can hear a pin drop, but the only thing I hear is the beating of my heart as it echoes in my ears. "I know who the baby's father is."

I look around the room at the guys' faces, seeing if they are putting it together, and the only one I know for sure is Chase, who just chuckles. "I'm the baby's father." The words come out of my mouth without me even knowing they left.

"What?" Michael is the first one to say something.

"What the actual fuck?" Dylan swears, looking at me and then at Abigail. Who slips her hand in mine to show him we are united.

"I'm sorry," Justin says, shaking his head, "I don't

think I heard what you actually said."

"He said he's the baby's father," Michael says the words slowly, not reading the room.

"Shut up." Max hits his shoulder.

"What the hell is wrong with you?" Matthew hollers, jumping up. "This is the second woman you've knocked up. Why aren't you using condoms?"

"We used protection," Abigail declares, "but obviously, it isn't always one hundred percent." She looks at Michael. "You should know something about that."

"Wow, what did I do?" he asks. "Why are you picking on me?"

"I just wonder how all you smart men didn't put two and two together when she said how far along she was." Chase sits looking at everyone with a cocky look on his face. "Didn't you do the math?"

"Who the hell opened their calendar and went back?" Michael shoots out at him.

"I think everyone needs to shut the fuck up," Justin says, his voice tight. I look over at him as he sits back on the couch, and I wonder if he wants to jump up and punch me in the face. I don't even know how I would feel if the roles were reversed. "You left her alone, pregnant, by herself." The words gut me to my soul.

"That is on me," Abigail says loudly. "I never told him. I found out, and well, I didn't know how to tell him so…"

"You kept it from him," Dylan states. "What is wrong with you?"

I hold up my hand, not willing to let him talk to her like that. "I'm going to say something." I look at all of them, and they just stare at me. Xavier nods his head at me for support,

"There is no one else in this world I want to have a child with." I squeeze her hand tighter in mine as the tears sting my eyes. "I never thought it would happen again like this." I smile at her. "But there is no one else I would want to be the mother of my child more than Abigail." Her own tear escapes, and I move my free hand up to her eye to wipe away the tear. "There is no one else who will be a better mother." She smiles, and I can't keep up with her tears. I look over at Caroline, who has her own tears running down her face. Justin comes over and sits beside her, putting his arm around her shoulders, and she turns to quietly cry on his shoulder.

"I know mistakes happen, but my, our son, will never think he was a mistake." My own tear escapes, and it's Abigail's turn to raise her hand to wipe mine away. I bring up our joint hands and kiss her fingers, her face filling with a smile. I know, no matter what comes next, it'll be okay.

Twenty-Eight

Abigail

I LISTEN TO his words, and every single time I see how devoted he is, I regret not telling him before. I know now isn't the time to let him know why I kept it from him, but I also know that he'll know the truth by tomorrow. The whole truth.

His lips touch my fingers, and I hold up my free hand to his cheek. "Thank you," I say as my thumb rubs the scruff on his face. I don't even know I'm leaning in to kiss him until my lips touch his.

"Did you just say your son?" Matthew is the first to say something. "Are you having a boy?"

"I am," I say, laughing through my tears. "We are."

All the men look over and high-five each other like they are welcoming one to the club. My mother puts her arms around me and pulls me to her. "A boy."

"A boy," I repeat, feeling Tristan hold my hand tighter, his thumb rubbing over my fingers.

"So what happens now?" Dylan asks, looking straight at Tristan. I'm not going to lie. When I saw all the men rush in, I almost threw up on Tristan's shoes yet again. But it turned out so much better than I thought it would be, but it's still too early to celebrate.

"For one, we need to tell Penelope," I speak up for him.

"Then, after that, we need to discuss a couple of things privately," Tristan says, looking at me, and I get nervous thinking about how this talk is going to go.

Everyone laughs, including me.

"It's like he hasn't been around the family," Matthew declares. "I'm going to come right out and ask the question everyone is scared to ask."

"Of course you will," Max says, "because, heaven forbid, you don't know what everyone else is thinking."

"One." Matthew puts up his finger. "When are you guys getting married?"

I just shake my head. "Not everyone needs to be married, Uncle Matthew." I don't even bother looking over at Tristan. "People co-parent all the time."

"Can we not put them on the spot right now?" my mother advises. "They are having a baby together. Let them figure it out."

"But what is he going to do?" Dylan now speaks up. "How will you take care of her?"

Tristan doesn't miss a beat. "She's my responsibility, and so is the baby."

"Why are we giving him the third degree?" Chase speaks up. "He found out about Penelope and jumped right in. Do you think he's not going to do that for his son?" He gets up and shakes his head. "I was promised dinner."

"Yes, let's get some dinner," my mother redirects, getting up. "I ordered food."

Dylan gets up first, coming over to us. "Don't think I'm going to let you off easy," he says to Tristan, who gets up, not letting go of my hand. "You still slept with my sister."

"Yeah, not easy to swallow," Michael teases. "Welcome to the club."

We all laugh as they hug Tristan and me before walking into the kitchen. "How you doing?" I ask him, and he just smiles at me.

"Like a weight has been lifted off my chest," Xavier says for him, and I roll my lips. "You're a dick." He points at Tristan. "I'm not talking to you. Do you know what it was like on the plane for three hours?" I can't help but laugh at him. "It's all fun and games until you're keeping the biggest secret from your in-laws."

"Thank you." Tristan slaps his shoulder and squeezes, but he shrugs it off.

"Fuck you," he grunts, going to the kitchen, and I look down and laugh.

"Are you okay?" Tristan asks, and I look up at him.

"I wasn't the one in the hot seat," I remind him, and he just smiles slyly.

"As long as you're okay, I don't give a shit what they

do to me," he admits as he lets go of my hand. Instead, he pulls me in for a hug. My arms wrap around his waist, and I just lay my head on his chest.

"Is this your lucky shirt?" I ask, looking up at him but still keeping my arms around him.

"It's the shirt that we, you know," he says, smirking as he pushes the hair away from my face. "So I guess it is my lucky shirt." He cups my face and then kisses my lips. I close my eyes, enjoying his lips on mine.

"They are making out in the living room!" Dylan yells. "She's already with child, so I don't think they can make it worse." I laugh and put my head forward as Tristan kisses my forehead.

I finally let my hands slide from his waist as we walk into the kitchen and eat dinner. We only stay for an hour since everyone wants to get back home, so instead of leaving at ten like we planned, we leave at eight.

The plane ride back home is more hectic than the one coming here since we borrowed Uncle Matthew's plane, and all of us are aboard instead of just the two of us. I sit down on the couch, and Tristan sits next to me. My hand rubs my stomach as we take off. "Why don't you lie down," Tristan suggests, and I just shake my head.

"I'll be fine," I reassure him, and ten minutes later, I close my eyes for a second and only open them when the plane bounces down when we land. My head is on Tristan's shoulder as he has his arm wrapped around my shoulders, keeping me in place, "I guess we're home?" I ask.

"We are," he confirms as I sit up and stretch my arms

and my back before getting up. We are the last two on the plane. He lets me go first, and I see everyone walking toward their respective cars. "See everyone tomorrow," Chase says, and everyone mumbles the same thing.

"Make sure you take care of my sister!" Dylan orders, and Michael pushes his shoulder.

He slips his hand in mine, and I don't question it or read too much into it. "Are you okay?" he asks as we walk over to his car, and he opens the passenger door for me.

"I'm not going to lie," I admit, "I'm really hungry."

"What do you want to eat?"

"Cheeseburger," I answer him honestly, "with fries and ketchup."

"Your wish is my command," he replies, and all I can do is smile before getting in the car. He stops at a drive-through, getting me a burger and fries. When he drops me off, he just looks at me. "Do you want to come to my house tomorrow night so we can tell Penelope?"

I nod my head. "That sounds good," I tell him, not wanting the night to be over but knowing I have to let him go. I get out of the car and wave behind me as I walk into the house. Luckily, Gabriella is out, and when I wake the next morning, she is already gone.

I'm getting out of the shower when my phone rings from my bedroom, and I run in to answer it, seeing it's Tristan. "Hello," I answer right away.

"Hey, it's me," he says, and I can hear he is in the car.

"Hi, you." I smile when I hear his voice.

"I just left practice. Do you want me to swing by and

get you?" he asks, and I can tell something is bothering him from his tone.

"Yeah, that sounds good," I say softly. "Is everything okay?"

"Not really, but I'll talk to you about it when I see you."

I sit down on the bed with my stomach aching. "If you want to cancel tonight and tell her another night…"

"No," he says right away. "I'm pissed I haven't seen you today, and it feels like I haven't seen you in a week." I can't help the smile that comes over my face.

"It's been a little more than twelve hours," I remind him. "I'll be ready in ten minutes."

"See you then," he says and hangs up. I shake my head, getting up and walking over to the closet to grab another dress. This one is a baby blue; it's the only thing that is easy to wear these days. I slip on a pair of slides, walking downstairs at the same time I hear him pull up in the driveway. Grabbing my bag, I walk outside and see him getting out of his car when he sees me. "Hi," he greets me, walking toward me, and for the first time, he hugs me when he sees me. I'm engulfed by his smell as my hands wrap around his waist.

"Hi." I look up at him, and he bends his head to kiss my lips, another thing he's never done, but I'm totally okay with.

He walks me to the car as my head screams that I want to kiss him again. He opens the door for me, and I get in. I watch him walk around the car, and I swear I think I swoon. He's wearing stuff I've seen a thousand times before, but just looking at him, knowing he held my hand and kissed me, he just looks hotter. "Are we getting Penelope?" I ask when he starts driving.

"She has dance, so I have to pick her up at five," he informs me. I look at the clock and see it's just past three. "I figured we can go home and talk."

I look out the window nervously as I think about what I'm going to say. I've practiced this speech in my head a million times, telling him I am in love with him. But I never thought I would say the actual words. When we pull up to his house, we both get out at the same time. His hand finds mine as we walk into the front door. I slip off my shoes and dump my bag before following him into the house. "Do you want something to drink?"

"Water would be good," I answer, hoping it can help push down the flutters in my stomach. He hands me a water bottle and then grabs my hand, pulling me into the living room.

"Okay," he says, sitting me down and then sitting down beside me. "I have to say something, and I want you to be completely honest with me." All I can do is nod. "I woke up this morning," he starts, and my hands hold the water bottle, not sure what the hell he's going to say. "Scratch that." He shakes his head. "I came home last night, and I was miserable." I can't say anything because my heart is lodged in my throat. Was he miserable because of me or my family? "Move in with me," he urges, looking into my eyes, and I think the blood drains from my body.

"I want to see you every day and help you." I swallow, wondering if he's asking me to do this because of me or the baby, but not because he feels like I do. "I want to be there for you and the baby."

I clear my throat. "You will always be there for the baby," I say. "Even if I'm not living here, you can come over any time you want."

"That's not the same, and you know it." His voice sounds like he's pleading with me. "I want to get you pickles and ice cream in the middle of the night. If that is what you need."

I put the bottle of water on the table in front of me. "I need to tell you something," I finally cut him off. "Something you should know. Do you know why I didn't tell you I was pregnant?" I hold my hands to stop them from shaking. "Because I was afraid you would tell me you didn't want the baby." I wipe away the tear as he tries to say something, but I stop him by holding up my hand, knowing I have to have this out there so he knows.

"I was afraid you would tell me to get rid of it, and I would end up hating you. That all this love I have for you would be tossed away in one moment, and I don't think I could have handled that. That the baby I am carrying, who I love more than I love myself, would be pushed aside. That you would look at the one night we spent together, which was hands down the best night of my life, as a mistake." I look down at my fingers. "And that would kill me because I've been in love with you since you walked into the hospital room to meet Penelope. Every single time I saw you, my love grew for you, watching you become the father you are. I fell in love with you because of the love you have for Penelope. I fell in love with you because there is no one else in this world I can see myself with besides you, and trust me, I've tried to change my mind," I finally say.

I smile through the tears because sometimes it feels good to speak your truth, and this is my truth. "So to answer your question…" I stand, not sure what I'm going to do or where I will go after I say the next words. "I can't move in with you because me moving in with you would mean a whole different thing than you want." I can't help but smile at him. "You want me here for the baby, and I get it. But I don't think my heart could take living with you and not have hope." I grab the bottle of water. "So, for that reason, I will not move in with you." I swallow down the sob. "I have to use the restroom." I turn and walk out of the room as fast as I can.

Twenty-Nine

"I HAVE TO use the restroom," she says before she turns and walks out of the room, leaving me with my heart so full it could burst out of my chest. My eyes stay right where I last saw her retreating back. I take a second before I turn my head around and sit down on the couch, the thumping of my heart settling down as I replay the words in my head over and over again. *I've been in love with you since you walked into the hospital room to meet Penelope.*

That day is etched in my mind forever. Walking in and seeing Penelope in Abigail's arms is something I will remember until my last breath. My legs start to move up and down with nerves, replaying all her words. My head was spinning as she stood there with tears in her eyes, and all I wanted to do was kiss her and make sure she was okay.

My legs move before my head tells me to give her space, except I can't not go to her. I walk to the bathroom, hearing the water running. My hand comes up to knock on the door instead of waiting for her. The water turns off. "Abigail." I whisper her name softly, wanting nothing but to look at her. "Are you okay?"

"Yes," she mumbles, but the door doesn't open. "I'll be right out."

"Okay," I say, walking back to the couch and waiting for her, thinking about what to say to her. Knowing this is the only chance I'm probably ever going to get.

I hear the bathroom door open and then look over at the hallway where I know she will walk out. She walks to me with her shoulders back and her head held high. Fuck, I keep saying she's beautiful, but she's so much more than that. "How are you feeling?"

"Good," she replies, avoiding looking at me as she comes in and sits next to me on the couch.

"Abigail…" I start saying her name, and she shakes her head.

"Please don't," she says softly.

"If not now, then when?" I ask, and she looks at me. "If I can't tell you how I feel now, then when?" I smile at her and can't help but hold up my hand to cup her cheek. "Before anything, I want you to know one thing." I swallow, and so does she. "What I'm about to say has nothing to do with the fact that you are carrying our child." My thumb rubs her cheek. "And everything to do with me and you. When I found out you were pregnant,

I was crushed. Physically, emotionally, and mentally crushed. I had my chance with you. I had that one night with you, and I ruined it. I got up when I heard the guys talking about you and walked out of the room. I couldn't stand it. It was as if someone reached inside me and yanked out a piece of my heart."

She licks her lip as her blue eyes turn even more crystal, and I hope I can spend the rest of my life looking into them as more than just her baby daddy. "I fell in love with you two years after I met you," I admit to her, and her mouth opens. "I can even pinpoint when it was. It was after a hockey game, and I came to find Penelope, and she was in your arms sleeping. You sat by yourself rocking my daughter in a corner, refusing to move when someone called you over." She gasps. "I watched you from the door. You were the most beautiful woman I had ever seen. You are even more so now." I try to laugh at the correction. "I've been in love with you for years. Watching from afar." I shake my head. "Trying not to be the creepy guy who is caught watching. I thought you were so far out of my league, and I came with baggage. I just couldn't do it to you."

"She isn't baggage," she quickly counters.

"Reason five million twenty-seven thousand as to why I love you." I get closer to her. "You are the first girl I've been with since I got Penelope." She gasps. "You are the only one I want to be with. I can't explain it, but I feel complete when you and Penelope are around. Like it was always meant to be us. Asking you to move in with us was more about my need to have you close than anything else." She smiles through her tears, and I can't not move in and kiss her. My lips fall onto hers so softly I can taste her tears. "Please stop crying. I don't like it."

"Okay," she says before she leans in and kisses me. "I'll try." Her tongue slides into my mouth, and I swear I moan out loud. I'm about to turn my head to the side and take the kiss deeper when my phone rings. I let go of her lips. Going over to my phone and grabbing it, I see it's an alarm to go pick up Penelope.

"I have to go get Penelope," I tell her, and she gets up.

"What if she hates the idea of a sibling?" she asks in a low voice. "What if she hates me for coming between you two?"

I walk over to her and grab her face in my hands. "She could never hate you." I smile at her. "Never."

"I really hope so," she says as I kiss her lips one more time before slipping my hand in hers and walking out the front door. "Should I stay here?" she asks when I get in the car. "Should I give you guys alone time?"

"Hey," I say, turning to her, "you know she loves you just as much as she loves me, right?" Her face fills with a smile.

"I love her just as much," she declares as I reach over to her and grab her hand in mine. The drive doesn't take us long, and she's out of the car before I am, walking over to the chain-link fence where kids are playing.

Penelope must spot her right away because she squeals her name, "Abigail!" She runs to her, and Abigail has her arms open for her.

She wraps her arms around Penelope and kisses her

head. "Did you get taller?" Penelope looks up at her, and the look they share is filled with love.

"Yeah," Penelope says, walking over and grabbing her backpack, and swinging it over her shoulder.

"Is it me, or does she look like a teenager?" Abigail asks, and I just nod my head. I want to slip my hand into hers or put my arm around her, but I don't know if she will be okay with it.

"Are you staying for dinner?" Penelope asks Abigail when she slides her hand in the same hand I've been itching to hold.

"I'm not sure," she says, looking down at her.

"Dad can make your favorite dish?" Penelope looks at me, and I nod my head while she looks back at Abigail. "What's your favorite dish?"

"Well, this week, it's burgers," Abigail says. "Bacon cheeseburgers."

"Mine too," Penelope says. "Dad, can we have bacon cheeseburgers?"

"Anything," I tell her, opening the back door for Penelope, who stops in front of me. "Hello, by the way." I lean down to kiss her head.

She laughs and gives me a side hug. "Hello." She tilts her head back and scrunches her nose, just like she used to do when she was a baby. "What do you put on your burger?"

For the whole car ride home, she talks about what she did at school. Who she sat next to, who is friends with who. I don't have a chance to get a word in.

She dumps her bag in the office as soon as we walk in

and then walks to the kitchen and grabs an apple. I look over at Abigail, who is wringing her hands. "Hey, P." I use the little nickname I sometimes call her. "Why don't you come here so I can talk to you?"

She heads over, her ponytail going back and forth as she walks to the couch where we usually have our discussions. I wait for Abigail to follow her. She sits at the far end of the couch, and I sit next to her, facing Penelope. "What happened?" Penelope asks as she looks at us.

"Nothing happened, per se," Abigail says to her, trying not to sound nervous, "we just have something to tell you."

"Are you guys getting married?" she asks, clapping her hands together, and I just look at her shocked. "Can I be a bridesmaid and not the flower girl? I'm too old."

"Um…" Abigail says, looking at me with the help me look on her face.

"We are not getting married." I chuckle and don't add yet because I still want her to move in with me. "But we are having a baby."

Penelope gasps. "Is that your baby?" She points at Abigail's stomach, and I just nod my head. "You guys had sex."

"Um…" Abigail says, her eyes going big as she looks at me, but I'm too shocked to even think about anything except what she just said.

"Hold on." I hold up a hand. "Who told you about sex?" Even saying the word with her, I want to throw up.

"Laura's mom was pregnant last year. She came to

school and said her mom and dad had sex to get the baby in there when Carver said the stork brought her brother," Penelope states like it's nothing.

"Do you know what sex is?" I ask her, and Abigail holds up her hand.

"Why don't we table that discussion for another time?" She smiles tightly. "Maybe focus on the fact Penelope is going to be a big sister." She turns back to Penelope. "Are there any questions you want to ask us?" Penelope looks like she's about to ask her something. "That don't have to do with sex or how the baby got in me."

"Where is the baby going to live?" Penelope asks, and I see Abigail wring her hands. I bet she's wishing now that she hadn't asked that question.

"I was thinking that maybe Abigail could move in with us," I finally chime in, "but it's Abigail's decision. But whether she lives with us or not, the baby will be here as much as he can." Just thinking of not being there every step of the way with another child has me blinking away tears.

"Your dad and I still have a couple of things to talk through," Abigail explains, reaching for my hand, "and some logistics to work through."

"Are we going to have a room here for when the baby comes over?" Penelope asks.

"Yes," I say without thinking twice. Regardless of where the baby lives at the beginning, he's going to know he's always got a place here.

"Can I help decorate?" she asks Abigail.

"Of course," Abigail says right away, "we can choose

whatever you want."

"When do we find out if it's a boy or girl?" Penelope asks, and I'm about to answer when Abigail shrieks.

"Oh my God." She brings my hand to her stomach. "I think I just felt a kick."

Penelope flies out of her chair and comes to us. Abigail grabs her hand and puts it next to mine, and I swear I feel the softest movement ever. "That's it," Abigail says. "Did you feel it?"

"Yes," I say, blinking away the tears and looking at Penelope, who laughs when she feels it again.

"Hi." She moves down to talk to Abigail's stomach. "I'm your big sister." I don't know if it's her voice, but we both feel the baby kick again.

"He loves his big sister," Abigail whispers with tears in her eyes as she wraps an arm around her. "You are going to be the best big sister ever."

"It's a boy?" Penelope questions. "Can I have a sister after?"

"How about we take this one baby at a time?" Abigail suggests, and I just look at her.

"We can always try for a girl next." I wink at her and lean in and kiss her, and when I do, our son kicks. I'm not sure if he's for this plan or not.

THIRTY

ABIGAIL

"WE CAN ALWAYS try for a girl next." He winks at me, and I swear my face gets flushed, or at least that is what it feels like. He leans in and kisses me, and when he does, our son kicks again, this time harder than ever.

"Oh, I felt it again," Penelope says, getting even more excited. "It's me," she declares proudly, "he likes me the best."

I can't help the tears that spring to my eyes. "Of course he does, beautiful girl." I was so scared she would hate me for having a baby. I was so scared she would feel like she had to fight for her father's attention. I was so scared for so many things that if I'd just said what I should have it could have been so different from the start. It's at that moment my stomach decides to let out the biggest groan I've ever heard.

"Someone needs food," Tristan observes. "You two want burgers?" I just nod my head. He walks over to the kitchen where he grabs his iPad and pulls up, I don't even know what. He stands there in the middle of his kitchen, looking down at the iPad in one hand while he reaches up with his other hand to scratch his neck. His shirt lifts a bit and the flushing feelings start again. I just stare at how hot he is before he puts the iPad back on the counter and looks over at us. "Food is going to be here in thirty minutes." He looks at Penelope. "How are we doing with homework?"

"I have some reading to do." She gets up, leaving me by myself as I watch them with their afternoon routine. I get up and walk to the island, pulling out a stool next to Penelope, not to intrude on their time but to be with them. I watch as Penelope pulls her things out of the school bag. She starts getting her things ready when Tristan walks over to my side of the stool.

"I like having you here," he states softly, and I can't help but smile because I like being here also. I take that back. It's not that I like being here. I like being with them. "I also would like to know if it's okay to kiss you."

"I would like that very much," I reply shyly as he rubs his nose on mine. My hand comes up and holds his cheek while he kisses my lips softly. My stomach flutters every single time he kisses me. When dinner comes, he brings the brown bags into the kitchen, making plates for Penelope and myself, but nothing for him.

"Are you not eating?" I ask him, and he walks over to the stove where he takes out his prepared meal.

"I am," he confirms, coming over and sitting next to me as we eat. I thought after telling Penelope about the baby, it would be weird. I don't know why, but it's nothing like that. It feels like it did all this time.

I shoo them out of the kitchen when I know it's time for her to get ready for bed. Grabbing my phone before going into the kitchen, I FaceTime Gabriella, who answers after one ring.

"I don't even care that you haven't spoken to me in two days." She pretends not to look at the phone. "I don't even care you went home to tell Mom and Dad about your baby daddy and didn't think to tell me." I just watch her. "I don't even care."

"I'm sorry," I tell her softly, "everything just happened so fast."

"Too fast to call your twin sister?" she shrieks, looking at the phone. "You just wait until something happens with me, and you find out through Christopher." Her voice goes even louder. "Christopher, who didn't even give me the right information." I just shake my head. "He told me you are getting married—"

"I'm not getting married," I finally interrupt. "Don't you think I would tell you if I was getting married?"

"I thought I knew you," Gabriella says, "and then you jump on a plane with my nephew."

"We told Penelope," I say softly as I clean up the kitchen and look over to see Gabriella waiting. "She took it so much better than I thought."

"Obviously, she did. She's amazing." Gabriella shakes her head.

"She did ask me if the baby was going to have a room here," I share, looking toward the stairs to make sure I'm alone. "Actually, Tristan asked me to move in with him."

"What did you tell him?" Her face comes even closer to the phone.

"I told him I couldn't live with him because I was in love with him, and he just wanted me for the baby."

"Boy," Gabriella groans, "you are so dumb sometimes." I just roll my eyes. "You have been the only one not to see what he feels for you." I look at her, shocked. "You are getting everything you've ever wanted." I swallow when I think about it. I'm having a baby with the love of my life. "Don't get all in your head."

"I'm not all in my head," I deny, but I am all in my head. "I have to go."

"Are you coming home tonight?" she asks. I want to say yes, but to be honest, I have no idea. "I'm leaving tomorrow to go visit a couple of friends in LA."

"For how long?" I ask her, and she cocks her head to the side. "I said I was sorry."

"Yeah, whatever," she says. "I have to go. *Below Deck Down Under* is starting, and this new captain is so hot." She wiggles her eyebrows. "I'd like him to go down under."

She hangs up the phone, and I move around the room, making sure everything is clean. I turn the light off and walk into the living room. I sit on the couch, curling my feet under me. "Hey." I hear Tristan when he walks into the room. "You didn't have to clean the kitchen."

"I most certainly did," I tell him as he sits next to me,

draping his arm over my legs.

"How are you feeling?" he asks. I try to tell him I'm fine, but a yawn escapes me. He gets up, holding out his hand. "Let's get you to bed. You can crash in the guest bedroom."

"I want to say no," I remark, grabbing his hand to get me off the couch, "but I'm honestly so tired."

He laughs at me as he walks me upstairs, very much like he did the last time. "You call me if you need anything."

"Do you have a T-shirt?" I ask him. "I don't want to sleep in my dress." He walks toward his bedroom as I make my way into the guest bedroom. My feet sink into the plush carpet as I turn on the bedside lamp. I sit on the bed waiting for him as he comes back in with T-shirts in both hands.

"I don't know what you wanted, so I brought you two," he offers, holding them out for me.

"Thank you." I get up and reach for them.

"You let me know if you need anything else," he says, and I nod. "Good night, Abigail," he says softly and leans in to kiss my lips gently.

He walks out of the room, and I can still feel his kiss on my lips ten minutes later when I'm getting out of the shower and drying myself off. I grab the white shirt that reaches right under my butt, covering everything. The minute I put it on, I smell him all around me. Slipping under the cover, it takes me a second to fall asleep, only waking when I need to pee and I'm suddenly so thirsty. I finish in the bathroom and tiptoe out of my room. Seeing

Penelope's door half closed and Tristan's open but in the dark. I try not to make any noise as I walk down the stairs toward the kitchen.

Pulling open the fridge, I grab a water bottle when I hear someone coming down the stairs. I see Tristan walking into the kitchen. He's rubbing the sleep out of his eyes as he sees me with concern on his face. "Are you okay?" He walks to me wearing just his black boxer briefs.

"I was thirsty," I reply, my mouth drooling at the sight of him. I turn away, afraid my face is flushed again. "You can go to bed."

"I'm not leaving you alone," he states, and then he leans against the counter. "You look really fucking good in my shirt."

My nipples suddenly peak, and because the shirt is white, it's very evident. "Thank you," I say awkwardly before I walk to him, standing in front of him. "It smells like you."

He pushes the hair over my shoulder, stepping even closer in front of me. "I'm trying really hard right now," he says, his voice thick with need, "to not push you."

"What if you weren't trying?" I put the bottle of water down on the counter, wanting to have my hands free. "What would you do?"

"First, I would kiss your neck." I move my head to the side, giving him access, and he doesn't wait for another invitation. He bends his head and kisses my neck softly before trailing his tongue out and then sucking.

"I'm okay with that," I assure him, my eyes closing as

he moves from my neck to my ear. "What else?" I try to swallow, but my mouth is dry.

"Then I'd move my hand under the shirt and see if your nipples are as hard as they look." I'm so freaking on edge that I moan at the thought of him doing this. I arch my back and feel his hands slowly moving up over my stomach to my tits. He groans out when both hands graze my nipples, and the minute he rolls each nipple at the same time, my head falls back, and I moan and shudder. My hand comes out to grab his cock, which has been hard ever since he came down the stairs.

I don't know who moans the loudest. I don't know whose hands go where, but all I can think about is sucking his cock. "Ever since the first time," I say, moving my hands into his boxers and feeling his hard cock in my hand. "I've thought of doing this again." There in the middle of the kitchen, I squat down so my face is right in front of his cock. I don't think he's expecting me to do this, so he's just watching as I pull his boxers down and take his cock into my mouth. I moan as I fist him, moving my hand and my mouth at the same time.

"Fuck," he mutters, his hands going into my hair, and it makes me even wetter knowing I'm giving him this pleasure. "That mouth," he says as his hips thrust, "I've dreamed about it every single day since."

I lick the tip of his cock. "I played with myself thinking about you," I admit to him. "That and your mouth on me." His eyes look into mine as I take his cock into my mouth again. This time he fucks my mouth while we watch each other. I can feel when he's close because his thrusts are shorter, and his breathing starts getting faster.

"I don't want to come in your mouth," he tells me, and I almost cry when he moves away from me.

"Why not?" I ask him, and I swear it sounds like I'm whining.

"Because I want to come in you." He picks me up and places me on the counter. "Because after having your mouth on me, all I can think about is sliding into you."

I open my legs for him to stand in the middle of them, and we are at the perfect height. "I want to do so many things to you." He pulls the shirt up, and at this point, I just need him to touch my pussy. I put my feet on the counter, opening more for him. "Fuck," he says when I lift the shirt over my head, but I don't take it off my shoulders.

I'm sitting on his island with my tits aching to be touched and my white lace thong drenched. I move my ass closer to the counter's edge so he can get better access to my pussy. "You're wet," he states as he drags a finger up my slit over my panties, and I just nod. He moves the thong to the side and then slides his cock into me. "Fucking hell," he swears softly, leaning down and taking a nipple into his mouth. I come on his cock so hard I'm shivering and moaning loudly, "Sshhh, baby," he hushes, his mouth falling on mine as his tongue plays with mine, and he fucks me.

I come over and over again, losing track of the number of times until he rams into me one last time, and I'm the one swallowing his moan this time.

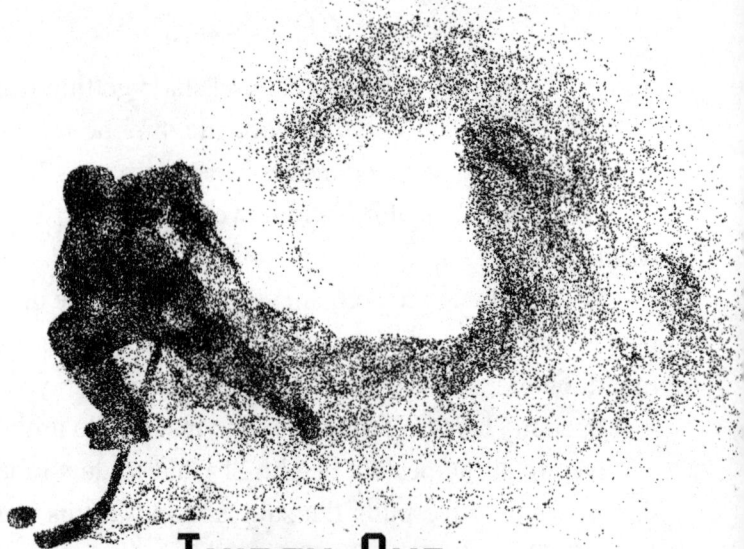

Thirty-One

I COLLAPSE ON her chest as she leans back on her elbow. "Did I just fuck you on my counter like a barbarian?" I say the words out loud instead of just in my head. My breaths come in pants as I try to get my breathing back to normal.

"I really hope this isn't another dream," she says as she runs her hand through the back of my hair. I look up and see her looking down at me. "If it is a dream, I'm not sure I want to wake up from it." She bends her head, and I raise mine to kiss her. "Also, you might have to get off my belly," she urges, and I jump off her, making her laugh. "You weren't hurting me; I just have to pee."

I look at her pink cheeks as she sits up. Her tits are bigger than they were the last time. Her belly is fucking beautiful, and I lean down and kiss her stomach. "Hi, baby boy," I say, rubbing her stomach, and it just makes me so fucking happy. "It's your dad."

"Who was just inside me." Abigail rolls her lips when I glare at her. "What? I'm just telling him in case he's wondering who poked him in the eye." She smiles so big her eyes light up. "I'm kidding. You probably didn't even feel it."

"How sure are you?" I ask her as she pulls her shirt over her head, and I want to stop her.

"I'm one-thousand-percent positive the baby can't feel you." I tuck my cock back in to my boxers and grab her by the waist.

"I love you." I say the three words I was so scared to say before, but now I feel the need to tell her all the time. "Let's get you to bed." I kiss her softly, picking her up and putting her on her feet. "Do you want to sleep in my bed?" I ask her, holding my breath. I wanted her to come to my room before, but I didn't want to push her. But now after having her again, all I want to do is keep her close.

"What do you think Penelope will say?" she asks, not sure.

"Well, considering she said we had sex," I remind her, "and I'm really fucking hoping she didn't google sex when I wasn't here."

"I don't want her to feel uncomfortable," she says softly, and I just walk into my room.

"I'll set the alarm early so she doesn't see you in my bed," I suggest to her, walking to the king-sized bed. "I'm going to be honest with you," I tell her, tossing the cover back. "Penelope is the only one I've ever shared a bed with. I don't know if I move a lot or not." She walks to me and kisses me under my neck.

"Do you think you can set the alarm for ten minutes before so we can have…" I smirk at her.

"Like I need ten minutes," I joke with her, and she laughs quietly before turning and looking around. "Bathroom is through there." I point at the door in the corner.

She turns and walks toward the bathroom, and I walk over to Penelope's room to make sure she's still asleep. She's spread out in the middle of her bed like a starfish. I get back into the bedroom at the same time as Abigail is coming toward the bed. "I had to clean up. What side do you sleep on?"

"The middle." I chuckle. "I'll be right back," I tell her, walking to the bathroom and cleaning myself off. When I slide into bed five minutes later, she's in the middle of the bed waiting for me. I slip in behind her and kiss the back of her neck.

"That got you in trouble before," she mumbles as she yawns. Even though I would love to take her again, I let her sleep. I don't know when I fall asleep, but I do it with her in my arms. When the alarm rings, I blink open my eyes, but all I see is hair in front of me. I turn over on my side to silence the noise.

"Morning," she mumbles, snuggling into me even more. She kisses my neck before she closes her eyes again.

"Morning." I hug her, pulling her even closer to me.

"I love this."

"What?" she asks, looking up at me, and I feel the baby kick. "Whatever it is, I think your son likes it too."

She rolls toward the edge of the bed. "I'll go to the other room," she says, and I get up, walking to the walk-in closet to grab the robe.

"Here." I hand it to her. "I'll meet you downstairs. I'll make breakfast."

"Are you getting dressed?" she asks. I smirk at her as I grab her hand and pull her into the bathroom with me, locking the door behind us. I place her on the counter, and just like last night, I slide into her. It's fast, just like last night. "The next time we do this," I tell her as I pull out of her, "we are doing it in a bed."

"Is that so?" she asks, getting off the counter and pulling off her clothes as she starts the shower. "Does this mean we are dating?" She piles the hair on top of her head.

I chuckle. "I want to do more than date you." I kiss her lips. "But let's just take it in baby steps."

She steps inside the glass shower as the water rains over her. "What does that even mean?" She grabs the bar of soap and lathers her hands.

I lean against the counter I just fucked her on. "It means I want forever with you, but I have to earn you." She stops lathering her hands and just stares at me. "Now finish your shower, and I'll meet you downstairs."

"Okay," she utters softly as I walk out of the room, really fucking hoping Penelope is still sleeping. Her alarm goes off as soon as I take two steps down the hall, and it rings five times before she turns it off.

"Pancakes or waffles?" I ask her, waiting on the step.

"Waffles and fruit," she mumbles right before I'm sure she goes back to sleep until the alarm rings again. I start making the waffles when Abigail walks into the kitchen wearing my robe.

"It smells good in here," she says, coming behind me and kissing my shoulder. "What can I do to help?"

"Can you cut up some fruit?" I ask her, and she walks to the fridge, grabbing some strawberries, raspberries, and blueberries.

"What does your week look like?" I ask her as I pour more waffle batter into the machine before closing it.

"I have four night shifts in a row," she states as she washes the fruit, "then I'm off five days." She grabs a knife to cut the tops off the strawberries. "What about you?"

"I leave today for four days, and then I'm back," I tell her. "Do you think you'll be okay to see me when I get back?"

She looks over at me, smirking at me. "I think I can squeeze you in."

I don't say anything else to her because Penelope comes into the kitchen. "Morning, beautiful girl," Abigail greets her, and she just grunts as she grabs some orange juice from the fridge. "You never were a morning girl."

"It hasn't changed," I say to her as Penelope pours herself juice and then drinks some. "That's not true. She's fine on the weekend."

"That's because I don't have to get up at the crack of

dawn," she huffs, walking over to the sink and grabbing a couple of strawberries. Abigail smiles at her and leans over, kissing her head. "Morning," she mumbles to Abigail, and the two share a smile. Then she puts her hand on Abigail's stomach. "Morning, little bro."

I can't help but smile at them. They eat side by side as I make a protein shake and run up to get dressed. When I come down, the kitchen is clean as Penelope runs to get her bag. "Bye, Abigail." She walks over to her and hugs her. "Can I call you tonight?"

"You can call me anytime," she tells her, kissing her forehead. "I work tonight, so I might not answer, but I will call you back when I can."

She runs to the front door while I walk over to Abigail. "I'll be back in thirty minutes." I kiss her lips. "I have to be at the rink in an hour."

"So no hanky-panky." She rolls her eyes. "Got to go put my panties back on then."

My cock goes immediately hard. "I have to go out to the car with a boner," I scold, trying to adjust myself. "How am I going to explain this?"

"Tell her you're having an allergic reaction," she teases, trying not to laugh at me. "Go or she's going to be late."

I rush out of the house, and thankfully, Penelope is already in the car. I drop her off quickly before returning home and having to rush to get in a suit. "I can take an Uber," Abigail volunteers when I walk out of the walk-in closet and she finishes making the bed.

"Not a chance in hell." I side-eye her, putting my tie

in my side pocket.

"You look very handsome," she compliments, smiling at me, "and I get to kiss you."

"If we had enough time, you could even kiss my—" She stops me from talking. We walk out of the house with my hand holding hers and the other hand holding my luggage.

"I'll call you tonight," I tell her, and for the first time, I'm uneasy about going away. It also happened at the beginning when I had Penelope. I would worry every second of every day until I got back and made sure she was okay.

"Okay, if I can't answer…" she starts to say, and I just nod my head. She leans over and kisses me. "Be safe." She smiles, leaving me with one last kiss before leaving the car.

The next four days go by at a snail's pace, or at least that is how it feels. The nights are usually spent waiting for her to call me back, and the days I don't call her because I know she sleeps all day long. When I finally walk off the plane at home, I rush to my car and get in. I didn't tell her what time I was coming home, hoping it would be enough time, but there was an issue with the landing gear or something. I just hope she's not still sleeping by the time I get to her.

I ring the doorbell once, and I'm about to walk away when I hear the door unlock. She opens the door, and I see her squinting at the sun, but her whole face lights up when she sees me. She throws open the door and jumps into my arms. "You're here!" She buries her face in my neck, wrapping her legs around me. I walk into her house with her attached to me, but the minute I take two steps in, my phone rings in my pocket.

"I hate your phone," she mumbles as I reach into my pocket, pull out my phone, and see it's the alarm to go and get Penelope.

"Sorry, I thought I was going to get here earlier," I tell her. "But the plane was delayed."

She unwraps herself from me. "How fast can you get dressed?" I finally look down and see she's wearing the white shirt she wore the last night she slept over. "That's my shirt."

"It is," she confirms, walking up the steps to her bedroom. "I borrowed it," she says over her shoulder. "Give me two minutes." In less than two minutes, she's coming back down wearing yoga pants and a white tank top. Her bump definitely got bigger. She puts on a button-down shirt when we get to the front door, as she picks up a big duffel bag. "I figured I'd be staying over at your place," she says and then looks away. "I should have asked."

I walk to her and turn her head toward me. "We'll start with one bag at a time, and hopefully, after a while, you'll have everything at my house." She laughs as we walk out.

"Can we keep the bag in the car when we get home?" she asks when we pull up to Penelope's school. "I don't want her to feel like I'm just barging in."

"Do you know the first thing she asked me every single night when I called her?" I ask her, and she just looks at me. "If you were moving in." Abigail opens her mouth and then closes it. "Let's go, baby." I kiss her neck. "You look very sexy," I tell her, and she gasps.

"Can you not talk about sex in a school parking lot?" she hisses, walking with me. Penelope comes running out of the door, straight to me. She jumps in my arms, just like she's always done when I'm away more than two days.

"Hey, you." I wrap my arms around her and kiss her about ten times, making her giggle at me.

"Stop, Dad," she says, squeezing down her neck to make sure I don't kiss her. "Can we have ice cream?"

"We can," I agree as she walks over to Abigail and hugs her also.

"How's the baby?" she asks as we walk to the car.

"He had the hiccups this week," she shares with us, "and I felt them." I open the car door for Penelope and then for Abigail.

I don't think I've ever been happier until my phone beeps, and I see a text from Xavier.

Xavier: *Hey, have you seen this?*

He attached a link to an Instagram page where the gossip from the team is. I spot my picture right away. Clicking on it, I see the caption.

Sources are saying that Tristan Weise is expecting another baby.

I feel like I'm going to throw up when I see the comments.

How many baby mommas is this?

Two kids, two moms?

The last comment makes me want to throw my phone. **I wonder if he knows who the woman is this time?**

THIRTY-TWO

ABIGAIL

I WATCH HIM look down at the phone, seeing the color drain from his face. I'm putting the plate in the sink, my eyes never leaving his. His fingers grip the phone so hard his knuckles are turning white. "Is everything okay?" I ask him, turning to clean up the rest of the dinner plates. I wait for him to answer me, but the only thing he does is shake his head.

He turns his phone down and slams it on the counter. I look over at Penelope to see if she is looking at him, but she's too engrossed in her show to care. I wipe my hands on the dishrag before going over to him. His hands are outstretched on the counter in front of him as his head hangs down. My hand goes to his lower back when I get close enough to him, "What happened," I whisper.

"I was supposed to protect you," he says, his voice

filled with anguish, and I just look at him confused. "Through all this, I promised to protect you, and I'm fucking failing."

My heart speeds up so fast it's almost like I'm panting. "What the hell are you talking about?" I hiss.

He picks up his phone and hands it to me. "It's bad." My head spins as I look down, not sure what I'm supposed to be looking at. My eyes find his picture and I read the caption and I pfft, tossing the phone down. "What the hell are you doing?" he asks shocked.

"I'm not going to read garbage," I inform him, turning and walking back to clean up the rest of the plates from dinner. After the ice cream shop, we came home and when he went to the trunk to grab his bag, he grabbed mine at the same time. Penelope didn't even notice, in fact, nothing fazed her about me being here or having dinner with them. It's almost as if it was always the three of us.

"It doesn't bother you?" He walks over, standing next to me at the sink as the water runs.

"What bothers me is that people have no idea what they are taking about, so they make stupid-ass comments," I admit to him.

"But—" he starts to talk, and I hold up my hand.

"Do any of those people who commented know you?" I ask him, and he folds his arms over his chest, leaning against the counter, crossing his feet at his ankles. "Do they actually know, know you?" He doesn't bother answering me, so I continue, "Because anyone who knows, knows you knows that you are the best dad. You put her first before anything else." I turn to put the plate in the dishwasher. "If anyone should be talked about, it's me," I admit to him and he glares at me. "If I would have told you at the beginning, would you have turned me away?" He doesn't have to answer me. "Exactly, so I'm the one who kept it from you."

"So it doesn't bother you that they are saying I have two kids and two baby mommas?" he says, and I have to chuckle when he says baby mommas.

"No." I shake my head. "Cooper has two baby mommas. Does it bother Erika?" He just rolls his eyes at me. I turn the water off, grabbing the dishrag again before turning and walking over to my purse.

Pressing dial, I put the phone to my ear. "What do you want?" Gabriella answers after one ring.

"Can you come over here?" I ask her, and I can already hear her moving around the house. "And bring me a nice sports bra and matching panties. Oh, and your camera."

"What the fuck for?" she asks.

"I'll tell you when you get here," I tell her. "And like a black sweater."

"See you in fifteen," she states, hanging up the phone and I look over at Tristan, who is still just looking at me.

"I need to go and get ready," I tell him. "I'll clean up when I'm done."

"What are you getting ready for?" he questions me as I walk over to the stairs.

"You'll see," I tell him, walking up the stairs to his room. I take out the little makeup case I brought, putting on some stuff just to make me look a little bit like I'm glowing instead of exhausted. The last four night shifts have been brutal and sleeping has been wishy-washy. Plus, the baby has decided that now he knows how to kick to do it all the time, especially when I lie down to sleep.

I'm applying my lip gloss when the doorbell rings. I can hear voices when I walk out of the bedroom and toward the stairs. "I'm here," Gabriella announces, looking at me and then turning to look at Penelope when she comes to the door, probably wondering who it is.

"Hi, Gabriella," Penelope greets her, walking over to her and giving her a side hug.

"Did you get taller?" Gabriella asks, and she just nods her head.

"Okay, so what am I doing here?" Gabriella asks, holding up the two bags she has in her hands.

"We are going to take a picture for a baby announcement." I walk down the rest of the stairs to the door, grabbing the bags from her.

"What?" Tristan asks, looking at me.

"Well, we never announced we were having a baby, and people are all gossiping, so we'll give them something to talk about." I look at him.

"If you start to sing the song," Gabriella groans, "I'm leaving."

"I'm going to go get changed," I tell him. "Can you put on a black shirt and black pants?" Then I look over at Penelope, who is just watching. "Do you want to be in the picture also? If it's okay with your dad?" She looks at me and then at her dad, who just shrugs.

"Okay, so meet back down in five minutes." I turn to walk up the stairs. "Everyone, wear black."

"Are you in mourning?" Gabriella asks me, and I stop walking up the stairs.

"Okay, fine. Everyone, wear white." I shrug, walking up the stairs and to the duffel bag where my stuff is in. Grabbing the white tank top dress I brought over, I walk to the bathroom and change. Walking out, I see Tristan come out of the walk-in closet wearing blue jeans and a white T-shirt.

"Gabriella says for us to be in jeans and a T-shirt," he informs me, and I just look at his blue eyes.

"Are you okay with Penelope being in the picture?" I ask him quietly. "I want her included, but I don't want you to be uncomfortable about it. She's part of this journey with us," I remind him, "and she needs to be front and center also." I smile. "But I also don't want to exploit her."

"I love that you love her as if she was your own." He walks to me, grabbing my face in his hands, bending his head to me to kiss me softly. That is the way Penelope finds us when she walks in the room, wearing the same thing her father is wearing.

"I'm ready," she announces, not even caring she caught us kissing.

"Okay," I huff, "let's get the show on the road." I slip my hand in his and then in hers and we walk down together.

"Look at how cute you guys are," Gabriella gushes. "Okay, so I have a couple of ideas. The sun is almost going down, so can we get outside to take some shots in the yard?" She walks to the backyard. "Do you guys have an ultrasound picture?"

"Yes," Tristan says, walking over to the living room and grabbing the frame on the fireplace mantel. I didn't even see it there beforehand.

We walk outside, my hand back in Tristan's. "Okay, so I want Tristan and Abigail in the back and Penelope in the front." We get into our places. "Penelope, I want you to hold the frame in your hands and hold your hands out in front of you." She grabs the camera around her neck as she snaps some shots. "Okay, you two in the back, kiss each other." I look at Tristan, and all I can do is smile, and I hear the clicking sounds when he leans in and kisses my face. "That's good." She looks around for a bit before instructing us on the next picture. "Okay, I want Tristan to hold the frame." Penelope hands him the frame. "And I want Penelope to stand beside Abigail with your arms around each other." I put my arm around Penelope's shoulders, and she wraps her arm around my waist. "Now, Penelope, put your hand on Abigail's belly and, Abigail, put your head on Tristan's shoulder. Tristan, look down at the baby and the frame."

I can hear the clicking every single time she takes a shot. She looks down at her camera, making sure she got some shots.

"Can I go now?" Penelope asks us, and Gabriella just nods at her. "I'm going to watch my show."

I watch her skip into the house and then look back at Gabriella. "Okay, this is what I want next." She looks at us. "I want you two to look at each other; put your forehead on hers," she instructs Tristan, "and then put one hand on her stomach. Abi," she turns to me, "hold the picture in your hand." We do as she tells us, and I look into his eyes, "Abi, put your hand on his neck, around his shoulder."

"You're beautiful," he tells me, and I just smile at him, leaning in and kissing him.

"Did I tell you guys to kiss?" I hear Gabriella. "You're lucky it's a good shot." We laugh at her.

"Okay, Tristan, sit on the grass with your legs open, and Abi, sit in the middle of his legs." I get down on my knees before turning to sit with my back to his chest. "Put your hands on her stomach," she tells Tristan as she comes over and props the frame up beside us. "This is good," she says, and I lean my head back on his shoulder and look up at him smiling as he leans forward and kisses my temple.

"Okay, I think I got it," Gabriella turns to walk inside. "I'll be ready in ten minutes." She closes the door behind her, and I just sit here for a second in his arms.

"Have I told you I love you?" he asks, and I look up at him, the smile on my face getting even bigger, making my eyes almost squish closed.

"Not lately," I reply honestly.

"I love you," he repeats, and my heart literally flips in my chest. My hand comes up to hold his cheek as he bends his head to kiss me. My tongue slides into his mouth, the both of us needy. I turn in his arms, getting on my knees in the middle of his legs. My hands go from his chest up to his neck, while his hands go from my hips to my ass, pulling me into him. He turns his head to deepen the kiss when I hear Penelope yell from behind us.

"Gabriella says stop making out and come see the pictures!" I let go of his lips, looking over my shoulder for Penelope, who isn't even there anymore.

"One of these days," Tristan vows, getting up now and holding out his hands to help me up, "I'm going to make out with you and fuck you without worrying about being interrupted."

"Promise?" I say, standing and slipping my fingers with his.

"You can bet on it," he kisses me softly, and I believe him.

Fifteen minutes later, we both post on Instagram at the same time. Two pictures, one of the four of us and the other one of just the two of us.

My caption reads, **Baby makes four.**

I hand him my phone, and he hands me his as I read his caption.

Made for Us.

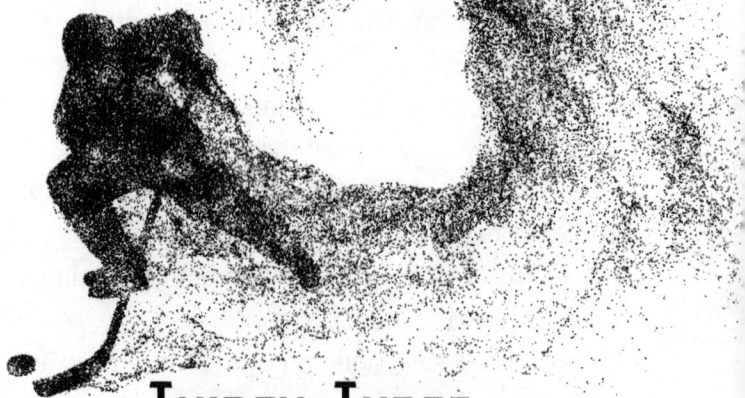

THIRTY-THREE

TRISTAN

I TYPE OUT the words for my Instagram and press enter.
I watch the circle on top to make sure it's posted before I
look over at Abigail, who is still typing. She looks at me
and hands me her phone while I hand her mine. I look
down and read her caption.

Baby makes four.

I smile at her as she looks down at mine and then
looks back up with tears in her eyes. "Yours is so much
better than mine," she sniffles, wiping the tears from
her eyes. The phone pings in her hand nonstop. "People
are commenting on your post." She hands me back my
phone.

I look down and see I already have two hundred and
seventy-one comments. I open the app just to see if
they are nasty comments. They are all polite, except for

Christopher, who put a comment.

Are you going to put a ring on it also?

I laugh and show Abigail, who looks over and laughs, shaking her head. I'm about to answer him when Matty chimes in.

I thought they were engaged already.

I don't have a chance to type anything because the phone rings in my hand, and I look down to see it's Dylan.

"Hello," I answer, putting him on speakerphone. "You are on speakerphone, and I'm here with your sisters and Penelope."

"Hmm," he growls, "so I can't yell at you."

"Why would you yell at me?" I ask him, putting the phone down on the counter and walking over to the fridge, grabbing a water bottle while Gabriella is on her laptop doing something with the pictures. Penelope is on the couch watching television, and since she doesn't have school tomorrow, she has no bedtime.

"Did you guys just announce you were having a baby?" he asks, but doesn't give me a chance to say anything else, "before announcing you were getting married?"

"Well, for one," Abigail declares, "we aren't getting married."

"Yet," I say, winking at her, as she just stares at me with her mouth hanging open.

"Before she agrees to marry him, she has to agree to move in with him," Gabriella hollers from the counter without even looking up. Abigail glares at her. Gabriella finally looks over at Abigail and shrugs when Abigail holds up her hands, saying why.

"What do you mean she has to agree to move in with him?" Dylan questions, shocked. "Of course she is moving in with him. Where the hell is the baby going to live?"

"We could co-parent," Abigail suggests out loud, and now I'm the one glaring at her. "Cooper does it."

"And he hates every second of it," Dylan shares. "You liked him enough to have sex with him and have a baby. Why not move in with him?"

"We are not having this conversation right now," Abigail says between clenched teeth, "Penelope is here."

"Does this mean you're selling your house?" Dylan asks.

"I'm still living in it, asshole," Gabriella retorts. "You act like she's been living alone."

"How am I supposed to know you're not jet-setting around the world?" Dylan states. Gabriella gets up from her stool and walks over to the phone and presses the red button, disconnecting the call.

"You're welcome," she gloats, walking back to her computer and closing the laptop, "but you still didn't answer the question." She looks over at Abigail. "Are you moving in here?"

"I don't know," Abigail says, looking at me and then at Penelope to see if she has something to say.

"Penelope," I call her name, and she looks over from the television, "should Abigail move in with us?"

"Yes," she replies, turning back to watch her show.

I look at Abigail, who slaps my arm. "What was that for?"

"How could you just ask her like that?" she asks between her clenched teeth.

"How else did you want me to ask her?" I walk over to her and put my arms on her shoulders while she holds my hips. "Move in with us."

"You might as well just say yes," Gabriella pushes. "You know you want to, plus…" She holds up her finger. "I think he likes you." She winks at me, and I squeeze my eyebrows together. "See, he didn't even fall for my charms."

"She's pregnant with my child!" I shriek. "Why the hell would I fall for anyone's charm?" I look back at Abigail, who is trying really hard not to laugh. "What do you say?"

"Ugh," she grunts. "Fine, I guess I'll move in with you."

"Like it's that much of a struggle," Gabriella teases. "Hey, P," she calls her name, "want to come over to my house and do manis and pedis?" Penelope jumps off the couch.

"Dad, can I?" she asks, and I look at Abigail, who nods. She jumps up and down. "Is this a sleepover?"

"We can," Gabriella says, "there is a room that no one has been in." She grabs her stuff from the counter. "Someone has to sleep in it."

"Are you sure?" Abigail asks Gabriella, and she just looks at me.

"How hard can it be? She can talk and goes to the

bathroom by herself," Gabriella replies, "like she literally can take care of herself." She looks over at Penelope. "Isn't that right?"

"I can Uber my own food," she announces, crossing her arms over her chest.

"You do not order your own food," I retort, rolling my eyes. She shocks me when she picks up her iPhone and shows me the Uber Eats app. "What credit card is that?"

"I don't know. I took one from your wallet," she admits. "You told me to the last time."

"When?" I ask her, shocked.

"When you were in bed, and I was hungry," she reminds me. "It's fine. I only used it a couple of times."

"You know what would be funny?" Gabriella asks. "If you ordered like three hundred dollars' worth of cupcakes for fun." She puts her arm over Penelope's shoulder. "Do you want to bring a change of clothes?"

"I'll go get my bag," she says, running up the stairs.

"Don't you dare let her watch any of your shows," Abigail warns in a whisper.

"Define shows," Gabriella pushes.

"*Love Island,*" Abigail fires right away. "No *Love Island.*"

She rolls her eyes at her. "That was on already at three o'clock, so she's safe."

Penelope comes back with her bag. "Bye, Dad," she says to me, getting on her tippy-toes and kissing my cheek when I lean down. "Bye, Abigail." She walks over and hugs her.

"If you want to come home, all you have to do is call

me," I remind her as she turns to walk out of the room.

"Take care of you and the baby," Gabriella says to Abigail, giving her a hug, then leaning down and talking to her stomach. "Bye from your favorite aunt."

"You know how the baby got there?" Penelope asks, and I close my eyes. "They had sex."

Gabriella looks at her and then back at us. "You don't say?"

"Yeah, that's how babies get in the stomach," Penelope informs her.

"Well, not exactly," Gabriella replies and Abigail jumps forward.

"Okay, that talk is for another day," Abigail grumbles between clenched teeth as we walk them out the door.

We stand on the porch. "She's going to be okay, right?" I look over at Abigail, who just shakes her head.

"We can hope," Abigail replies. "I mean, she'll protect her with her life. But I'm not sure about her mouth."

"We are kid free," I remind her. "Well, almost kid free." I put my hand on her stomach.

"What will we do with all this free time?" she asks with a twinkle in her eye.

"Well, the first time we are going to do it, I'm going to eat some dessert." I walk her into the house and up the stairs immediately. "Then you're going to have some dessert."

"I think I'm full." She rolls her lips at me, and I pull her to me to kiss her. I take her in the bedroom, and she does actually eat dessert. Twice.

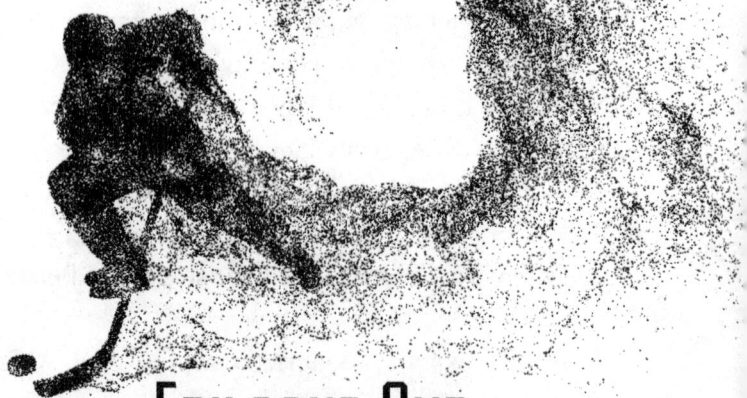

Epilogue One

GABRIELLA

Two Weeks Later

"I CAN COME to you." I put the phone on my shoulder as I walk over to my planner and open it. I'm still old-school. No matter how technology is, I always, always write my appointments down. "How is next week?" I pull out the red pen, ready to write the lady's name in it.

"That works. My name is Geraldine," she repeats like she didn't tell me this five times already, "and it's a boudoir shot." I close my eyes, dreading saying yes to my aunt, Alison, when she said her friend's mother wanted to take some portraits of herself. I don't think anyone thought it would be a boudoir.

"That works," I confirm, writing her information down. I'm just finishing writing her phone number down when the doorbell rings.

I hang up and walk to the door, not thinking anything of it, unlocking the door and opening it. I never expected the green eyes to be staring back at me. His hair is pushed back, and he's wearing a leather jacket, jeans, and motorcycle boots. Romeo Beckett in all his Hollywood glory "What the fuck are you doing here?" I shake my head. "Forget it. I don't even care." I slam the door, but he sticks his boot inside the door.

"Gabriella," he says my name as almost a whisper. It's been eight months since I last laid eyes on him. "We need to talk."

She's wrong.

It's time to win her back.

EPILOGUE TWO

TRISTAN

A few months later

"THIS HAS BEEN the longest road trip of my life," I grumble, unbuckling my seat belt when the plane finally touches down. We have been away from home for the last seven days, which usually isn't that bad, but Abigail is officially a week late and I was scared she would give birth when I wasn't there. Nico had the plane on standby, just in case, but I also knew she wouldn't want to bother me so she would pretend she was always okay.

"Just feel lucky her water didn't break and you had to go to her," Dylan says, getting out of his seat. "It would have been the longest plane ride of your life."

"Wow, you should go into motivational speaking," Michael deadpans. "And right before you start, you should kick them all in the balls."

I laugh at the both of them as they bicker like always. "Okay, see you guys later." I grab my bag and literally run off the plane.

It takes me record time to get home and the minute I walk into the house, I know something is up. "Hello," I say when I see Gabriella waiting at the bottom of the stairs. "What's wrong?"

"Why would something be wrong?" she replies, trying not to make me freak out.

"Well, then what's wrong with your face?" I ask her and she glares at me.

"What's wrong with your face?" she counters.

"Where is she?" I put my hands on my hips. "Abigail!" I shout her name and she walks out of our bedroom. Well, she actually waddles out of our bedroom wearing a long dress. Her face looks like she hasn't slept all night and the worry sets in.

I move around Gabriella and take the steps, two at a time. "What happened?"

"Nothing happened," she says in a low voice, "I'm just having some contractions."

"Some?" Gabriella says from downstairs. "It's been going on for thirty-six hours."

"What?" I shriek and look at Abigail. "Why didn't you call me?"

"There was nothing for you to do," she tells me and I walk to her. "I can't even go to the hospital because the contractions are seven minutes apart."

"Where is Penelope?" I ask, looking around.

"My mother took her," Gabriella informs me and I nod. The last thing Abigail would want was for her to worry about her being in pain.

"Did you call Dr. Emmy?" I ask her as I hold her face in my hands and kiss her. I thought I loved her before, but watching her grow with my child in her, it's brought me to a whole other level. There are no words to describe it, even if you asked me to.

"I did, it's my body preparing itself." She tries to calm me down, but then she closes her eyes as she starts her breathing exercises from when we took the Lamaze classes.

I rub her back. "In and out," I urge softly as she groans. "When was her last one?" I ask Gabriella who takes out her watch.

"Two minutes ago."

I'm about to yell at her when I look down as I hear a gush come out of her and splash onto my shoes. "Oh my God," she cries, "my water just broke."

"Jesus, I thought you peed yourself," Gabriella says and then picks up her phone. "Alert the press, her water just broke." She puts the phone down. "Car is packed. All we need is for her to get into the car."

"I'm not getting into the car like this," Abigail gasps. "I'm leaking all over the place."

"Who the hell cares?" I question, not even caring I'm wet.

"I care." She turns and waddles back into the bedroom. "You change, I'll change, and then we can go," she says calmly, "Gabriella!" She yells for her sister. "Can you bring me the underwear with the pads?"

"I never in my life want to know what that is," Gabriella states, coming into the room as I kick off my shoes.

"It's on the chair." She points to the chair with a change of clothes, as if she knew this would happen. She plans for everything every single time,

"Oh my God." Gabriella picks up the cream-colored thing in her hand. "This is underwear and a pad all I one."

"Yes," Abigail says, pulling her dress over her head. "Bring it to me."

I pull off my socks and toss them in the corner and I'm about to say something when Abigail yells out in pain. "Get in the car!" I yell to Gabriella. "Have the car running"

I walk over to Abigail. "I need you to lift foot." I hold the underwear on the floor.

"I can do it," she retorts, grabbing it from me and quickly putting them on. It takes thirty seconds to get her into the car.

I sit in the back with her, my arm around her shoulders. "I'm having another one," she announces to me, putting her head on my shoulder as she tries to breathe through the pain, but this time she moans out.

"You got this," I soothe her and by the time we reach the hospital, she is having them every single thirty seconds on the nose.

Gabriella parks at the entrance and jumps out, running into the hospital, while I start to get out of the car. We have to stop while she has another contraction, this one is more intense than the last one because she moans the whole time. The breathing is out the window at this point. "I'm not one to complain, but this shit hurts," declares sitting in the wheelchair.

"You have a human person coming out of your ho ha," Gabriella reminds her and I glare at her. "What? Like she doesn't know a human is going to come out of her?"

"Listen, as much as I love to hear you guys bond," Abigail says, "I need to get in there." I hold on to the wheelchair and push her into the elevator.

I put my hand on my forehead. "We forgot to call in," I admit to her. "That was like the number one thing on my to-do list." I look down at her as she tries to smile but then put her head back and groans out as she clutches her stomach.

The door of the elevator swings open and Dr. Emmy is there waiting for us. "Well, if isn't it my favorite couple." She smiles at me and then looks down at Abigail. "How far apart?"

"She just had one," I say as I wheel her out and she groans again, "that's been like maybe ten seconds ago."

"Let's get her hooked up to a monitor." Dr. Emmy grabs the wheelchair from me and briskly walks down the hallway and into a room. With the bed in the middle of the room, I walk with her, holding her hand, and when she gets up, she stops midway to groan again. "I need an IV in here," Dr. Emmy says, "now." Her voice sounds calm but I can see the nurses assess the situation. "Contractions are one after another and I think she's going to be ready to push."

"What?" Abigail says, standing up straight. "No, I don't think so." She walks over to the bed. "Besides, I need the epidural." She looks over at me and I can tell she's scared. "We talked about it." She blinks away the tears that are forming in her eyes but one escapes.

My hand comes up to wipe it away. "It's okay," I tell her softly as she turns to get into bed and groans again, this time her body shaking. I look over at Dr. Emmy who looks at Abigail.

"When did this start?" she asks her. I watch Abigail now start to shiver and her teeth start to clatter together.

"A couple of days but I thought it was fine," she admits and I just stand here shocked. She looks at me. "I didn't want you to worry." I put my head back and tell myself she doesn't need me going crazy right now. My body fills with rage that she was in pain and didn't say anything because of me. "It's fine." She walks out of the room quickly and I look back over at Abigail.

"We need to move quickly," the nurse declares, coming to stand beside me. "We need her out of her clothes and into the hospital gown." I nod at her and watch Abigail move side to side to get the dress off of her. But she has to stop at least twice when contractions come on.

I move out of the way when the nurse comes back and starts an IV and, in a matter of minutes, she's hooked up to the monitor and the sound of the baby's heartbeat fills the room. Dr. Emmy comes back in and she's in blue scrubs. "How we doing?"

"Not good," Abigail says between clenched teeth and it's the first time she's shown that she isn't okay. My head whips to her and I see the tears in her eyes now, leaking down her face. "It's burning and there is a lot of pressure." She looks at me and it breaks my heart that I can't do anything for her.

I rush to her side, wiping the tears off her cheek as she closes her eyes and puts her hand on her stomach, groaning out in pain. "You got this," I say, my heart speeding up as my whole body goes cold. "Breathe, baby," I urge, putting my forehead to her temple as she cries out.

"Okay, let me see what is going on here," Dr. Emmy states calmly and Abigail opens her legs. I spot the blood right away and my eyes fly to Dr. Emmy, who smiles at me reassuringly. "This is all normal."

"It hurts," Abigail moans as she moves her head side to side and starts to shake in my arms.

"Okay, Abigail," Dr. Emmy says, her voice is firm now. "I'm going to need you to focus on me," she orders her. "We need to get your baby out."

Abigail shakes her head side to side, "I can't do it. I need the epidural."

"What did I miss?" Gabriella asks, rushing in the room and then looking at the bed. "Ouch, that has to hurt." She points to Abigail.

"Gabi," she calls her name and Gabriella rushes to her side, slipping her hand into hers. "Tell them I need them to get me the drugs," she pleads with her, and I see Gabriella look down at her, trying not to sob. "I just need something."

Gabriella looks at me and then at Dr. Emmy. "You

have to give her something."

"It's too late," Dr. Emmy says, "Okay, Abigail, when your next contraction comes, I want you to bear down and push." The nurse comes over and places one of her feet into the stirrups and then does the same thing with the other foot. "Looks like it's coming."

There is a lump in my throat that feels like it's the size of a baseball. "Okay, here we go," the nurse says. "Push, Abigail." Abigail bends her head forward as she pushes, the sounds of her yelling fills the room. I want to tell them to stop it all, I want to tell them she needs to be given something. I want to tell them this is all too much and I can't stand to see her like this. "One, two, three…" the nurse says as I count with her until ten.

"Okay, stop pushing," Dr. Emmy says. "You are doing great."

All I can do is rub her head and all I want is to do is pull her into my arms. "You are doing amazing," I praise her and look over at Gabriella, seeing her quietly sobbing as she nods her head. "You are so strong." I'm silenced by Dr. Emmy, who tells her it's time to push again. Every single time it feels like it's going longer and longer. It feels like it's been forever, but it's only be four minutes.

"I can't do this," Abigail says exhausted, as she collapses her head back.

"You can do it," I urge her and she looks at me. In that moment I know what I need to do.

"Marry me," I say the words before I even think about it.

"Did you just ask her to marry you while she's pushing

out your child?" Gabriella gasps. "She still needs a push gift."

I glare at her then look back down at Abigail. "I've loved you for so long." I push back the hair that has fallen onto her forehead. "Living with you these last couple of months has been a dream come true." I smile at her. "I want to see you with my ring on your finger. I want to grow old with you. I want to know that every single day you know how much you're loved and I want to be the one who tells you." My own tears are running down my face. "I want to make more babies with you."

"More babies?" she questions, smiling at me through her tears. "Like in a couple of years maybe."

"Whenever you want," I tell her, kissing her lips then Dr. Emmy gets our attention.

"Okay, you to time to meet your son," she says to us.

"Wait," Abigail says to her then turns to me. "Yes," she confirms, smiling and then I can see pain on her face. "I'll marry you."

"You guys are so freaking weird," Gabriella says. "Can we just focus on one thing at a time?"

"You can do this," I tell Abigail, who nods at me. It takes her four more pushes before the doctor places our son on her chest. She wraps her arms around him and cries, I can't even stop the sob from coming out of me. My chest is so full of love, I have no idea how I've ever lived without the two of them. I put my hand on top of her and look down at our son, who is just looking around at us.

"Dad," Dr. Emmy says, "time to cut the cord." I stand

up and she hands me the scissors and yet again Abigail has given me a first.

"He looks so much like Penelope," Abigail observes. "Hi, baby boy," she coos kissing him.

"Are you okay?" I ask Gabriella, who just holds her hand to her mouth.

"I love him so much," she says between sobs, "and I'm his favorite."

I just laugh at her as the nurse comes and takes the baby off of Abigail, who looks at me with panic in her eyes. "You follow him and you don't leave him."

I nod at her. "Tristan," Gabriella says, "you know the movie *Taken*?" My eyebrows just pinch together. "You fucking kill anyone who touches him." She uses her thumb to mimic slicing her neck.

"What is wrong with you?" I ask her and she just rolls her eyes. I walk toward the side where the nurse puts our son, who is now just looking around.

"We have a big boy," the nurse declares, "nine pounds fourteen ounces."

"It's a turkey," Gabriella says, "your cooch is going to be like loosey-goosey."

"Can you leave." I look at Gabriella. "Go call the family."

"Mom is going to be pissed," Gabriella warns, coming over and taking a picture of him. "What's his name?" she asks us and I look at Abigail.

"Penelope chose his name," Abigail says. "His name is Payton."

MADE FOR ROMEO

Gabriella

Moving to LA was my dream since I was thirteen.
By the time I was twenty, I was sought out by some of the most beautiful people in the world to take their pictures.
No one cared that I came from a hockey dynasty.
Everything was perfect.
Then I met him.
It was supposed to be a one-time thing.
But it ended up being more. So much more.
Until he betrayed me.

Romeo

Growing up in LA, everyone knew I came from Hollywood royalty.
Following in my father's legendary footsteps, I learned early on not to fall for the shallow shine of this city.
When I met her, I didn't know she was what I'd been looking for.
In one night, I ruined everything.
She left without a second thought.
I've spent every day since becoming the man she deserves.
She thinks it's over.

Printed in Dunstable, United Kingdom